SlipTime

A Sam Buckner Adventure

By

Leo J. Audette

This book is a work of fiction. Names, characters, places and incidents either are products of the author's imagination or are used fictitiously. Any resemblance to actual events or locales or persons, living or dead, is entirely coincidental.

Edited by Dolores Garon.

www.leoaudette.org

Cover picture: courtesy of Imaginary Foundation
www.imaginaryfoundation.com

Dedicated to

This novel is dedicated to Mark and Adrienne, my son and daughter. I'm proud of both of you and will always love you.

Other books by the author:

The first two of the Sam Buckner Adventures:

The Osiris String

The Divine Formula

      (Available at Amazon)

"The day science begins to study non-physical phenomena, it will make more progress in one decade than in all the previous centuries of its existence."

Nikola Tesla

SlipTime

Prologue

The patient was lying on a narrow bed, in what looked like a hospital room. He couldn't be sure of that, or for that matter, of anything else.

As he gazed at his surroundings, the fog in his mind prevented him from fully focusing on some of the details, such as the single, small window perched up high; or the stainless steel toilet in the far corner; or the metal door with a peek-through window.

He could only move his head from side to side and seemed to be paralyzed from the neck down. Every few moments though, he felt the restraints on his wrists and ankles, which accounted for his immobility. Then he would float back into the fog.

The patient had been found wandering on the 375 not far from Tikaboo Peak in Nevada, delirious, making little sense of who he was or where he had come from. Because he was well, if not strangely dressed, the police did not consider him to be a vagabond. He had no identification on his person and no form of currency in his pockets.

Without grounds to charge him with any crime, they had decided to take him to the closest large hospital in Las Vegas for observation, and to determine what was wrong with him. The doctors had checked him over and diagnosed him as being healthy and uninjured. Aware that they should not simply release him onto the streets, they had called in a psychiatrist to evaluate his mental state.

Five days had elapsed since he had turned up and, still, the physicians could not make heads or tails of the condition of the man whom they called Patient Joe.

The most remarkable aspect of this occurrence was that, on the same evening, the police had found a woman displaying similar characteristics, wandering down the same road. She had been sent to another hospital and it had taken a few hours for the health system's medical database to correlate both events. She had then been moved to the hospital where Patient Joe had been admitted, in order for medical staff to simplify and compare their evaluations and treatment.

Patient Jane was now in a private room and suffering delusions identical to those of the male patient, a couple of floors below.

In the cafeteria, down the corridor from Patient Joe's room, two psychiatrists were drinking coffee and discussing the corresponding incidents.

"Yes, I agree with you. The cases are definitely related, but I'll be damned if I can explain their symptoms," said Doctor Young.

"Simon," added the Head of Psychiatry, Doctor John Lawson, "I believe the way they were dressed when found and the strange vernacular they used, has to be the key to understanding what has happened to the pair."

Doctor Young responded, "You make a good point. We're going to have to think like detectives as well as like doctors to solve this case."

He paused a moment and continued, "There is a little light at the end of the tunnel, though. Patient Joe has had an ever-increasing number of lucid moments. Though they are short in duration, I feel his mind is slowly reasserting itself and will begin to make some sense of what he is going through. Has your patient displayed the same signs of returning to clarity?"

"Yes, she has, but her moments of reality have only begun to exhibit themselves today; hence, the reason for our meeting now."

"How would you propose we proceed with these patients?" asked Simon Young.

"I believe we need to continue monitoring their progress and keep each other informed about the frequency and duration of their periods of lucidity. Then, when they both have reached the thirty-minute threshold of clarity, we should show them photos of themselves and of each other and assess their reactions. If they prove to be positive and, if and when they fully recover from their state of stupor, we will bring the two together. Perhaps the pictures or their meeting will jog their memories and we might be able to understand what has happened to them. Then, and only then, will we be in a position to help them with the correct course of treatment."

Young considered the course of action for a moment. As he rose from the table, he nodded in the affirmative and said, "I agree with you. There isn't much we can do for them until they can

4

manage to give us some feedback on any of our questions. Thank you, Doctor."

Then, with a grin, Lawson added, "Might I suggest, Simon, that the next time we meet, we discuss the state of our patients over some well-aged Scotch."

"That's a great suggestion," responded the junior psychiatrist.

Doctor Young returned to his wing and looked in on Patient Joe. As he watched the man on the bed, he wondered yet again what type of trauma could have produced his bout of psychosis.

He then headed to his office to continue the detective work he had spoken of with his colleague. He went to the closet and pulled out the clothing Patient Joe was wearing on the evening he had been delivered to the hospital.

Looking at the style of the articles and material of which they were made, he walked over to his desk and sat down, depositing the clothing on its surface.

He then waved his hand over the right corner of the desk and the hologram of a computer screen appeared before him. He touched a few virtual buttons and a search page came up.

He uttered a command, "CASS, display twenty-first century men's apparel."

He leaned back in his chair and began watching the images and videos that materialized before his eyes.

Chapter 1

(The year AD 2016)

The door to the Roosevelt Room in the West Wing flew open and then crashed behind President Alexander as he stormed out, walking angrily to the other door which led directly into the Oval Office, on the opposite side.

He was quickly followed by the Chairman of the Chiefs of Staff, General Baxter. As he entered the Oval Office, Alexander turned to him and growled, "Why did you wait until now to inform me about this?"

The general didn't flinch.

"Sir, it was a need-to-know issue, and until we knew you weren't going to be a one-term president, there was no need to chance that too many people would become aware of it: national security and all. No first-term President has known or been told of the situation. Orders not to inform them were given by President Eisenhower himself."

The general had never seen Alexander in such a state of rage. He had always been a cool, calm and collected individual. Nothing ever seemed to faze him. This briefing, however, had burst the dike. Even the veins on the President's forehead were visible.

The general understood the President's reaction. He, too, had behaved in an almost identical fashion when he had learned of it, some ten years prior. There was only a handful of people who were privy to the information: himself, the executive director of the President's Council of Advisors on Science and Technology and the executive director of the National Science and Technology Council, both sitting in the Roosevelt Room. And now, President Alexander.

Three other Presidents had also been brought up to speed on the issue, but they had all passed away, taking the secret to their graves.

Alexander wasn't finished. In a less threatening tone, he continued.

"Harry," addressing the general informally, "What do you mean, an issue of national security? This extends way beyond our borders. It could affect all of mankind. How and why would the people involved keep this a secret, and for so long?"

Before the general could respond, Alexander gestured for him to sit down.

He was regaining his composure and was ready to discuss the briefing and the revelations which had been disclosed to him.

"I want to see the *thing* myself."

The general nodded yes.

"I assumed you would, sir. Whenever you want, I'll make the arrangements."

Alexander rose from the sofa and walked over to the door leading to his assistant's office.

Mildred looked up at him as he peeked in.

"Yes, Mr. President?"

"Do I have anything pressing tomorrow?" he asked.

She quickly brought up the President's schedule on her computer monitor.

"You have a meeting with the secretary of state at one o'clock and one with the ambassador of Ecuador at four."

"Reschedule both. I'll be out for the day. Also, inform Captain Graves that I'll need Air Force One ready to go by seven in the morning, tomorrow."

Mildred was used to these sudden changes in routine and simply replied, "Will do, sir. Any preferred dates for the new meetings?"

Alexander pondered for a moment and responded, "No, not yet. I'll know better when I return tomorrow evening."

Chapter 2

Sam was walking to the new apartment he and Melinda had been able to secure, again at the Watergate Hotel. Her first suite there had been a one-bedroom, and though larger, as was each one in the complex, than the average unit found in other buildings, it was still better suited to one person than to a couple.

This one happened to have been previously occupied by Placido Domingo. Situated on the top floor and in the centre of the C-shaped South Watergate building, it provided the new tenants with a fantastic view of the Potomac River from its expansive living room, as well as from its master bedroom. Large floor-to-ceiling windows allowed for the unobstructed vista.

The cost of the unit, though, topped the amount of housing allocation Homeland Security could give Melinda, at her pay scale. On the other hand, the royalties Sam had begun receiving for the sale of his research paper, The Divine Formula, were more than enough to afford them the amenities and space this apartment provided. When the world learned about Sam's involvement during the assassination attempt on the President's life, his became a household name and the sales of his book went through the roof making it a number one bestseller on the New York Times list of *must-reads*.

Above and beyond this, the fact that he was now married to an American citizen enabled him to apply for and obtain a Marriage-Based Green Card, and granted him permanent residency in the US.

He was also given an H-1B visa, allowing him to work anywhere in the country. Cambridge University had accorded him a tenure track position, in part because of his contribution to science and in part, unbeknown to Sam, because of a few discreet phone calls made by Secretary Fleet to some of his former colleagues at the university. It meant he had to divide his time between giving lectures at both the University of Toronto and at Cambridge, but his schedule was more than manageable.

Sam was starved and sweating. He had just returned from the complex's health club, where he went every day he was in town. The amenities offered by the Watergate were amazing: everything from full-time concierge service and twenty-four-hour room service, to restaurants, rooftop terraces and swimming pools.

Life could not get better, he thought. Well, maybe, was the reply to his internal monologue. The fact that he was coming home to Melinda propelled his state of happiness and contentment to a whole different level. How could he be so lucky?

"Hey, where are you, Ms. Gordon?" he called.

Sam and Melinda had discussed the issue of her taking his name, but they had decided that, due to her position, it might be wiser to leave things as they were. They knew they were married and that was all that mattered.

"Where else? I'm in the kitchen, where a proper wife should be while preparing a proper dinner for her man," Melinda responded with a tinge of sarcasm.

Sam hurried to the kitchen area and poked his head around the corner.

There was Melinda, standing over the stove, wearing a red kimono-style silk housecoat, stirring a pot of Beef Bourguignon.

"Wow, that smells good," Sam said, as he walked over to her and held her from behind, caressing her neck.

"It should," she replied. "It has the better part of a bottle of Beaujolais in it. But it won't be ready for at least half an hour."

Sam let her go and started making his way to the hallway which led to the bedroom section of the unit.

"I need to take a shower. I had a good workout at the gym."

Melinda tasted the stew and thought it might need a little more salt. She then covered the pot and reduced the heat to simmer. Setting the timer, a mischievous smile lit up her face.

As she headed down the hallway, she caught a glimpse of a naked Sam entering the bathroom and disappearing to his right.

She couldn't help but think how nice an ass he had.

She heard the shower door open and the faucets turn on.

Melinda strutted to the bathroom, slowly undoing the belt on her kimono and letting the cloak gently slide off her shoulders, exposing her Nubian-like skin and her curvaceous and slender body.

She too was naked by the time she reached the entrance to the bathroom.

The whole shower cavity was filled with steam and she could barely see Sam for the mist. She opened the door, allowing cooler air to flow in, magically revealing her husband who was leaning, arms outstretched against the wall, his head under the rainfall shower fixture.

It was her turn to embrace him from behind, pressing her breasts against his back.

The shower filled with steam once more, and the two disappeared from view.

Twenty minutes later, they emerged from the stall, patting each other dry with their towels.

"I could almost use another shower after that," Sam commented, "but I'm really hungry now. The stew smells amazing.

"You know," he said with a grin, "it's nice when we can have dessert before the main course."

Melinda laughed and tapped him on his behind.

"Who says that was dessert? Think of it as more of an appetizer. And after supper, you'll know you've been served dessert."

The two kissed as they walked out of the washroom.

Chapter 3

Later that evening, Melinda's cell phone chirped. She and Sam were sitting holding a bowl of popcorn and watching a movie they had rented.

She reached for a napkin, quickly wiped her hands and picked up her phone. She looked at the number of the caller and turned to Sam.

"It's my boss. I wonder what he wants.

"Hello, sir."

"Hi, Melinda. I hope I'm not calling at an inopportune moment?"

"No, sir. Sam and I are just chilling out at home."

"I'll get right to the point. I've just spoken with the President and he would like to see you first thing in the morning."

With a surprised look on her face, Melinda tried to cover the microphone with her hand and mouthed to Sam that the call concerned the President.

It was his turn to look surprised.

She returned to her boss.

"I'll be there. Did he say why?"

"No, he didn't. Actually, he said he couldn't even tell me, but that I'd be brought into the circle before long. All very cryptic."

"And he wants to speak with *me*?" Melinda added, totally puzzled.

"It would seem so. He said I would understand when briefed.

"You know, if I was an insecure person, I'd start worrying about my job; regardless, I trust the man and won't read into this. Oh, and he asked that Sam come with you."

Melinda's eyes grew even larger as she gaped at Sam.

"That won't be a problem. I'm sure he'll look forward to seeing the President again."

Now Sam found himself mouthing, "What?"

Melinda gestured for him to hold on a moment.

"At what time and where, sir?"

"He wants you there at seven a.m., in the Roosevelt Room." He paused a moment and then added, "Whatever the scenario, it sounds important. He usually doesn't schedule meetings before ten. My curiosity is piqued with this one."

"As is mine, sir," responded Melinda.

"OK, then, I won't keep you any longer. Fill me in when you're able to with whatever information you're allowed to share. Good night."

The line went dead at the other end.

Melinda turned her phone off, putting it down slowly, deep in thought.

"What was all that about?" quizzed Sam.

"I'm not sure. We've been summoned to the White House for a meeting with the President."

"It sounds like something big is up," responded Sam, "and your boss isn't in the loop. Is that normal for Washington?"

Melinda thought for a second.

"No, not really. Someone at my level is seldom made privy to information their boss isn't aware of. It's all very intriguing."

Sam checked his Emopulse watch.

"It's getting late. Why don't we hit the sac and try to get some sleep?"

Melinda looked at Sam and added, "I have a feeling it's going to be a long night."

All Sam could say was *yup*.

Chapter 4

When Sam and Melinda were escorted to the Roosevelt Room by a sharply dressed Marine, they were surprised to find they wouldn't be the only ones attending the meeting.

There, sitting on one side of the long boardroom table, were the executive directors of the President's councils on science and technology, and General Baxter.

Before them, on the opposite side, were three other individuals, none of whom was familiar to Sam or Melinda.

The general rose to greet them with a firm handshake.

"So good of you to join us, Under Secretary Gordon and Doctor Buckner."

He turned and pointed to the two chairs beyond the three strangers.

As they were settling into their seats, the general began the formal presentations.

"Allow me to introduce you to the other attendees the President has invited."

Gesturing to the people next to whom he had been sitting, "Doctor Frank Miller, Executive Director of the President's Council of Advisors on Science and Technology and, this is Doctor Judith Armstrong, Executive Director of the National Science and Technology Council. Some of you may know them . . ."

It surprised Sam that three of them, including Melinda, nodded in the affirmative.

Then, facing those across the table, ". . . and this is Doctor Marvin Lewis, a professor at Harvard University's Physics Department."

Sam leaned over to Melinda and whispered, "I recognize the name. He won a Nobel Prize two years ago."

"Next to him," Baxter went on, "is Doctor Nancy Fitz, professor at the Massachusetts Institute of Technology.

"And beside her is Commander Harvey *Howey* Johnson, the head of our NASA Propulsion Research Department."

Pointing to Sam, he continued with the introductions.

"Doctor Sam Buckner is a professor and researcher at the University of Toronto's Biogenetic Department. And finally, may I present Melinda Gordon, Under Secretary of Homeland Security, Office of Intelligence and Analysis."

In spite of the nods from everyone in the room, Sam reasoned correctly that all but the two individuals opposite them had no clue why they were there and why people of such different disciplines would be asked to convene at the White House. The sombre look on the faces of the two executive directors was not reassuring.

Just then, the door opened and in walked President Alexander, prompting General Baxter to stand at attention and salute.

"At ease, General, and thank you for tending to the group until I could join you."

Without a smile, the general took his seat.

The President pulled out and sat in the leather chair at the head of the table. Looking at the people to his left, he began.

"You must be wondering why I would request your participation in this meeting."

The expression on their faces confirmed the statement.

"What you are about to hear can never leave this room. As well, as of now, you may not communicate with anyone without permission and must be willing to commit yourself to being sequestered for an unknown amount of time."

The President peered into each person's eyes for any sign of doubt.

"If any one of you cannot agree to these terms, I ask you to say so now, and you will be free to take your leave."

The comment dumbfounded the five of them, to say the least. Nevertheless, rather than discerning any indication of concern, the President was rendered a collective look of steadfast acceptance on the part of the group.

The President smiled.

"I gather your silence means you accept?"

They all nodded yes.

Alexander carried on. "I expected nothing less from each one of you.

"Now, let's get down to business."

14

Glancing at the general and the two executive directors, he pressed on. "Recently, I've been made privy to some information that could alter history."

That comment elicited signs of puzzlement from each of the *guests*.

"Though I will not give you the details now, I will ask you to wait a little while longer to get the particulars. I would like you to trust me just long enough to fly to a site which will also remain confidential. All your questions will be answered when you arrive at your destination."

The group now displayed more disappointment than concern or bewilderment.

Alexander proceeded, scrutinizing each of the invitees in turn.

"I suppose you are also wondering, why you?"

Their body language indicated he had expressed the question they all had in mind.

"You were selected by my two executive directors. They pored over hundreds of names, only to come up with the five of you."

Their body language now changed to show surprise as they visually questioned each other and then the President.

Looking at Doctor Lewis, he explained, "Your area of expertise is the study of the physics of soft condensed matter, materials which are easily deformed by external stresses, electric, magnetic or gravitational fields, or even by thermal fluctuations."

The President chuckled and looked at Director Armstrong.

"Did I get that right?"

She smiled and remarked, "I couldn't have said it better or more succinctly, sir."

The President turned back to the first scientist.

"Now, if I understand correctly, you work with both synthetic and biological materials?"

"Yes, sir, that's right. We try to probe and understand the relationship between mesoscopic structures and bulk properties."

The President shot him a quizzical look.

Lewis quickly added, "Mesoscopic structures are at the atomic level, while what we call bulk matter can be as large as molecules. So it is the properties of their structures that interest us."

Without making any more comments, the President moved on to Doctor Fitz.

"Your field is Inertial Navigation Systems?"

Nancy Fitz indicated that that was correct.

"These systems use computers and rotation sensors to continuously calculate position, orientation and velocities of moving objects, am I right?"

"Yes, sir. The inertial instruments we have developed are a huge leap ahead of those used even five years ago. The military has purchased our technology for some of their new projects."

"Yes," pursued Alexander, "I remember the battle in Congress to get the funding approved."

Turning now to Commander Johnson, he smiled and forged ahead.

"Howey, you are head of our propulsion research lab in Houston and I believe the title explains what you do. Nonetheless, even you will be astounded and, I dare say, flabbergasted by what you will learn."

Then, looking at Sam, "Doctor Buckner. Please don't consider yourself an afterthought. Your expertise in genetics could be critical to this mission."

Though the President wanted to thank Sam yet again for having been instrumental in saving his life, twice, Alexander knew it wasn't necessary, and Sam understood this.

"And finally, Under Secretary Gordon, your presence here is due to the resources you can bring to bear in this project and, your job, assuming you accept, will begin the moment that door . . ." Alexander pointed to the door leading out to the hallway, ". . . opens and we leave the room. Your task will be to coordinate measures to ensure the security of the group and to provide an absolute information blackout, both crucial to this mission."

Melinda calmly said, "Yes, sir. Understood."

The quiet assent of the individuals before him had Alexander smiling inwardly and congratulating himself, for he knew that he had hooked them.

He cleared his throat rather loudly, indicating he was almost finished and then added, "Ladies and gentlemen, I can only say you will not regret your decision to participate. I hope you won't be too surprised to learn that you will be leaving in roughly two hours on the flight I spoke to you about."

Surprise was an understatement, and before the five could respond, the President addressed General Baxter.

"General, I leave it to you to get them there safely."

Genuinely relieved, the President smiled broadly and announced that he had another meeting and would see them upon their return. Four seconds later, he was gone.

General Baxter rose to get the attention of the small circle which was now voicing concerns about the lack of time to prepare.

"Don't worry about your apparel. Since we anticipated your eagerness to be part of the project, we took the liberty of retrieving some of your effects and articles of clothing, suitable for where you will be going and for the duration we project."

The group was stunned, but didn't dare ask who had indeed retrieved their things or how they had managed it. To some extent, they felt their privacy had been violated. On the other hand, they also understood the gravity of the undertaking the President had thrust upon them.

"Moreover, all of you, other than Under Secretary Gordon, will be allowed to make one call, which will be monitored. You may only confirm that you are well and that you will be on government business for a period of time. Under Secretary Gordon, I believe you will have many more calls to make. Then, I'm afraid you will all have to surrender your cell phones, tablets and any communication devices you might have with you."

As he spoke, the door opened once more and several Marines walked in, dragging a series of suitcases, each labelled with the name of the intended owner.

Looking at Melinda, the general added, "While the others make their calls, may we speak? I need to share some information which you will require to assume the responsibility of coordinating security."

Sam drew Melinda close to him and whispered, "What have we gotten ourselves into? Conversely, I'm really pumped about this whole affair. What about you?"

She looked at him, smiled and said lovingly, "As long as we're together, sweetheart."

Sam knew better than to kiss her under these circumstances. Still, he did wink at her discreetly.

Chapter 5

Pursuant to the plan, the group was lifting off the runway exactly two hours later. They had been driven in a small convoy of black SUVs which Sam was becoming familiar with, after the wild rides along the Gardiner Expressway and Queen Elizabeth Way, when he had first become involved in the hunt for Dr. Al-Eissa and then again, when they had gone after and almost found the doctor in Frankfurt.

They rode from the White House, along US Route 1 and transferred to the extension of the George Washington Memorial Parkway, which led directly to the Ronald Reagan Washington National Airport.

Much to his surprise, the grey military plane they were led to, a Boeing 777 was not in a secluded part of the airport. It had docked at one of the minor gates in the main terminal. Contrary to the departures of the other flights, though, there was no boarding call or any announcement stating its departure time and destination.

Sam concluded that being plunked amid a crowd of planes made their craft   inconsequential if not imperceptible.

Three hours into the flight, the engines slowed noticeably and the plane began to dip forward. The captain announced that they were beginning the descent for the landing at their destination, ETA twenty minutes.

During their travelling time, General Baxter had isolated himself at the front of the plane, working on his laptop and taking calls on his cell phone. Melinda had opted for a seat at the rear of the plane, where she was also on her cell phone, communicating with her office staff, giving instructions for the work they would need to do in her absence.

The four scientists, of course, were huddled together. Marvin Lewis was sitting next to Nancy Fitz, while Harvey Johnson and Sam were literally draped over the back of their seats in a kneeling position, in order to face the other two. They had been engaged in an animated discussion, trying to guess what could be the nature of the *project* the President had spoken of, and what they might possibly be able to bring to it, all in an effort to try to figure out what they had agreed to get involved in.

Sam saw Melinda coming to the centre of the plane to join them. He decided it was time to sit with his wife. He excused himself from the others and had to climb over Howey in order to get to the aisle where he took her hand and led her a few rows ahead. Finding two empty window seats wasn't a problem, since, other than the team and a few military personnel, no one else was on board the four hundred-plus passenger airplane.

He looked out the porthole and then commented to her, "We've been flying west for a while now. It's nothing but desert beneath us. Any idea where we're going?"

"No, not really. The military has so many bases in the west of the country, it could be anywhere."

The captain suddenly announced that the plane was in its final approach and asked that all passengers be seated and buckled in.

As they banked to the right, Sam was able to get a glimpse of the two runways and a taxiway leading to a series of buildings to the southwest of the airport.

The landing was flawless, much to the credit of the pilot, and once at the end of the runway, the aircraft turned to head toward the terminal.

The plane had barely stopped, than General Baxter was up and heading to the door. A soldier stood at attention next to the hatch, saluting the general as he arrived. A knock from outside the fuselage told them the stairway to the plane had been positioned and it was time to open the door.

By then, the rest of the group was waiting behind the general to deplane. When the door opened, they were all hit by bright sunlight and a blast of hot, dry air.

The general faced his flock, smiled and said, "Welcome to Area 51."

Chapter 6

Several of the scientists seemed genuinely surprised. As for Sam, his face lit up with an expression of giddy happiness, like someone just learning the answer to a long sought-after secret.

He squeezed in closer to Melinda and whispered, "How cool is this?"

They stepped down to the tarmac and followed the general, while looking around at their surroundings, trying to compare the legend to the reality they were encompassing.

There wasn't anything sinister about the airport: a bunch of old and plain-looking buildings and a dozen or so World War II hangars. They didn't see any evidence of much air traffic either, other than the plane from which they had just disembarked, and certainly no UFOs.

As they arrived at what seemed to be the terminal, a two-storey wood-clad structure with blistered white paint and a series of large windows to the front, the general explained that he wanted the party to meet the base commander, General Hanson.

Walking into the building provided a bit of a shock to their systems. The cool air from the air-conditioning unit greeted them with welcome relief from the abusive heat outside.

The front room did not resemble any terminal they had ever seen. It was, rather, nothing more than a large living space, with a series of sofa chairs clustered around several modest tables.

The general gestured to the small gathering, beckoning them to sit. He then addressed one of the two guards standing at attention by the opening of the hallway leading to the rear of the building.

"Soldier, would you inform the general of our arrival and ask him to come and meet the group?"

"Sir, yes, sir," snapped the soldier who crisply saluted Baxter and disappeared down the hallway.

Facing the assembly again, the general explained, "I'll be leaving the briefing to the base commander. He is thoroughly intimate with the operations here and will be able to answer all of your questions, but, only those which pertain to your project."

Sam couldn't help himself. He had to ask.

"General, since we are at Area 51, this whole undertaking wouldn't have anything to do with the Roswell flying saucer, would it?"

There was a chuckle from the others, excluding Melinda, followed by a moment of quiet anticipation.

Baxter leaned forward toward Sam and was about to reply, when Lieutenant General Hanson entered the room.

"Ladies and gentlemen, welcome to Area 51."

As they stood, he walked over to Baxter and extended his hand.

"Harry. It's good to see you again."

Baxter responded, "The pleasure's all mine," and quickly added, "May I present the new sets of eyes the President has sent. I have informed them that you would fill them in on the mission."

After introducing each of the members, he asked, "Do you think we could get to our assignment ASAP?"

Hanson laughed and answered, "Harry, you've always been such a task master."

Glancing at each person, he simply said, "If you are ready for a mind-blowing experience, please follow me."

Hanson walked to the door, never doubting that they would be right behind him.

They stepped out into the heat and walked around the building to the side. There, a military Humvee was idling while waiting for its passengers.

Hanson stopped and pointed to the series of old hangars which dotted the vast area of the complex.

"Though the base is remote, we sometimes get unwanted guests trying to fly by or who attempt to hike it over the hills you see in the distance. They rarely have much to detect other than these buildings. They hope to 'encounter' flying saucers . . ."

Sam thought the base reminded him a little of some of the movies he had seen about World War II fighter plane bases, teeming with Flying Tigers, Mustangs and B-17's, with armies of mechanics maintaining the crafts. The buildings here were similar, but there were no planes. And for that matter, no personnel either.

Hanson pressed on, ". . . but we do our best to disappoint them. In spite of that, we still test our experimental planes here, but these flights only occur after a massive sweep of the area for any observers and, most often at night. But enough for now. Please hop into the vehicle. You'll find it a little more comfortable."

He was right. For the minute or two they had been outside, all were sweating through their shirts in the thirty-five-plus-degree Celsius temperature.

Thankfully, the Humvee's air-conditioning was on and they were grateful for the relief from the heat during their five-minute drive between the hangars and their destination.

They arrived in front of what looked like the oldest hangar in the complex. Its roof was large and curved, and much of the white paint which covered it was either blistering or had already peeled. The actual hangar measured about thirty metres wide and its interior was protected by four sizable sliding doors. Two huge pocket doors flanked either side, making the hangar look even bigger.

The base commander ordered the driver to honk his horn.

The tension the general's guests were feeling was extreme. Behind their cool and silent demeanour brewed a million and one questions. What was hidden behind those walls? What secrets would be uncovered there?

Suddenly, the doors began to move and pull apart. The sunlight made it difficult to make out the interior of the dark, cavernous structure.

The vehicle started up and entered the building.

When their eyes adjusted to the dim light within, they saw that the cavity was empty. Sam and Melinda looked at each other and their faces expressed disappointment.

The Humvee moved slowly toward the centre of the structure and then stopped.

Hanson smiled at his guests.

"I know what you are thinking; but, please be patient for a little while longer."

He pulled out a small object from his shirt pocket and clicked a button. The vehicle shook for a moment and then they were moving, downward, on a large-scale elevator platform, similar to the type one would see on an aircraft carrier. The only difference is that they were not going down just one flight, but were already on level two, according to the sign on the wall, and still dropping.

Of course, the general expected the group to be surprised if not amazed.

"As I was saying earlier, any interloper trying to figure out what we do here would be greatly disappointed. All they would see are old buildings and little activity on the grounds.

"What they want to see and can't, is actually below ground. You may be surprised to know that ninety percent of the base is in effect beneath your feet. That is where the twelve thousand or so military and technical personnel are housed and work."

Before the platform stopped, they had descended to Level Seven, as indicated by the large numbers painted on all four metal entrances which faced them, one on each side of the elevator floor. Every one of these boasted two doors measuring six metres high and six metres wide.

Sam leaned his head against the vehicle's window to look up. A series of similar entryways could be seen, leading toward the surface, each, in decreasing order, with the floor number painted on it. Sam wondered how many more were below them.

Hanson turned to the driver and said, "Corridor C."

The driver acknowledged the order, put the Humvee in gear and drove around to the door directly behind them. As the vehicle made its U-turn, Sam noticed that each one had a small letter painted in the upper right corner, ranging from A to D.

The general's guests all sat still in silent disbelief. Only General Baxter had engaged in quiet discussion with Hanson on the way down, indicating that he was obviously very familiar with the surroundings.

The transport stopped short of the door marked 7C. The barrier split in half and the fifteen-metric-ton blast portals swung inward into the large Quonset-like hallway behind it.

The site was amazing. The semicircular, brightly lit corridor rose above and beyond the width of the two halves of the opening. The walls were concrete and painted white. A two-lane road stretched far ahead and curved gently toward the left.

General Hanson resumed his explanations and from the nods of his guests, he remarked, "I see you are all somewhat surprised."

Harvey Johnson was the first to speak.

"Who wouldn't be? I'm used to large structures at NASA, but this facility can easily rival them. And all underground!"

Hanson smiled smugly and responded, "Just to give you a bit of added trivia, each level and each corridor leads to a different project the government is funding, this being the twenty-eighth and lowest in this facility."

Well, that answered Sam's question: They *were* on the deepest level.

He did venture another question: "I assume the government has more of these facilities across the country?"

Hanson responded, "Yes, it has. Some are as much as three times as deep. We call them D.U.M.B. sites, or Deep Underground Military Bases. This is the original, of course."

Sam leaned over and whispered to Melinda, "I don't know about you, but I'm feeling a little claustrophobic."

She squeezed his hand in agreement.

The Humvee drove on for about a minute, passing several offshoot hallways. Finally, it turned right into the one labelled 'Project Warehouse 1'. A few metres farther, it came to a halt in front of a tall garage-type corrugated roll-up entryway.

Hanson jumped out and opened the door on his side of the vehicle to let the passengers out of the second row. The driver did the same on his side, folding down the back of the seat and flipping the seat itself forward, to allow those from the third row out.

They all congregated around the generals as the Humvee started up and reversed to leave.

Looking at the group, Hanson seemed to hesitate and gather his thoughts, as if he was about to reveal a secret he had never spoken of to *outsiders*.

"Ladies and gentlemen, General, I need to take a moment here before we enter. Needless to say, what you are about to see can never be spoken of outside this facility. Ever!"

The tension in the group was electrifying.

"In 1947, an incident occurred, in the desert, not far from Roswell, New Mexico."

Imperceptibly, each of the scientists and Melinda cringed at the mention of Roswell, especially since the word was being uttered here, at Area 51.

"And the myth of flying saucers was born. It was said that a craft and several alien bodies had been found and brought here.

"The military responded with a counter campaign to dispel the stories which had hit the newspapers. Luckily, at the time, Operation Mogul was underway. It used high-altitude balloons with sensitive microphones, sent up to detect the sound of Russian atomic bomb tests. Pieces of one were found at the site of the so-called saucer crash.

"The legend persisted and the government had to launch Project Blue Book, which as you probably know, was set up to investigate all the credible stories of alien sightings. As you may also know, the thousands of incidents investigated were, for the most part, debunked."

The general paused for a moment, turned and walked to the wall next to the door and pressed a red button. A bit of a rumble was heard and it slowly began to rise.

With an air of seriousness, he added, "Though most of the stories were proven to be fakes, the first of these, was not."

A collective audible gasp emanated from his party as each one of them crouched slightly to try to get a glimpse of what was beyond the barrier, before it was up all the way.

Melinda again squeezed Sam's hand, this time tightly enough to make him wince.

Hanson gestured for them to follow him through.

As they entered the large rectangular room, there in the centre, tied down by guy wires and surrounded by a myriad of pieces of electronic equipment, as well as four fully armed soldiers, appeared a strange-looking, somewhat oval-shaped, emerald-green object.

Chapter 7

The awe-stricken look on the faces of the team was reminiscent of that of the scientists and technicians in the film 'Close Encounters of the Third Kind', as the aliens had finally landed before them on Devils Tower, in Wyoming. They were utterly speechless.

The configuration of the object was strange indeed. It was egg-shaped, about three metres high and seven metres long, with a relatively flat bottom. It hovered a little more than a metre above the floor, similar to an inflated helium balloon. And though it didn't shimmer, the deep green hue made it look like a huge, smooth-surfaced emerald.

Now, it was General Baxter who spoke up in order to bring back some sense of reality, as little as there was, to this setting.

"This is what the President has asked you to come see and as a result, hopefully formulate answers to all the questions the government has been asking since '47."

He nodded in the slightest to General Hanson who picked up on the cue.

"That's correct. We have been probing the E.G.G. or, Extraterrestrial Gravitational Gizmo, as one of our more imaginative scientists called it, when we first brought it to the base. The acronym stuck."

The comment brought some chuckles from a few of the guests and proved to release a great deal of their tension.

"In the past, we have brought in some of the most notable scientists in a variety of fields, but to no avail. Our President feels you might be able to come up with a better understanding of what this is and how it works.

"Each one of you is from a relatively new area of research and it's hoped that what little data we have compiled, along with your observations from studying the craft in person, might bring about some insight. If not, don't be hard on yourselves: Many have tried and all have failed.

"You must have questions to ask?"

No sooner were the words uttered, than a barrage of questions were fired at him.

"Do you have any idea of the composition of the shell? What have the spectrometers indicated concerning its density? Have you entered the craft? Any notion why it's green? Why is it tied down and how can it be floating like that? Have you detected any form of radiation?"

The general was pleased with the reaction.

"Let's sit down over there by the equipment, and I'll give you some of the information we do have. It will be up to you to propose what *you* might be able to bring to the project."

Everyone followed the general to a table and chairs situated next to a piece of equipment that looked remarkably similar to that used by Doctor Fitz in her lab at MIT.

She was the first to inquire about it when they were all seated.

"Sir, how is it that you have *this* accelerometer?" pointing to a particular apparatus. "It's like the one I developed and built no more than six months ago."

"Yes, Doctor Fitz. We had one built according to the specifications you submitted when you requested funding for its development. We were hoping it could help us in our investigation of the EGG."

You could tell the doctor was miffed, better understanding the meaning of *Big Brother*.

Hanson tried to smooth her ruffled feathers.

"Please recognize that every request for funding for equipment which could be useful in our search for answers to our problem is brought to my attention and decisions are made as to whether or not to replicate such equipment. Only the top one percent of the requests meet our criteria and yours did just that. Please take it as a compliment."

Fitz seemed satisfied with the response and replied, "So taken, General."

"Now," Hanson proceeded, "let me tell you what we have tried and the results we have achieved during the past sixty-eight years.

"We have probed and prodded the EGG with every known piece of technology at our disposal and obtained few or no results.

Radar, ultrasound and even electron microscopes have been used to try to determine the composition of the shell of the ship, but to no avail. Acid, diamond drill bits, bullets, blowtorches, you name it: Nothing has affected the surface.

"We haven't located signs of an entrance or propulsion method. That being said, we did discover a few characteristics of the craft.

"When we try to use any form of locator, such as radar, we find that we can see it, it's there on the radar screen and, a nanosecond later, it isn't. Then, there's the question of the surface of the thing. . . ." He paused and then uttered, "Rather than tell you, I'll let you experience it for yourselves."

Hanson gestured to the four soldiers to disconnect the guy wires caging the object. They pulled the wires off and the oval shape remained floating about a metre above the floor of the room.

Hanson rose from the table and summoned them to examine it themselves.

They moved towards the craft and then stopped a few metres from it, to look at it from a closer perspective.

General Baxter spoke up, "Dr. Fitz. You're the expert of rigid body inertia. Why don't you touch it? Oh, and no, Howey, we haven't detected any form of radiation. It is safe."

Fitz hesitantly approached the craft and slowly raised her hand, extending her middle finger to feel the object. Her eyes grew large with incredulity. Even though she barely stroked its surface, the object moved as though it had zero mass.

She quickly withdrew her hand, amazed at the effect of even the lightest pressure.

"My God," she exclaimed, "it's as though it's a balloon filled with helium. It barely exhibits the properties of mass. And yet, I was able to touch it."

Hanson responded, "That's correct. We have determined that it has no mass. There, and yet not there, as I've said before."

In the meantime, Howey was circling the EGG, looking for any evidence of a propulsion system.

He looked at those on the other side and said, "I can see why that scientist called it the Extraterrestrial Gravitational Gizmo. The only means of levitation could be antigravity. That's evident from the fact that it seems to be floating with no obvious system of external propulsion."

"Doctor Lewis," Hanson continued, "I would like you to go beneath the EGG and feel the surface."

Lewis followed the instructions and crouched to get under the craft. He reached for the surface above him and firmly passed his hand on it. To his surprise, the surface seemed to give in to his touch, rolling back along the path where his hand came into contact with the surface.

"Holy cow! It doesn't seem solid. Can you see this! It gives when I touch it."

Again, General Hanson tried to recapitulate. "You're correct. We've found that if you touch it from below or from above, the surface seems pliable, whereas, when touched on the sides, it moves as though it is weightless. The President thought you would find that interesting, based on your field of study. We're hoping you will be able to explain the phenomenon."

Hanson looked at Sam and saw that he seemed to be awaiting his turn, but not so Melinda.

"Doctor Buckner, by all means, go ahead and feel the surface. I would suggest from beneath. We don't need to go running after this thing to get it to stop floating away."

Sam looked at Melinda and smiled with glee at the prospect. She shrugged forward, encouraging him to go ahead.

He eagerly crouched and positioned himself under the object and raised his hand to emulate Lewis' motion.

As his skin pressed lightly against the craft, a bright pulse of light emanated from it, almost giving him, and the others, a heart attack.

He threw himself forward beyond the oval shape, sliding onto the floor, trying to get out from beneath it.

Everyone else, reacting instinctively, pulled back and away from the EGG. The soldiers raised their rifles and pointed them toward the craft in what, afterward, seemed to be a ludicrous reflex.

Melinda's first thoughts were about Sam and whether or not he was safe. She couldn't see him, in part because she had been somewhat blinded by the light and because he was hidden somewhere on the other side of this bizarre object.

She cried out his name, "Sam, are you OK?"

"Yeah, yeah, I'm fine. Don't worry."

General Hanson was also caught by surprise, but quickly regained his composure. He ordered the soldiers to stand down and told the others not to be afraid, and to relax.

Clearly shaken, the group slowly gravitated toward the general, as though he could provide a bubble of safety.

Sam found comfort in hugging Melinda.

Hanson glanced over to his counterpart who seemed to be as bewildered as his charges.

Then addressing the others, he tried to downplay the situation by explaining, "Listen to me. You don't have to panic. This has happened before. Actually, twice."

Everyone gaped at each other in a combination of amazement and confusion.

"Let me clarify," pursued the general. "Back in the '50s and then again in the '80s, it was reported that two of the scientists analyzing the object elicited the same reaction when they touched it. The consequences of the incidents were scrutinized and no ill effects were experienced by anyone in the room. Additionally, none of the instruments monitoring the event indicated any change from their normal state, other than the light meters which were evidently impacted, I suppose, due to the blinding light. So, I can say that this is probably not different from those incidents."

Pausing a moment, he then carried on. "That said, I think we need to look at this rare event and try to figure out a probable cause for its occurrence and what this body, of sorts, might be. Do you agree?"

It was obvious to Sam and the others that the general was attempting to regain control in a chaotic and frightening situation, while trying to refocus them on their mission.

He looked at his watch and decided to wind things down. "I think this day has been unlike any other you have ever experienced. I have to admit, this event has been unique for myself, as well. May I suggest we wrap things up for now. I want to allow you to have supper, rest and absorb what you have experienced. A good night's sleep will enable you to tackle the task the President has handed you. General Baxter and I will meet with you tomorrow morning, at 0800 hrs, in meeting room 7C-H. We have military personnel at your disposal with transportation to any area you need to travel to: that is, within the confines of this research pod."

"Anywhere?" Sam quizzed.

"Almost anywhere."

He winked and added, "Trust me, you'll know when you shouldn't try to enter an area."

The general nodded to one of the sentries who immediately used his com to relay a message. Sam assumed it was to call for the transport the general had mentioned.

Hanson continued, "We've made arrangements for your stay with us. Unfortunately, the number of guest quarters is somewhat limited down here. So, Howey, I hope you won't mind bunking with Dr. Lewis."

Johnson shook his head no.

"Dr. Fitz, you have a room to yourself, and Dr. Buckner and Madam Under Secretary, you might be relieved to know that you will have your own *suite*."

That brought some laughs from the group. And, yes, it was a relief for Sam. He had pictured himself being housed in some large barrack, with countless bunk beds and worse, segregated from Melinda.

By then, several electric golf carts had arrived in the bay just outside the laboratory door.

Informed by the sentry who had summoned them, General Hanson motioned to the group to head toward the exit which would take them out of the room and away from the EGG.

It was obvious that the scientists were reluctant to leave. They had so many questions they wanted to ask--no, *needed* to ask. It was then that they began to realize the enormity of the mission they had signed up for.

As they boarded their transportation, their grins revealed the anticipation each felt at the opportunity they had been granted.

Melinda, on the other hand, was more sombre. She was mentally planning how to keep a lid on the story, not so much while they were down there, but once the group left the project and were on their own, going on with their daily lives. For the moment, their cell phones had been confiscated, and she knew that even if one person was able to access one of them, they were too far down to get a signal.

She needed to study their personalities to assess their ability to keep the information from everyone in their sphere of influence forever, or at least until the President made the information public. And that, she thought, would never happen because of the effect it could have on the world.

The group had travelled about two minutes, driving swiftly and quietly down the long tunnel, before they took a left turn. They soon came to another small parking bay. Ahead of them was a set of oversized glass patio doors.

Hanson stepped off his cart and invited the group to huddle around him.

"I'd like you to remember the name of this hallway entrance: 7C10. This is where you will need to direct any driver to take you when you want to return to your living quarters. There you'll find," pointing beyond the doors, "everything you will need during your time off from the project. The general and I will leave you here and you will be welcomed by First Lieutenant James. He'll look after you from here."

Just then, the doors slid back and out walked a soldier dressed in a perfectly pressed uniform. The nametag on his breast pocket revealed the name John James.

"Ah, here's the lieutenant now."

James quickly asserted, "We're not too formal here. You can call me JJ."

Hanson looked at the group and said, "You'll be in good hands."

Addressing General Baxter, he added, "Harry, I think we have a few things to discuss."

They shook hands with everyone, hopped on one of the carts and were gone.

First Lieutenant James smiled broadly and instructed them to follow him.

Once beyond the doors, the atmosphere changed dramatically.

Though the hallway was wide, the space looked more like a classy hotel than quarters in a military facility. Instead of a high and wide dome-shaped corridor, the walls and ceiling in this area had the more normal structure you would find in most resorts: walls nicely painted in a warm beige, artwork adorning them, and a floor of concrete as the only concession to practicality.

"OK," he began, "this area of the pod houses about half of the three hundred personnel working on the project. We have a cafeteria, bedrooms, meeting rooms, a chapel and activity rooms. About two kilometres of hallways, leading to each area, run through this wing."

He turned to point to a series of Segway PT Sliders, two-wheeled, self-balancing, battery-powered, single-person electric vehicles, parked along the wall to their right.

Fitz spoke up, "Do you want us to use those?"

"Yes, ma'am. Of course, if you prefer walking, you are welcome to do so, but you will find it easier to get around on one of these. They are surprisingly simple to use and to get used to. Let me show you."

Whispered comments could be heard from the scientists: "Cool." "This is going to be fun." "I've always wanted to try one of these."

He brought the group over to their *vehicles*, and stepped up onto the platform of the first in line.

"All you need to do is turn the key to switch it on and then simply lean into the direction in which you want to go."

He demonstrated by holding onto the handlebars and leaning back somewhat. The Segway moved slowly backward about a third of a metre.

He leaned forward a little and it responded quickly and quietly, moving ahead until he leaned back, bringing it to a stop.

"The only suggestion I would give you is to take it slowly at first and don't overlean. It will react precisely and in proportion to the weight transfer. Other than that, stand upright with your feet apart slightly."

Each stepped up onto a machine and got it started by using the key.

JJ moved backward, well out of the way of the others and asked them to ride out, one at a time and to try to get into a single file, with Howey at the front.

After several attempts and a lot of teasing for the awkwardness of some of their movements, they finally got into the formation requested by the lieutenant.

"OK, let's move ahead. I'll describe what you'll see as we get deeper into the wing."

As they advanced along the hallway, some comical comments and grunts could be heard, as they each adjusted to the Segways.

"Oops! . . . Damn! . . . Alright! . . . Oh crap! . . ."

On the whole, they seemed to be learning as they went. They also noticed a substantial increase in the number of military personnel, also on Segways, passing them by in both directions. This started to feel like an inhabited area rather than an empty science lab.

All the while, JJ pointed to and explained different aspects of the complex. As they passed a few of the side hallways, he directed their attention to various signs: Recreation Room One, Small Gym, 7C Office area.

"All right, now. We'll be coming up to the Cafeteria Two section, through the next right turn. So, I would like you to slow down and stop in the parking bay."

Howey, who was at the front, made his turn and began to lean backward ever so slightly to slow down. Lewis, just behind him, failed to see Howey slowing down. A few seconds later, he realized his mistake and quickly emulated Johnson's move, but he leaned back too far and too quickly.

The tires on his Segway squealed as they reversed direction and sped backward. The move surprised Lewis which prompted him to try to compensate. It took him a fraction of a moment to remember he was being followed by Fitz.

The two collided with a thump, almost toppling Lewis off his vehicle. No one fell over or was hurt, other than Lewis' ego.

A round of laughs followed and his colleagues uttered a series of chides about his driving abilities.

Though they had only known each other for a few hours, they had bonded during the plane flight. Further, the magnitude of the revelation they were made privy to had cemented their new friendship, much like that of a military squad after a particularly gruelling mission. Lewis took no offence to the jokes, but rather interpreted them as a sign of camaraderie.

They parked their Segways behind other ones, obviously left there by members of the base personnel. All were neatly arranged in compact rows, each vehicle touching the other in order to take up as little room as possible. Evidently, there was no question of ownership: One simply took whichever Segway was last in line.

As they followed the lieutenant into the short hallway leading to the cafeteria, Sam and the small gathering continued to giggle and give Lewis friendly pats on the back.

The ice had been broken and the tremendous stress they had all experienced was dissipating. Only the scope of the task ahead remained heavy on their shoulders. What they now felt was a shared sense of commitment.

****

They walked through another set of large glass sliding doors which automatically opened for them. A short distance later, they entered an immense and warmly lit circular room, measuring about seventy metres in diameter. The ceiling was domed, with soft light pouring out of what seemed to be skylights, naturally flooding the area in a bright glow.

Sam leaned over to Melinda, pointed up and commented, "You'd never know we're about three hundred metres underground."

The centre of the space provided the serving counters circling the kitchen equipment, reminiscent of the way the old settlers used to arrange their buckboards for protection. A concrete driveway ran all around the periphery of the enclosure, obviously to allow for the flow of Segways. Perforating the outside wall were hallways leading elsewhere.

There were about fifty soldiers and lab technicians sitting at tables around the core of the refectory, all busy talking and eating.

When they became aware of the newcomers, the level of noise dropped dramatically, making it evident that they were not used to strangers showing up.

When the military personnel realized First Lieutenant James was with them, they stood and snapped to attention.

Without even blinking, JJ yelled, "At ease! We'll have company for a few days."

The soldiers took their seats and resumed their conversations as if nothing had happened.

The smell of food warming was a welcome and comforting sensation. It had been almost seven hours since any of the group had eaten and their hunger hit each one with a vengeance.

Howey asked if they could grab a bite to eat.

JJ replied that he needed another five minutes of their time and they would then be free for the balance of the day.

"I'm required to give you a few more instructions. Now, if you'll notice the area in the centre, that is where all your meals will be served. It's open 24/7. Then, if you look around the circumference of the room, you'll notice a series of twelve hallways. Each one leads to a bedroom wing.

"Your group has been assigned quarters in the Caf2D wing, just on the other side of the cafeteria."

He reached into his shirt pocket and retrieved several plastic key cards. Verifying the names on each, he handed them out to the appropriate recipients.

"All your belongings have already been delivered to your designated accommodations. Over to your left, you'll see the wing identified as Caf2G. That will bring you to several boardrooms. Number Three will be where you will meet Generals Hanson and Baxter at 0800 hrs tomorrow morning. Of course, if you choose to meet this evening, you can simply find and use whichever space is not occupied. Any questions?"

Each of the guests looked at one another and at JJ with facial expressions and shoulder shrugs which indicated they had none. Well, not that they didn't have questions regarding their venture and the EGG, but at the moment, satisfying their hunger seemed to be a greater priority.

Chapter 8

The group found adjoining tables in a secluded area of the cafeteria, where they sat to devour their first supper in the centre. They were surprised at the quality and variety of dishes available to personnel. They could choose items ranging from T-bone steak, trout and soup to the conventional fare of hamburgers and hot dogs. There was even a bar menu with offerings of beer, wine and various alcoholic drinks.

They ordered their food, along with a couple of pitchers of beer. It felt as though they were back in university, sitting around a table in a pub with friends. They had to admit, the beer went down nicely.

They eagerly ate their meals, all the while talking in animated fashion about the experience they had shared that day. The shocking effects of what they had been shown had by now dissipated and the scientist in each of them was asserting itself.

The doubt and speculation they might have harboured about the myth of Roswell had been dispelled. They now knew it was true and that certainty became the basis of their new reality. Presently, they needed to build on this and bring their areas of speciality to bear in order to try to make sense of it.

They each considered how they planned to approach their research into the EGG to solve the puzzle--a feat, it would seem, no one had been able to accomplish for more than half a century.

Sam admitted he felt a little uneasy about the notion that the experiments tended to lend themselves more to physicists than to biogeneticists such as himself. The others were quick to try to bolster him by indicating that his training, and the fact that he could bring totally different views to the problems, would be critical to figuring things out, or at the very least, to providing them with potential leads to follow.

They bounced ideas back and forth off each other for almost two hours. When the discussion changed to the ramifications on history which would be incurred as a result of what they had seen, the general consensus was that everyone now understood the President's wilful vagueness about the project. None at the table felt the pertinence of the assignment and appreciated the need for discretion regarding it more than Melinda.

There had been a great number of theories put forth in the past about extraterrestrial visitations. She remembered, as a young girl, renting the movie *Chariots of the Gods* on VHS, which had revealed fairly convincing images and arguments for such visitations. There had been a lot of controversy about the ideas conveyed, but it had blown over for lack of concrete evidence. Now, there was proof! And her job was to keep it quiet.

Sam looked at her and sensed that there was something wrong. He turned to his colleagues and suggested that they put an end to their deliberations for the time being and resume their discussion the following day. It had been a long one and they all should simply try to decompress. He didn't add that he was aching to talk to Melinda in the privacy of their room. It was one thing to ponder over the events with fellow scientists, but quite another to share his innermost feelings with them. That was reserved for Melinda and the need for closeness and intimacy with his wife became his sole focus.

Chapter 9

Sam and Melinda parked their Segway next to the door whose number matched the number on their key card. As they entered, the lights came on automatically. The room took the two aback.

Sam whistled and remarked, "This place is full of surprises, isn't it?"

Melinda responded, "You're not kidding. This is really nice."

The couple had expected a stark, military-style barrack room. What they were looking at was nothing short of luxury accommodations.

"It rivals any Hilton I've stayed at," commented Sam.

The suite was spacious, painted in soft pastel colours, with what looked like large windows flooding it with natural light. There was an inviting living section to the left, complete with a corner sectional sofa, coffee and end tables, a nice grey-oak laminate floor, a fifty-inch flat-screen TV. Sam walked over to the wall unit framing the TV and opened a few of the doors adorning it to discover a bar fridge behind one of them, fully stocked with small bottles of wine, spirits and sodas.

To the right was a well laid out, self-contained galley kitchen, and ahead, a short hallway to what they assumed were the washroom and bedroom.

"I think I could move in permanently," Sam added.

Melinda had walked to the corridor and opened each of the doors.

"The washroom is a little tight, but you'll like the bedroom."

Though sparsely furnished with a large armoire, two nightstands and a king-size bed, one would swear it had been decorated by a professional designer. On the bed were a half-dozen matching and contrasting cushions, strewn over an off-white down-filled duvet. Above the padded headboard hung a large stylized seaside scene, reminiscent of Cape Cod.

Peeking in, Sam took Melinda's hand and drew her back into the living room area.

"This is incredible and completely in keeping with the day. We need to talk."

Melinda seemed to be shocked back into reality. She too had been overwhelmed by what they had been made privy to just a few hours ago.

"You're right. But I think I'll need a little wine to help me unwind and regain enough of my composure to make sense of it all."

Sam told her to find a spot on the couch while he searched for glasses in the galley cupboards. Heading over to the wall unit and opening the small refrigerator, he turned to her and stated, "You have a choice between a Chardonnay, a Pinot Grigio or a Valpolichella. Which one?"

Melinda glanced back at him with a befuddled expression and said, "One of each, I think."

That made Sam smile and he responded with, "OK, a *Chard* for you and the *Valpo* for me: for a start."

He brought the glasses over to her, twisted the screw caps off the small bottles and poured the two wines.

He settled comfortably on the sectional next to her and took a sip.

"I've been aching throughout the day to talk to you about all of this. My head's swimming with questions, ideas and wonder. It's hard to describe how I'm feeling."

"I'm right there with you. I'm only now coming to grips with the President's vagueness about the affair and the reason for the secrecy."

Appearing to be puzzled, she queried, "And, why didn't he include my boss instead of me?"

Sam nodded in the affirmative and then shook his head to indicate he didn't have an answer for her. Subsequently, he went off on his own tangent.

"This changes EVERYTHING! Our whole concept of who we are and what our place in the universe might be. Two hours of brainstorming with the others and no clue about any of the questions we are being asked to answer."

Melinda put her hand on his, trying to soothe him.

"That is nothing for you to be upset about. They've been trying to solve the problem for almost seventy years."

He perused her face for a moment and then leaned in to give her a kiss.

"You're right. I have to slow down a bit and approach all of this like any science project: step by step. The first fact is that this *thing* is real. No more speculation or rumours. That's huge."

He paused for a few seconds and then gave Melinda what she interpreted as a look of disappointment.

"What is it?" she asked.

Again he hesitated and then answered, "If you're wondering why you're involved, what about me? The others are clearly here because of their expertise in physics. I'm a biogeneticist. So, what value do I bring to the project?"

She gently took his face in her hands and kissed him softly on the mouth. Then gazing deeply into his eyes, she replied, "Listen, there has to be a motive. I can't believe the President didn't have his reasons for the selections he and the directors made. This is only the first of many days, I'm sure. Let's do as you suggested and take them as they come, one at a time."

He smiled back at her and said, "I'm so lucky to be married to you. You always know exactly what to say to make me feel better."

He checked the time on his watch and remarked on the speed by which the past few hours had flown and how draining they had been.

"I don't know about you, but I think the wine is having an effect on me. Are you tired?"

She nodded yes.

He took her again by the hand and slowly led her toward the bedroom. He looked around and remarked that this was definitely not your typical army barracks.

Tired or not, the wheels were still spinning.

He absent-mindedly voiced one of the questions whirling around in his head: "Why do you think the EGG is green?"

Chapter 10

As per their instructions, the small group arrived at Room 3 promptly at 8 a.m. the next morning. The last to meet them in the hallway was Howey. All commented on and ribbed him about his apparel. He had decided to wear his favourite beige cargo shorts, sandals and a bright and colourful silk shirt, covered with palm trees and toucans.

Sam and Melinda had awakened two hours prior, refreshed and unable to sleep any longer. They had showered and after dressing, made their way to the cafeteria for breakfast.

By the time of their arrival, most of the military personnel were already leaving to head off to their respective posts.

Sam had recovered from his short-lived bout of anxiety and state of doubt. Now, everything seemed possible. He wasn't sure if that was due to the smell of the coffee and bacon and eggs he had ordered, or to the wave of eagerness that had overtaken his being.

As a scientist, he had been given the gift of a lifetime and he wanted the team to succeed, even though he knew that no one would ever find out if they did. The irony of this situation resided in the fact that it was his wife's job to make sure no one ever would.

After breakfast, the small gathering walked into the boardroom and found the two generals already sitting at the large table, neither of them getting up to greet the scientists, but Baxter did comment on Howey's Floridian look. "Whoa! That is bright. If you're looking for the beach, go to the end tunnel you first came through and turn right."

There were more jokes made at his expense. He loved it.

"So," Hanson began, "Madam Under Secretary, Dr. Fitz, Gentlemen, please take a seat. We have much to discuss. But first, I trust you found your accommodations satisfactory?"

All agreed that they had been more than pleasantly surprised at the comfort and luxury of the suites.

The general explained that because the staff resided below ground for such long periods of time, the military had decided it was important to make all the living spaces feel like home. The labs were more utilitarian, again reflecting what they would find in any university laboratory.

"And, as I mentioned," he continued, "it may surprise you that many of the other D.U.M.B. sites, though not all, are constructed in a similar aspect. One recurring problem is that we constantly have to refuse requests from our soldiers to remain for a further tour."

Dr. Fitz asked, "Are military spouses allowed to visit their partners?"

"No, they aren't. That is to ensure security and to act as an incentive for personnel to return home."

That drew laughs from everyone.

General Baxter stepped in.

"OK, then. Let's get down to business. We would like you to proceed directly to your experiments on the EGG. Before each of you are sealed folders in which you will find a summary of every experiment carried out by your predecessors . . ."

Everyone picked up the folders, stamped *Top Secret* on the cover, and broke the seals to look inside.

". . . in order to give you the upper hand or at least a slight lead and to allow you to leapfrog to present-day information, in an effort to figure out how this ship works. In particular, the information found here will allow you *not* to repeat the experiments already conducted on the EGG and which revealed no concrete results."

All of the participants looked at each other and nodded, silently agreeing that this would be a good starting point.

Dr. Lewis asked if they could get a list of the equipment at their disposal.

Hanson replied, "Absolutely. We'll provide you with it within the hour."

Sam queried, "If a piece of equipment isn't on the list, can we put in a request for it?"

"By all means. If you think of something we've overlooked and you need equipment not included in our inventory, we'll source it out and have it brought in."

Baxter then instructed them to start reading the documents and after lunch, to meet once more to give him their recommendations for the next stage of the project.

His comments were as much an ending to their meeting as they were their marching orders for the morning.

The two generals rose to leave the room.

Melinda got up as well and asked General Baxter if he had a few minutes for her. She wanted to discuss the security procedures they had introduced to date, in order to allow her to formulate her own.

"Certainly, Madam Under Secretary."

"Please, General, call me by my first name. I don't think that formality is necessary down here."

"As you wish, Melinda," was his response.

Just before walking out of the room, Melinda looked back, only to see the group had already begun reading the data, totally immersed in the information which had been provided for them.

She smiled and shook her head, thinking, the kids are at play. Her heart skipped a beat as she glanced at Sam, and then the door closed behind the trio.

Chapter 11

After the generals' and Melinda's departure, the four scientists spent at least an hour and a half reading the information in the folders. And, as promised, a list of the equipment available to them was delivered.

The rest of the morning saw them partaking in intense and sometimes heated exchanges on the number and strengths of the experiments performed on the EGG. The methods used in each were dissected and analysed in order to try to determine why they had failed to produce results: Was it because of that era's less sophisticated equipment or because of flawed procedures?

Or was it that the craft was so alien that no one had come up with the correct experiment? This was the premise they had proposed in the end. Unfortunately, it was also the premise which put them back to square one and posed their greatest challenge. They had to create something totally new by thinking outside the box.

It didn't take them long to devise a strategy. They would first begin with experiments they were familiar with, in order to establish a baseline they could use to compare to the results of future experiments. Afterwards, they would start looking for similar or complimentary findings to see if they could then meld their results.

Sam felt comfortable contributing to the deliberations as they pertained to process and approach. But the subject matter seemed once more to be out of his area of expertise. That feeling of disappointment began to gnaw at him once more.

Lunch proved to be a slight distraction, with the discussions continuing in earnest. Once finished, they all returned to the boardroom, again to find the two generals waiting, along with Melinda.

Chapter 12

"Well, have we made any headway?" inquired Baxter.

They had decided that Howey, the person most familiar with spacecrafts, would be the group's spokesperson.

"To some extent we may have," he began. "We've studied the experiments that were conducted previously and the procedures that the scientists followed. Based on the time when they were performed, we have concluded that some of the equipment wasn't," he hesitated, "simply put, up to par with what we have available now. In others, the strategies of the experiments were flawed; for example, using diamond drills on the craft was ill-conceived and rather primitive."

The others chortled.

The generals' eyes grew wider and after glancing at each other, it was Hanson who spoke up, asking, "And you believe you can do better?"

Smiling, Howey looked at the other scientists, as if seeking their approval.

"Yes, we think we can. At least in terms of the approach we want to take and some of the equipment we will need to use."

Dr. Fitz interjected, "Sir, has the accelerometer the military copied from mine," voiced with an ever-so-slight hint of sarcasm, "been used on the EGG?"

Having expected the question, Hanson responded, "No, actually it has not." Then, he finished his statement on a somewhat apologetic note. "As you are aware, we've only had it for about five months now."

Howey resumed his explanation.

"We've prepared a short list of some of the items we will need. We can tell you where they can be found. The rest, you already have."

He handed the sheet of paper over to the general, who quickly read the list.

"I see no problem with this requisition. We will have the material ready for you to use first thing tomorrow morning."

Surprised, Marvin Lewis blurted out, "Jesus, even FedEx would be hard pressed to match you."

That brought a smile to Hanson's face.

"I see a request for carbon dioxide and oxygen monitors. Who is calling for that?"

Sam put his finger up to identify himself and added, "Just a hunch."

Howey pressed on, "Sir, we are eager to get back to the lab and the EGG. We'd like to set up and calibrate the equipment you already have and choose which we will be able to use."

Again, he looked at the others before uttering, "I think I speak for my peers when I say that this is the most important challenge we've ever been given and though what we did this morning was significant, it was also theoretical. We feel we now need to get our *hands dirty*."

Baxter smiled and finally concluded the discussion. "That is good to hear. If you want to change your clothing, you may do so. If not, we have overcoats in the lab. I'll have someone escort you back to the laboratory where you can begin your work. Thank you, all."

He looked at Hanson and nodded. The latter turned to Sam and asked, "Dr. Buckner, could you stay behind for a moment?"

That took the others and especially Sam by surprise.

"Certainly. Is there anything wrong?"

"No, not at all. Just an additional item I need to discuss with you."

Baxter did not give anyone time to react.

"That is it then," and he got up out of his chair, expecting the others to respond to the cue.

All but Melinda, Sam and General Hanson rose.

Again, Sam was dumbfounded by the fact that Melinda remained seated. He thought that maybe they would ask him to withdraw because he was a mismatch in the group.

Hanson kept silent as he watched the group leave and waited for the door to close shut.

Then, attempting to put Sam at ease, he quickly forged ahead: "I can imagine what you might be thinking, but don't worry."

Even Melinda had a hint of a smile on her face. She mouthed, "It's OK."

"Dr. Buckner, I have asked you not to join the others because I would guess you don't have too much to do in the laboratory for the moment. I have been authorized by the President to show you something. Let's say 'artifacts' that were collected during the course of the discovery of the EGG. For the time being, no one else can know about them, so as not to influence their experiments and results. Melinda has been brought up to speed, only because it will be her responsibility to keep everything under wraps once you all leave the base. Would you come with me now? Melinda will join you when you return."

Sam's mind was swirling yet again. Though he had butterflies in his stomach, he coolly got up from his chair and said, "After you, General. I can't wait."

As they left the room and began to walk down the hallway, back toward the cafeteria, Melinda took his hand, squeezed it and gently gave him a kiss on the cheek.

"I actually wish I could go with you, but it would add nothing to the mission."

Hanson pointed to two Segways up against the cafeteria wall and walked over to one of them.

"Come on, Doctor. You will not regret it."

Chapter 13

The two rode their vehicles out of the living pod area, to the parking lot next to the main road they had originally driven on when they had arrived the day before. That now seemed like a week ago to Sam.

There, a driver in a large electric golf cart waited for them.

"Hop on," Hanson said and added that the ride would not be too long.

The three drove along the Quonset-like tunnel for about a kilometre, passing several other corridors which bisected the one they were in.

The cart came to a halt next to a smaller tunnel called M-Lab, according to the sign above it.

General Hanson got off and ordered the driver to wait for them.

He then waved Sam to follow him. Sam peeked down the hallway, only to see a dead end. Then, looking more closely, he recognized the outline of what looked like a steel door, painted the same colour as the wall, thus causing it to blend into the wall and seemingly disappear.

The two walked to it, as Hanson reached into his shirt pocket and took out a key card which he swiped in the reader next to the door.

A series of clicks could be heard, each followed by tumblers sliding into the open position. The door popped out a couple of inches, forcing Hanson to pull it open completely to allow them access inside. The interior of the room was pitch black until, one by one, the lights in the lab turned on, revealing the first familiar surroundings Sam had encountered since his arrival on base. It reminded him of his laboratory in Toronto, comprised of several counters covered in black vinyl in the centre of the room and floor-to-ceiling cupboards with glass-pane doors lined up against the walls, displaying a huge assortment of beakers, test tubes and chemistry paraphernalia.

The general saw the look on Sam's face.

"I see you like it," he commented.

"Finally, a setting I can relate to," answered Sam.

"Good. The President thought you would be in your element."

Hanson led Sam toward the rear of the lab, which was relatively small when compared to the size of the rest of the rooms in the compound. There, stood another steel door, similar to the outside one with another card reader on the wall. The general had to use a second card to unlock this one.

Before pulling the door open, he turned to Sam and said, "What you are about to witness has only been seen by an incredibly small and select group of people. There are still many questions about the items you will observe and we hope you will be able to shed a little light on them. We know you are not a forensic pathologist, but perhaps you could give us another lead or set us on a different path."

Sam was taken aback by the comment. He half believed he knew what he might see. From the moment he'd been asked to accompany the general, he had tried to figure out why he had been chosen to do so. The only reason he could come up with was his medically related background. Still, his mind kept running back to the Roswell myths of alien beings supposedly kept there at Area 51. His heart was racing.

Hanson opened the door and walked inside the room. Sam followed into what felt like a refrigerator. There were three tall upright glass cubicles in the centre of the small cavity. They were lit from a set of spotlights in the ceiling of each enclosure.

Standing, or rather supported by thin metal rods, were bones arranged to replicate approximate positions or stances a body might assume.

"Holy smoke," whispered Sam.

"Are they what I think they are?" he asked.

"Perhaps," replied the general.

Sam, reducing his pace, walked around each cubicle, slowly surveying every detail of what was before him.

In the first, there were the bones of a right foot, femur, hip bone, parts of a spine and a lower jaw. The second displayed two thigh bones, and a complete but oddly shaped skull. Finally, in the third glass case there was only a right-side clavicle, arm bones and the left tibia. The eerie aspect of the scene was that the skeletons, or what was left of them, were only about one metre tall.

The general began to explain: "These bones were collected in the proximity of the EGG back in '47. There were not many left and it took searchers a couple of days to find them. We've been able to determine that they are parts of three separate bodies."

Sam finally pulled himself away momentarily to look at Hanson and ask, "Why only bones and so few?" He then turned back to the displays.

The general continued, "Good question and one that hounded Colonel Blanchard, who was then base commander and everyone since. By the time the base personnel were sent on July 7th, only a few days after a farmer located what he thought was a small craft crash site, these were all they found."

Sam spun around, a puzzled look on his face.

"Didn't the farmer see the EGG?"

"No, actually, it was found on the other side of a small ridge, out of the farmer's view."

"So what drew him there?" Sam pursued.

"According to the records, he saw a glint out in the desert, about half a kilometre from the road and some hundred kilometres north of Roswell. By chance, a high-altitude balloon equipped with remarkably sensitive sound-detecting equipment we were using to discern possible Russian nuclear tests, had deflated and crashed there. What he perceived and reported were pieces of the thin aluminium skin of the balloon and stainless steel equipment, something the poor country boy had never seen. Luckily, he didn't by any means catch sight of the EGG."

"OK, then, why aren't there complete bodies?" asked Sam, still walking around the cases and concentrating on the bone fragments.

"We believe the bodies must have been found by a mountain lion and finished by coyotes. If you look a little closer at the skull and then the tibia of the third specimen, you'll see clear signs of tooth marks, the first compatible with those a lion would leave on bone, while the coyotes would seem to be responsible for the rest."

Sam investigated more intensely.

"Yes, I see what you mean. But mountain lions?"

"It's not unusual for someone to be mauled by one in this area. We're aware of several people being killed in recent years within a two hundred-kilometre radius. And that distance is in easy range for such a cat. They will often carry the bodies off and even bury them to feed on later."

"Sounds like a gruesome way to die," Sam said before asking yet another question.

"Was there DNA testing done on them?"

The general nodded yes, but added, "Back in 1986, when that type of testing became available, the base commander immediately had the bone samples sent to be analysed, but the results were inconclusive and threw the project in a spin."

"How's that?" inquired Sam.

"The tests showed some human DNA was present, which had the investigators begin to doubt the beings came from the craft. Instead, they searched police records for possible multiple killings in the area."

Sam interjected, "Of children, you mean?"

"Precisely," responded the general.

"Did they find any?"

Hanson seemed a little deflated when he answered.

"As a matter of fact, just before the war, a local cult leader was accused of murdering several of the followers in his church, including children, but no bodies were ever found and he was acquitted. These remnants could possibly be what is left of them. So there is some doubt that the beings before you are indeed extraterrestrials."

"What you are saying, then, is that these could be alien remains and the DNA testing was flawed, or that they are the remains of human children who were killed and left to the elements in the desert? And that would mean, I suspect, that the aliens, if any exist, are still inside the craft?"

"That's pretty much our dilemma in a nutshell," admitted Hanson.

"Will I be able to look at them more closely?" asked Sam.

"Absolutely. What do you want to do with them?"

"Well, first, I would like to redo the DNA testing. The equipment and procedures we have today far exceed those of the eighties. And I'm struck by a few anomalies in these skeletons."

"What type of anomalies?" Hanson quizzed.

"I'm looking at the eye socket on the skull as well as the nasal cavity. The first seems a little large while the second is the opposite. I just need to get a closer look."

"I'll make arrangements for you to do so later this afternoon, if you wish."

"Oh, I wish," he answered, smiling from ear to ear, "and could I have the help of an assistant? Ideally, someone with forensic experience?"

"I'll check the roster to see if Dr. Lee is on the base, and if not, he will be brought in to help you. Anything else?"

"Yes. Do you think the DNA analysis could be expedited? I know where I would like to send the samples I'll be preparing."

"I'll make sure that wherever you want the samples sent, they will become that institution's top priority," responded the general.

"I wish I carried that type of clout all the time," replied Sam, chuckling.

"I would like to return to the lab as soon as possible to get started."

Hanson nodded but then added, "I need to remind you that nothing you have seen here and none of the information I have given you can be shared with the others. Again, because we do not want to bias their thinking, which in turn could bias their research if they were to work with preconceived ideas."

"I'm going to find it difficult because we stated in the briefing this morning that we wanted to work independently but share information which could give us new leads."

The general thought for a moment and then responded, "OK, I see what you're getting at. So, once you have any verifiable new data, you can inform the others."

Sam smiled at the concession he had been granted and added, "May I discuss this with Melinda?"

"That will not be a problem. She has already been made aware of the existence of the lab and the specimens. Her new duties require full knowledge of everything you people may come up with. So, yes, by all means."

They exited the lab and met the driver who was waiting exactly where they had left him, perhaps totally unaware of the history-making items just two walls away. If he was aware of them, he wasn't showing it.

Chapter 14

When Sam returned to their quarters, he found Melinda sitting on the sofa sipping a cup of tea.

"Hi! How did it go?" she asked anxiously.

"You wouldn't believe," he replied as he took a seat right next to her.

"Tell me everything.

"Oh, would you like a cup of tea first?" she added.

"No, thanks. I'm too hyped up to feel thirsty or hungry.

"Where do I start? How much did they tell you when you met with the generals?"

"Only that they had collected body remains at the site of the crash but that there were some questions as to whether or not they were of the passengers in the craft or of humans."

"That's about the long and short of it. I guess they want me to try to decide which is correct. So I'll be doing my own investigation, with a closer look at the few bone fragments they have and new DNA testing."

He paused a moment and then added, "Finally, something I can sink my teeth into."

"So what happens if you conclude that they're human bones?"

"That's a good question. If I do, then I suppose we could expect to find the alien bodies still inside the EGG. Getting in will become the most important job for the team."

"And if they are alien?" Melinda pursued.

"Then, we have the answer to the most important question science has ever asked: Are we alone in the universe?"

Just then, they heard someone knock. Sam rose to answer the door, and when he opened it, there stood a middle-aged major.

"Dr. Buckner?"

"Yes," responded Sam.

"I'm Dr. Lee."

The visitor was much shorter than Sam and of Asian origin.

"I was told," he continued, "to report to you ASAP. I'm to assist you in your investigation. Are you ready to head to the lab?"

"As a matter of fact, I am. Wow, it didn't take you long to get here."

Dr. Lee smiled and went on, "We're on a mission. There's a buzz on base about your arrival and it seems yours is the project of the hour, so my current tasks have been reassigned to others. I'm familiar with the lab and its contents: *all* its contents."

"Ah, I understand. That's good," responded Sam, "since I have no clue as to the whereabouts of anything in the lab."

Sam looked over to Melinda. He didn't have to ask.

"Yes," she said, smiling as though anticipating his request, "you go ahead. I know you're dying to get into the project."

He beamed back at her, much like a young boy being allowed to go play with his friends instead of doing his homework.

"You're the best and you're right: I really *need* to do this.

"OK, Doc, let's get this show on the road."

And they were gone, leaving Melinda to finish her tea and contemplate when and what she might have to report back to the President. She wasn't used to having to wait. She was a doer and loved to get a piece of the action herself. But in this situation, she knew the others needed time to accomplish what no one had accomplished before. The answers they were looking for could change the course of history itself: both past and future.

Chapter 15

Sam and Dr. Lee had been working in the laboratory for almost two hours. It took them about half that time to set up the equipment they would need to extract the bone material to have tested. Sam had decided to send a sample from each of the identified specimens, with the intent to determine that they were indeed three different entities. As well, with three samples, they increased the chances that though some of them might be from victims of a serial murder, one perhaps might be what they were hoping for: proof of intelligent life coming from elsewhere.

As Sam was sealing the test tube with the last of the chips he had drilled out of the bones, he asked Lee, "How long do you suppose it will take for the samples to leave the base and get to Toronto?"

"I was told," answered Lee, "that a jet was waiting to leave as soon as the samples were ready. I understand General Hanson ordered an F-15 Eagle to deliver the package."

"Is it fast?" Sam asked.

"It can reach and maintain Mach 2.5. That's over sixteen hundred miles per hour."

Sam glanced at him mockingly, smiled and said, "You know you're talking to a *Canuck* don't you? That would be about . . ." he quickly calculated, ". . . twenty-six hundred kilometres."

Lee laughed.

Sam whistled in wonder.

"That means it could be there in about an hour and a half. Incredible! Dr. Macdonald at SickKids Hospital could receive the samples about half an hour later and begin the testing."

Lee seemed somewhat puzzled by Sam's comment.

"What made you select SickKids Hospital? It doesn't sound like that's what they would do there."

"Ah, right. Don't let the name fool you. They have the Genome Diagnostics Laboratory where most of their tests include full gene analysis by DNA sequencing. Macdonald is an old friend of mine and is head of the lab. If anyone can do a proper test on these samples, he can. I also chose them because they can carry out the testing in a fraction of the time other labs do. They were instrumental in developing a web approach to the analysis process. They send their data to a host of other servers programmed to crunch the information simultaneously and return the results which are then compiled back at SickKids. What used to take two weeks now takes but a few hours."

It was Dr. Lee's turn to be impressed.

"So, it's 1600 hrs now. That means they could have answers for you as early as this evening."

Sam couldn't contain his excitement.

"You've got it. I'm jumping out of my skin I'm so anxious. By this evening we should know.

"So, would you be so kind as to take the pouch with the samples to General Hanson? I'd like to stay here to inspect the skull of that one body and try to get an idea of what it may have looked like.

"I'm having a problem not letting those alien movies influence my analysis. You know the ones: small, thin bodies, with large oval craniums and big black eyes."

Lee responded, "I know what you mean. I can't look at the bones without having the same picture come to mind. That was one of the unfortunate issues that emerged from the original investigation. An unknown party leaked some of the descriptions the investigators had recorded and somehow the media got wind of it. Their graphic artists just ran amok with the images and the moviemakers had a field day."

Sam picked up the femur from which he had extracted one of the samples. "Looking at this bone and especially the skull, it's easy to see how they would jump to conclusions. By the same token, there are several *earthly* explanations, if we assume the bones don't belong to an alien."

Lee picked up the bag holding the samples and headed off to the exit.

"I'll leave you to your research. I'll be back to give you a hand as soon as this is topside."

The door clanged shut and the electronic lock clicked into place. Sam was alone to do his thing. He walked into the cold room at the rear and opened the glass cage. He reached for the skull, gently removing it and cradled it tenderly as he headed to the main room.

He sat on one of the stools and held the skull in his right hand. He hunched over to peer more closely at the space where the eyes used to be. Deep in thought, he brought his left hand up to his chin. He happened to look up briefly and saw his reflection in the glass pane on the cabinet door before him.

The likeness he detected caught him by surprise. He laughed until he was almost in tears. It was the spitting image of the famous Thinking Ape statue, representing Darwin's Evolution Monkey, pondering the skull of a human being.

The irony wasn't lost on Sam. Could he be the equivalent of the ape appraising the skull of an advanced species?

He had to find the answer. He had to. . . .

Chapter 16

An hour flew by and Sam was startled by Dr. Lee entering the lab.

"Oh, hi! That was fast."

Lee looked puzzled but ignored the comment. He too had experienced those time lapses one sometimes has when engrossed in a project.

"So, have you solved the problem?" he joked.

"What?" responded Sam, still deep in thought.

Without any effort to try to explain or bring Lee up to speed, Sam simply began to verbalize his thoughts, mid-theory. "The skull doesn't display any sign of parental remoulding postnatally to create skulls that looked like cones, as was practised by some cultures, nor does it display evidence of two of the typical human cranial shapes, mesocephaly, and dolichocephaly. It does, albeit, seem similar to the brachycephaly-shaped skull: relatively symmetrical, but this one is much larger in the upper portion of the skull and more particularly the frontal portion. Would you agree?"

Lee nodded yes.

"And, nor are there signs of deformational plagiocephaly due to intrauterine crowding or positioning. At one point, I did consider the possibility that the deformations could have occurred in a single family, due to a uterine problem of the mother and the deaths would have been the result of the parents eliminating the evidence of said deformation."

Dr. Lee realized that Sam had reached the stage in his investigation where he was trying to establish the possibility that the skull was or was not human, based on known causes of cranial deformity in humans. He wasn't the first to have attempted this. But, Lee was impressed by the fact that it had only taken Sam an hour to reach this stage.

"I know you haven't been made privy to the reports on the remains, but you've attained the same plateau everyone else has. So where to from here?"

"I'm not sure," Sam admitted.

"I feel as if I'm back to square one, with two caveats. There is the EGG," he said, "and the DNA analysis which could give us a definitive response to the only question we truly have to answer: Are these the remnants of aliens or humans? If alien, then we have it. If human, we need to get inside the craft to see if the occupants are still there."

He checked his watch and put the skull down on the counter in front of him.

"I think I should take a look at my experiment on the EGG and see if the others have made any progress."

As he got up off his stool, Dr. Lee did the same and said he would help return the artifacts to their display case. It took them about fifteen minutes to do so and to place the equipment they had used back into the storage cupboards.

They left the laboratory and headed to the golf cart Lee had used to get there.

Sam commented, "What, no driver?"

Lee picked up on the jab and grinned as he said he was beneath the command threshold of authority which would have allowed him to have one at his beck and call. No, he had to do his own driving.

The two rode back to the cart parking area outside the room where the EGG sat, or rather floated.

As they walked into the space, Lewis looked up at Sam and chided him, "How's your holiday going, Sam? We peons seem to be doing all the work."

Sam laughed, but quipped back, "It comes with marrying above one's status."

Dr. Fitz was next to chime in.

"Gentlemen, you see here the perfect man. He knows that women are the dominant species and he is willing to admit it."

The others simply groaned and shook their heads in contradiction. Even the guards seemed to disagree openly.

Sam walked over to talk to Howey.

"So, any progress?" he asked.

Howey frowned and said, "No, not really. We have some new insights but nothing tangible yet. Fitz and I have been working on the principle which enables this thing to float the way it does. It doesn't seem to be using any repellent energy, like antigravity. The only thing that makes any sense is that it is following a gravitational plane or orbit, relative to the solid ground beneath it."

Sam looked at him questioningly.

"I can see what you're saying, but wouldn't that mean it has to be moving, much as the moon does, relative to the earth?"

"You have the concept right," said Howey, "although we can't explain how it can be moving in one spot. Still, we're working on it."

"How about Lewis?" Sam asked next.

"He's as baffled as we are. He's been scanning the EGG and his results would indicate the craft has some kind of phase or cycle change. For about a nanosecond, his sensors see the object and during the next, it doesn't exist. He thinks that could in part explain why the surface gives in to the touch of a hand. We could be displacing the molecular structure of the thing, where it instantaneously disappears and materializes at a slightly different place."

"Wow," said Sam, "these are some rather intriguing hypotheses. You've certainly made a lot of progress, I would think."

"Possibly," responded Howey, not wanting to seem too pleased with the comment.

"How about yourself? Any results from your experiment?"

Sam so wanted to let them know what he had been up to and the incredible experience he had had, assuming the DNA results could confirm the remains were alien.

He bit his tongue and responded nonchalantly, "That's what I'm here for. I'll take a look at the printout and bring it back to my room to analyse the data.

"Let's hope there's something there. In any case, General Hanson wants to be brought up to speed tomorrow morning. He's letting us sleep in, having scheduled the meeting for nine o'clock in the boardroom."

"I'll be there," responded Howey.

Sam walked over to the carbon dioxide monitor he had set up and picked up one end of the printout tape that recorded the levels of emissions from the EGG. He then stepped over to the oxygen monitor and repeated the action.

He compared the two as he analysed the printed squiggles. His eyes opened wide and the expression on his face went from surprise to sombreness.

Lewis had been watching Sam and asked, "Anything wrong?"

It took Sam a moment to respond.

"No, no. I'll need to see the result of the last twenty-four hours to be sure. It's probably nothing and I'd feel embarrassed if I told you about my hunch and it didn't pan out."

Lewis smiled in agreement. "I know exactly what you're talking about. It happened to me once, and *only* once. It's a sobering experience when you're before a group of a few hundred of your colleagues. Luckily, there are only four of us here. So when it's time, you'll know it. Looking forward to hearing about the hunch."

Sam was relieved he hadn't been pressed by Lewis to admit what he was now thinking.

He rolled up the paper tape and sought out Dr. Lee.

"Hey, Doc, do you think you could give me a lift to my quarters?"

"Like I said before, I aim to please."

With that, the two left the room, not missing the opportunity to make a few comments about the others having to stay behind in detention.

On the way back, Lee looked over to Sam and said, "You saw something, didn't you?"

Sam peered back at him with a semblance of fear on his face.

"I might have. Give me this evening to put it all together."

Chapter 17

Sam entered his suite, but this time found it empty. He assumed Melinda was busy doing her security *thing,* and decided that a shower would do him a world of good. Afterwards, he left to get a bite to eat.

He didn't want to be alone and yet didn't want to talk to other people either. So, he found the best of both worlds in a quiet area of the cafeteria.

Some twenty minutes after he had arrived, he saw Melinda come by on a Segway, motoring on the laneway along the outer wall of the room, heading toward the hallway entrance leading to their quarters.

He stood and waved to get her attention.

When she saw him, her face lit up in part because she had been anxious to hear what he might have discovered and in part because, well, it was Sam.

She parked her cart out of the path of other Segways and headed over to him.

Sam embraced her and hugged her tightly.

"Hi," she said, kissing him on the mouth. "How was your afternoon with the . . ." she looked around to see if anyone was within earshot, ". . . objects?"

They sat down and Sam was about to start, but stopped to ask if she wanted to get something to eat first.

"No, I'm too excited about hearing what you have to report. I can eat later."

"OK, for starters, let me say it's been incredible. I've had huge *highs* and a few *lows.*"

He spent the next hour describing the bone remnants, the procedures they followed to extract the DNA material to be tested. He described the speed at which the samples were to reach SickKids Hospital and how soon he could expect results. He spoke of the possibilities either answer could mean to the project. Then he told her about his experiment on the EGG and its implications.

Melinda was silent during the entire conversation, which was more a monologue than a dialogue.

"Sam," she finally replied, "I'm truly speechless. This is breathtaking. Did you discuss it with the others and how did they react?"

"No. I need to recheck the data and wait for the DNA results to come back. I'll have the opportunity to inform them at the briefing in the morning."

****

Three hours later came the ever-so-long-awaited knock on the door of their suite.

With great anticipation, Sam opened it to see Dr. Lee standing there with an expectant smile on his face.

"The results are back. I wanted to deliver them myself. May I join you?"

"Absolutely," said Sam. "Grab a seat and I'll get us all a glass of wine. One way or another, I think we'll need a drink."

Dr. Lee walked over to the upholstered chair next to the sofa, not wanting to invade the couple's space on the couch.

Sam returned holding a tray with three glasses of red wine. After setting it down on the coffee table in front of him and handing out the drinks, he sat next to Melinda. He picked up the envelope, hesitating to open it.

He tore one end of it in order to reach into it and pulled out a single sheet of paper.

As he read the contents, he smiled at first and then his face went completely blank.

Melinda became worried.

"What is it?"

Sam looked up at the two and said, "Well, James Macdonald sends his salutations. He says I owe him a case of beer for the favour he did me in cancelling all his appointments."

With that, Melinda relaxed and sat back.

Sam then glanced at Lee and continued, "They are human."

There was shock on the doctor's face, but then acceptance.

"We always thought it could be a possibility. The first DNA test conducted came up with the same diagnosis."

Sam resumed, "Human, but with anomalies. Some of the DNA sequencing shows evidence of mutations not associated with any of the abnormalities we discussed earlier."

Lee now seemed puzzled.

"So, presently, where does that leave us?"

Sam thought for a moment and then the smile returned to his face.

"Do you know what it might possibly indicate?"

Both Melinda and Lee shook their heads.

"They are human and they are not. What if this species is the result of crossbreeding between our direct ancestors and something *out there*?"

Chapter 18

The next morning, both Sam and Melinda were the first to arrive at the boardroom. On the table in front of them, Sam placed the report he had received from Toronto, the streams of paper from his carbon dioxide monitor and a series of pictures.

As the others made their way in, followed by both generals Hanson and Baxter, they took the same seats they had chosen on the first day there, almost out of habit.

Hanson opened the briefing by inviting each of the scientists to describe any breakthrough they might have made regarding the EGG as a result of their experiments or brainstorming sessions.

Howey began first, as expected, and explained that one of the conclusions they had reached was that this craft could not have been alone and on its own. Because of its relatively small size, the group determined there must have been a mother ship that came into the earth's orbit sending either a probe or a shuttle--the EGG--down to the surface. Something obviously happened to it and the mother ship had no other vehicle to replace it or of itself could not pursue into the atmosphere to rescue the craft that had crashed.

General Baxter intervened, "I would tend to agree with your conclusions. That has been one of the most hotly debated issues since the discovery. Anything new?"

Lewis and Fitz felt they should try to salvage the moment by describing their findings and hypotheses concerning the molecular composition of the craft as well as its ability to float as it did.

The latter prompted the two generals to peer at each other numerous times with a look of cautious surprise.

All the while, Sam felt uneasy with what he was about to reveal, wondering if he would be asked to leave the project for being so controversial.

It was now his turn, but before he could begin, General Baxter insisted he needed to inform the others of Sam's whereabouts the previous day.

The revelation startled them and Baxter had to apologize for keeping them out of the loop and the reasons why he did so.

Lewis quizzed Baxter: "So the rumours and stories about alien bodies being hidden here at Area 51 are true?"

"Yes and no," was his response.

He turned to Sam and said, "Dr. Buckner, could you fill the others in on your day with the remains?"

Hearing the word *remains* evoked many silent questions on the part of the scientists.

"Sorry guys, but I couldn't say anything until I had positive results to present. They only arrived after ten o'clock last night.

"As the general stated, I spent the afternoon studying what was left of three bodies found close to the craft."

He passed the pictures of the bones to his colleagues, who hungrily devoured each one with their eyes and pored over them again and again.

"I was most intrigued by the shape of the upper portion of the skull. As you can see, it is somewhat more voluminous than our own, but because the bodies are but a metre tall, the skulls appear to be huge. As well, the size of the eye sockets is substantial, indicating a mutation to larger eyes. I don't want to speculate on the reason for this at the moment, but that will constitute a major part of my research.

"The most important discovery, however, is what was concluded in the DNA testing I had performed in Toronto."

Fitz stepped in, "You mean to tell me you had it done and the results reported back to you within a day?"

Showing as much astonishment as Fitz, Sam replied, "Yes, that's what happened. Though that's another story and one which I'll share later over coffee. Suffice it to say that military speed and efficiency here are superlative."

Hanson and Baxter returned a look of thanks and satisfaction.

Howey couldn't wait.

"What were the results?"

Sam cleared his throat and continued, "They are human and more!"

His fellow scientists all sat back in their seats, trying to assimilate what Sam had just announced.

Lewis was the first to speak.

"Do you know what you are inferring?"

Sam knew they would pick up on the meaning quickly.

"Yes, these are the remnants of the occupants of the craft. Are they alien? Yes. Are they human? Yes. Well, at least at one time."

General Hanson interrupted Sam's description.

"So you have been able to confirm the results of the original testing as detecting the presence of human DNA?"

"Yes, sir. On the other hand, the rest of the sequencing from our testing does show signs of possible non-earthly origins. I'll let that sink in a little.

"But I have more information which may surprise everyone."

Howey blurted out, "More than the fact we have been visited by extraterrestrials?"

Sam shrugged his shoulders to indicate *maybe*.

"Let me start by asking if anyone thought the colour of the craft was strange."

Everyone looked at each other revealing that the concept had not occurred to them.

Sam carried on with his presentation. "I kept wondering, why green? I decided to go with a hunch and brought in the two monitors for oxygen and carbon dioxide. After a day's worth of testing, I realized that there was indeed evidence of absorption of one gas and the emission of water vapour."

Howey laughed and asked, "Do you mean from exhaust or farting?"

That helped break the tension and Sam continued with a little less apprehension.

"Something like that. But this is much more complex and notwithstanding what conclusions may come of it, I believe the EGG is indeed alive."

Chapter 19

Melinda sat back and watched the reaction Sam's comment had provoked. She had learned of Sam's findings the previous evening and she too had been astounded and confused. The revelation contradicted everything she had thought about the Roswell incident and technology as a whole.

Sam allowed the group to return to earth, so to speak, before he continued. When the pandemonium in the room subsided, he looked over to Hanson to see if he should proceed.

The general had to compose himself before he motioned to Sam to move on.

"It puzzled me that the craft would be of such a deep green. Why not white like our rockets? Then it struck me that plants are green. So, I questioned the soldiers who were guarding the EGG about whether or not there was ever any moisture detected in the lab. They told me that when the lights are turned off, they find the walls sweat slightly and dry up when the lights are back on."

Hanson stepped in. "Would that not just be caused by the fact that we are down deep in the earth, where moisture can accumulate on the outside walls and the lights can dry up the air and moisture when they are on?"

"Yes, that is possible, sir. Even so, I asked the guards to dim the lights at specific intervals during the day and night of testing."

Lewis chided Sam, "Yeah, made reading somewhat difficult but it was a relief from those bright lights. Thanks, buddy!" And then he smiled.

"Sorry about that, people, but I needed to see the interaction between the two monitors. What I found and confirmed last night was that the craft seems to act very much like plants do: more precisely, like cacti."

Melinda was smiling to herself at this point. She had found the theory ingenious when Sam had described it to her the previous evening.

Sam turned to General Hanson and queried, "Sir, has the craft been guarded ever since it was discovered and have the lights been on all the time?"

"Most of the time, yes."

"Cacti are succulent plants which have a particular pattern of transpiring and a particular mechanism called crassulacean acid metabolism or CAM, as part of photosynthesis. Transpiration, the process during which carbon dioxide enters the plant and water escapes, does not take place during the day at the same time as photosynthesis, but instead occurs at night. The carbon dioxide is absorbed and stored as malic acid, retaining it until daylight returns, and only using it in photosynthesis. Because transpiration in cacti only happens during the cooler, more humid night hours, water loss is significantly reduced."

Lewis commented at this point, "I think I see where you are going with this. You're saying that the lights act as the sun for this thing and that it emits water vapour when the lights are low or off."

"Right on," Sam responded. "My theory is that the lights act as would the sun and when photosynthesis occurs, the energy is not used to grow, but rather is converted into another type of energy to keep the craft running. When the lights are off or low, the craft absorbs the carbon dioxide in the air, mainly coming from the mouths of the soldiers guarding it and releases very small amounts of water vapour as part of the process."

Fitz added, "Hence, the moisture on the walls."

"Yes," Sam confirmed.

Baxter quizzed Sam, "If it's alive, why hasn't it contacted us somehow, or shown signs of movement?"

Trying to reconcile his own questions, Howey asked, "And how could it survive entry into the earth's atmosphere? Could it be why it crashed?"

Sam shook his head and continued, "I don't have answers to your questions. I'm as much at odds with the conclusions I've reached as you are. I can only say the evidence would support my hypothesis. At the moment, I have no idea how this could impact on your respective experiments, but I only ask that you keep an open mind and consider it as you continue your research."

Lewis put his hand up to add a comment.

"I, for one, think this has some merit. Consider the reaction to the touch. The skin is not rigid yet it is solid. It may not be coincidental that it feels a little like the surface of a cactus and has the same sheen. Its molecular structure could possibly have similar characteristics. That being said, I find it difficult to think of it as a flying vegetable."

Finally, a smile on the faces of the two generals.

Hanson spoke up.

"I would suggest the four of you return to the lab and brainstorm all the information presented this morning. I'm with Dr. Lewis that Dr. Buckner's revelations need to be considered, but I would advise you to continue to look at the other possibilities. In particular, we need to find a way to get inside the craft. That is still a priority."

General Baxter agreed and mentioned Melinda would have a lot to report back to the President. He suggested the briefing end at that point.

All were eager to get to the tasks they had been assigned.

As Sam was collecting the documents and pictures he had brought, he looked over at Melinda with eyes that asked, how did I do? She smiled back and as she always did to show her approval and her support, took his hand in hers and squeezed it gently.

Chapter 20

The four scientists were feverishly discussing the issues that had emerged from the briefing, especially the affirmations made by Sam.

Each described in detail the data they had collected from their own experiments, taking time to explain every step they had followed, accepting questions without any sense of defensiveness, in order to ensure that the procedures were sound and scientific. They were experts in their fields and true vertical thinkers when studying any and every thesis, comparing the antithesis and reaching their synthesis.

Then the group ran these results against the conclusions every individual had expressed during the briefing in order to see if there were any correlations which could possibly be found, to further broaden their understanding of what the EGG might be and where it came from. Horizontal thinking and this aspect of it gave them the most pleasure and satisfaction because it allowed them to see the interrelationship of their particular fields and the means by which they could build on their respective expertise as a group rather than as individuals.

Before having begun though, all of them had made a gesture which was totally not rooted in science, but more in humanity and what makes humans who they are. They had approached the craft and stroked its surface, perhaps in an effort to communicate with it in the simplest of ways, knowing that if it was alive, it might understand what they were trying to do.

Unlike when Sam touched it, none of them provoked the bright flash of light that had so startled them the first time. Perhaps it did understand.

The four refused to leave the lab other than to use the washroom. They had lunch brought in and barely slowed down in their deliberations.

At about one in the afternoon, Melinda walked into the lab and joined the group at their table next to the equipment.

Sam saw her enter and he rose to greet her with a hug. He pulled a chair for her next to where he was sitting.

"Well, I see your discussion is rather intense," commented Melinda and then asked, "Anything new since this morning?"

Dr. Fitz unceremoniously chimed in, "Oh, you missed a great session. It's been wonderful sharing ideas and yes, we think we are making headway on at least one issue. It seems Sam might be correct is his assertion of the thing possibly exhibiting some signs of what could be called life."

Sam smiled and while looking at Melinda, wrinkled his forehead a few times like Groucho Marx used to do, nonverbally saying, so, how about that, eh?

Lewis picked up the train of thought, "Yes, but this is so much more complex. Whatever civilization created the EGG, that civilization has been able to merge what seems to be organic material with non-organic. It opens up a multitude of possibilities for new fields of science and engineering, not to mention consumer products. And here I thought I was at the cutting edge of molecular science. I feel as if I'm only at the kindergarten level when it comes to this thing."

In the lull of the discussion, Melinda thought it could be a good moment to let them know the results of her conversation with the President.

"I've been in touch with President Alexander, to fill him in on the briefing results of this morning. He is absolutely elated and surprised. He wants me to congratulate the four of you for the progress. He is eager to hear any more of your conclusions and insights. He puts a lot of faith in your capabilities."

Howey responded by suggesting they might want to take a break from the work and that the beer was on him in the mess hall.

That brought a round of cheers from everyone. Only then did they realize how both draining and exhilarating the day had been. A period of respite, following words of praise from the President, would be a welcome treat.

As the others rose and began moving toward the exit to mount their Segways, Melinda got up and turned to look at the EGG.

Sam saw her stare at it and asked, "Do you want to touch it?" fully knowing it was killing her not to.

He took her by the hand and drew her closer.

He turned toward his colleagues and called out to them, "Hey, go ahead and start without us. We'll be right behind you."

The others waved and left.

Sam faced the craft again and put his hand up against the surface.

"See, it's fine."

Still holding Sam's left hand, Melinda smiled timidly and used her left hand to feel the EGG.

She stroked the surface, and as with everyone else, it softly gave in to the touch.

Just as she was about to comment on the feeling, a deep guttural vibration emanated from the EGG, travelling through their stomachs and causing both to jolt back in a moment of panic.

It took the guards by surprise, forcing them to once more come out of their state of complacency and familiarity with the situation, and bark orders at Sam and Melinda to move back, away from the craft and head to the exit for safety.

As they had done when the flash of light had escaped from the thing previously, the guards rushed, guns raised to surround the EGG while one of them called for a lockdown of the facilities. Another was yelling for everyone to leave the lab.

Sam and Melinda ran out of the room as the door was dropping, followed by the guards. By the time they reached the hallway outside the lab, the others were returning, stunned by the sound they had heard, knowing too well that it could only have come from the EGG. They were all asking if everything was OK with them and what on earth had happened.

Before the two could respond, and from out of nowhere, approximately thirty soldiers came rushing to the entrance of the lab, ushering the five into the large main roadway connecting all the areas of the research pod. Shortly after, drivers in a couple of golf carts appeared, in order to retrieve them and bring them to safety.

All of this happened within a matter of two minutes, a testament to the efficiency and efficacy of the troops there.

As they drove in silence to the pod wing leading to the cafeteria area, they could now see a soldier brandishing a rifle at every entrance area to the other labs and rooms along the roadway.

Chapter 21

Nearing the entrance to the cafeteria, the soldier leading them pressed the earpiece he was wearing and then turned to the group to say that General Hanson wanted them in the safety of the boardroom and that he was to take them there.

No sooner had they arrived and the door closed behind them, than Fitz quizzed both Sam and Melinda as to what had just happened.

"I really don't know," replied Sam. "We simply approached the EGG and both of us touched it, no differently than we had all done earlier. Then came this vibration and all hell broke loose."

Melinda added, "That sound, or rather feeling, scared the daylights out of me."

She looked at Sam and almost in a whisper, she asked, "Did I do something wrong? Was that my fault?"

Sam was surprised at the questions and realized that it was a natural reaction on her part.

He reached for her and gave her a long hug while reassuring her there was no fault on the part of anyone. For whatever reason, the EGG had reacted to them.

He turned to the others who were still standing around them and commented, "Why would that be?"

Lewis quickly understood Sam's question.

"Indeed, why would that be? What happened that was different when we touched it and the two of you did?"

Fitz's eyes widened and she remarked, "That might be the answer. It was the two of them, together."

She turned to the others and continued her line of reasoning.

"Can you remember if any two or more of us came into contact with the vehicle at the same time?"

They disbanded and made their way to the chairs around the table, all the while recalling their earlier session and interaction with the EGG.

Hanson mulled the question over and said, "Yes, I think we did examine it at the same time, but while doing so, we were palpating different areas of the craft. So, it probably doesn't need more than one person feeling it to react. And remember the fact that only Sam originally touched it when it reacted the first time."

Before they could continue, General Hanson walked into the room.

"Ladies and gentlemen, is everyone alright?"

He was looking at Sam and Melinda, but the group as a whole responded that they were.

"Well, you have created a stir, once again. Any idea what triggered that resonance? It was felt throughout the entire base."

"Not really," answered Howey, "that's what we were just trying to figure out."

Hanson had a strange smile on his face when he continued. "I think it will be important for you to try to come up with an answer to that conundrum. But in the meantime, I believe I have something you need to see. Could you accompany me?"

The group rose and followed Hanson, a little like sheep shadowing their shepherd, looking at each other questioningly the whole time.

Once more, a series of golf carts was waiting for them. The direction the caravan took confirmed they were returning to the EGG.

Getting out of his cart, Hanson waited until the party had surrounded him.

"For the second time, I find myself in front of this door, about to tell you yet again that what you will see will astonish you."

Hanson did something that struck the scientists as strange. In order to ensure that they not see anything inside, he ordered the soldiers to face forward, away from the door leading into the laboratory.

Melinda glanced at the general, who returned the look with a wink.

She moved close to him and said, "Thank you.

"What of the four guards? I want to interview them."

Hanson responded with, "I thought you would. They will be in quarantine until you meet with them and decide how best to proceed in order to contain what they witnessed."

He turned and waved the group through the door.

As on the first day, they followed the bottom of the door as it rose, trying to get a preview of what was supposed to impress them. They were all holding their breath.

There was the EGG, held down by the cables as it was before, but something was different.

"Oh my God!" exclaimed Dr. Fitz. "Look beneath!"

In the shadow below the EGG, there seemed to be something protruding from it. The rest of the crew finally realized that the object sticking out of the craft was what appeared to be a ramp with steps.

Lewis quickly turned to General Hanson.

"You opened it?"

The general shook his head and explained, "No, no one actually saw what happened, but after you left the lab and the rest of the soldiers entered to secure the area, they concluded the ramp had already descended into this position.

"When I arrived, I was apprised of the situation and we felt it would probably be safe to enter the vehicle. There had never been any radiation detected."

Sam asked the obvious question, "Did there appear to be anyone in it?"

Hanson responded, "No, and considering your finds yesterday, we were pretty sure the occupants would not be inside."

He continued, "I asked for a volunteer to inspect the vehicle and to the soldiers' credit, I got twenty. One was selected to enter. After a minute or so, he exited to let us know he had found nothing but three seats on the inside and had seen no one. I had to verify to confirm, so I checked it out and the soldier was correct."

Howey asked if they could see for themselves.

"I didn't think I could hold you back, which is the reason I decided to show you as soon as I could. I would like to give all of you the opportunity to scrutinize the interior. Even so, I would recommend only two at a time as it's a little cramped inside. You'll see. I would suggest sending the engineers first: Howey and Dr. Fitz. Take some time and then we can give Dr. Buckner and Dr. Lewis the opportunity to bring their expertise to bear. In the meantime, for those not in the vehicle, I propose that you try to come up with what made it open if we need to do it again."

You could see the excitement on their faces. What a stroke of luck! To be among the first humans to enter an extraterrestrial vehicle. They could not believe their good fortune.

****

Howey and Fitz had to stoop low in order to reach the steps. A short creature would have to duck just a little to get to them and then the climb inside would be simple.

The one-metre-wide ramp, now extending from the bottom of the ship was remarkable. It seemed to be made of the same material as the shell and without any sharp edges. The five steps leading to the interior were smooth and not green but a soft off-white. There were no hinges between the ship and the ramp; rather, it was simply an extension of the ship, seemingly shaped or moulded from the very fabric of the outer shell, forming one continuous entity with the whole, gently changing from green to white around the round edges.

Sam and Lewis tried to put their minds to the task the general had given them while waiting. Melinda sat with them, attempting to go over every second prior to the event and just afterward, to see if they could recall anything out of the ordinary. Sam could only conclude that it probably had to do with him or Melinda, or both of them in particular.

About fifty minutes later, Howey exited the vehicle, followed by Fitz.

"Incredible," he exclaimed. "It's basically empty."

That caught the others by surprise.

"What do you mean?" asked Lewis.

Howey looked at Fitz, as if to say: How do I describe it?

"Well, not exactly empty, but sparse. It's one room or cavity, with what seems to be a counter or ledge running around the circumference of the curved room. In the centre are three small chairs, or chairs that look like seats. There isn't a seam or right angle anywhere. Even the seats seem to be moulded from the floor, much like you can see with the ramp."

"What about instrumentation?" asked Lewis.

"We looked and probed every surface," said Fitz, "but found nothing. We speculate they might somehow form out of the skin of the ledge. We couldn't tell with what little time we spent in there. I hope you two can come up with some insight. We could end up investing as much time trying to figure out the inside as the military has trying to figure out the shell."

It was Sam's turn. He followed Lewis to the steps on which he had to put his hands in order to prop himself while he started to climb inside.

As his head emerged into the chamber, he was surprised to see how bright the interior was. Every surface seemed to glow gently, flooding every part of it with a soft light.

Howey and Fitz were correct. Sam could see no instrumentation. And, there were the three seats in the centre, all facing in the same direction. Lewis surmised that this setup might indicate that the blank, curving wall ahead of them and above the counter could be some sort of viewing apparatus.

Sam was curious about the chairs. He allocated quite a bit of time investigating their shape and design. They looked like elementary-school-size seats, each draping down to the floor from the small pad and then up to form the back, like a chair that someone had covered with a sheet. Only the sheet melded into the floor.

He turned to Lewis and joked, "And Goldilocks sat on Baby Bear's chair and broke it."

Lewis chuckled.

"Do you think they would mind if I tried their furniture?"

"You should have asked them when you were in the other lab with them."

"Touché," responded Sam.

He ran his hand over the seat and it too gave a little, like the outer shell. He readied himself and gently sat, trying not to put too much weight on it, afraid he might, in fact, break it.

Unlike the chair Goldilocks sat on, this one held his weight well. He settled into it and all of a sudden, he felt it move.

He yelled, "Whoa!" as he jumped off and stood back. It seemed to return to its original shape.

Lewis was dumbfounded and responded with, "What!"

"It moved."

"Moved how? Forward, backward, up?"

"No, I'd say outward. I think it was adjusting to me."

Lewis joked back, "As in adjusting to your *derrière*?"

"I believe so. I should try it again."

Sam positioned himself on the seat and sure enough, it then widened several centimetres.

With a startled laugh, Sam said, "I got to get me one of these. I wonder what would happen if I sat back."

As he eased into the back of the chair, it too took on a shape, but one which matched Sam's shoulders and torso. He was surprised again when his legs were being raised as if he was leaning back in a recliner.

Lewis was watching in amazement, seeing the material which was once the floor, morph and mould upward to support Sam's legs.

"This is absolutely stupendous," Sam remarked.

"It seems to know how to adapt to the sitter. Wait until the others hear about this. Why don't you try it? We'll see if it reacts to your size."

Lewis did and repeated Sam's moves. The chair changed to perfectly adapt to his girth.

"It's obvious Howey and Fitz didn't try the seats or they would have said something about them. Boy, did they miss out."

Sam's thoughts returned to the three occupants who originally brought the EGG to earth.

"The aliens certainly knew how to travel. So, I'm thinking the ceiling might be what they would look at, based on the position they would assume on these seats. Mind you, that doesn't tell us where the instruments to fly this thing are, but it's a start."

He looked over at Lewis who was still lying back comfortably and said, "I have a feeling we'll be down here a long time figuring this thing out. I hope you don't have too many people waiting for you back home."

"Nope," responded Lewis, "and I'm here for the duration. But right now, we have to inform the others."

The two got off their recliners and stood back. Sure enough, they re-formed themselves into their original shape.

Dizzy with excitement, they left the ship and joined the group.

Melinda was the first to ask, "Well, was it all you were expecting?"

The two looked at each other and laughed.

"You have no idea."

Chapter 22

The 'troops' spent the next three hours back in the boardroom, being debriefed by the base commander. General Baxter joined them in the reporting process hoping to ask his own questions. Every possible insight they were able to come up with, in spite of the relatively short period of time during which they had explored the interior of the EGG, was recorded by several cameras and microphones connected to who knows where.

Actually, Melinda did know where, since she was now responsible for keeping the most important secret in history from being divulged.

Wanting to show his appreciation, Baxter even had champagne delivered to the meeting room for a celebration which to some extent wasn't simply for the discovery that had been made, on his watch, but for the new star which he believed would be adorning his uniform before long.

Everyone decided to prolong the festivities by dining in the cafeteria and ordering the best the base had on the menu: T-bone steak, mashed potatoes and green beans.

By ten o'clock, Sam and Melinda had retired to their quarters, had showered and were sitting in bed, sipping wine.

"This day played out like something out of a sci-fi movie," he remarked, "but comparatively, I'm glad it happened today and not the first day we were here."

"I agree," said Melinda. "I think we needed time to adapt to these strange surroundings and get used to being close to the EGG. It's nothing short of surreal."

Sam put his glass down on the night stand and lay back onto his pillow, staring at the ceiling.

"Sweetheart, I can't help but wonder how boring my life would be if it wasn't for having met you."

Melinda looked down at him and said, "That's nice of you to say . . ."

Then she grabbed her pillow and hit him over the head with it, adding, ". . . and don't you forget it."

Sam laughed and reached up for her, whispering, "You want to play rough, do you?"

Melinda gestured for him to wait. "Hold on, let me put my glass down."

She leaned back and set the glass on the stand by her side of the bed and then turned to him, saying, "Yes, I do."

Their lovemaking was as intense as the day had been and an hour later, the two were lying under the blanket, panting with pleasure.

Sam joked, "Nothing like finding a spaceship to spice up one's love life."

She laughed and suggested that they should get some sleep, since the next day would be a busy one, for him as well as for her.

Sam pulled Melinda close to him and kissed her gently. She kissed him back and rolled over, placing her body along his so that they could spoon. It was their favourite way of falling asleep.

As he pushed himself up to find the light switch just above the bed, he happened to glance at his watch and then at the clock, both of which were set apart by the wine glass on the night table.

He turned the lights off and resumed his position next to Melinda.

He closed his eyes and whispered, "Good night."

No response. She was already out.

He lay there for a moment and then a thought came to him: Something isn't right.

He opened his eyes once more and checked the clock again. It displayed eleven o'clock.

Really?

He reached up and turned the lights back on. Melinda stirred and muttered something Sam couldn't decipher.

He grabbed his Emopulse watch to compare the two: It showed ten o'clock.

Sam's mind was racing. He knew his watch kept time accurately, down to the thousandth of a second. Maybe the clock was fast.

He tapped Melinda on the shoulder and said, "Hey, sorry to wake you, but what time do you have on your watch?"

Still half asleep, she raised her arm and brought her wrist closer to her eyes to get a better look at the time.

"I have eleven-oh-two. Why?"

Sam was trying to process the discrepancy between the two. Either he had to bring his watch in for repairs or attempt to find an explanation for the time difference.

Then it struck him like a lightning bolt!

He sat up in bed and said, "Hon, wake up, wake up."

"Huh? What for?" she responded.

"We've been looking at this all wrong," blurted Sam.

"Quick, get dressed. We have to talk to the others."

"Are you kidding?" Melinda asked.

"No, I have to confirm something. Quick."

He got up, put on his pyjamas and threw a housecoat over top. Melinda did the same, but with far less urgency.

Sam headed for the hallway and toward the front door, waving her on to follow him.

By the time they were in the brightly lit corridor outside their quarters, the two were fully awake.

"This better be good," said Melinda.

The first room off to the right of Sam's and Melinda's was Nancy Fitz's. Sam knocked loudly, spurring Melinda to suggest he keep it a little quieter. After all, they were out in a military base hallway, in their PJs.

"Yes?" said a voice behind the door.

"Nancy, it's Sam and Melinda. Could you let us in, please?"

"Sure. Just one moment."

They heard a little shuffling and then a clicking of the lock.

The door opened slightly and one eye peeked through the narrow gap.

"Hi. Just checking," Fitz admitted.

She drew the door towards herself, exposing the flannel housecoat she was wearing.

"Sorry, but I was just about to head to bed. What's up?"

Sam had an intent look on his face, while Melinda seemed to be in the dark.

"I need to get everyone together to double-check something. Would you mind coming with us to the men's quarters?"

Fitz was a little apprehensive but said OK.

The three walked to the next door and knocked on it.

Howey answered, still wearing his cargo shorts and loud shirt, holding a half- finished bottle of beer.

"Hey, guys. Are we having a party?"

He turned his head to look to his right and said, "Marvin, the gang's here for a party. Break out the beer."

He swung the door fully open and stepped out of the way.

"Enter," he said with a wide smile.

The small crew marched in and walked over to where Lewis was sitting on the sofa.

"To what, may I ask, do we owe the pleasure of your visit?" inquired Howey.

Sam suggested they sit down, while he remained standing, as though ready to make a presentation of some sort.

"Right. I know this is strange and you probably think I must be out of my mind. But I need to ask a question or two first."

Silence from the four before him.

"Who had a watch on when we inspected the EGG?"

While this question provoked some confusion on the part of every one, each gave an answer in turn. Both Lewis and Fitz admitted they did, while Howey told them he hated wearing watches, period.

Sam quickly glanced at their wrists. He noticed Fitz still had hers on, but Lewis didn't.

"Marvin, could you go get your watch?"

Lewis was back in a moment, holding the watch in his hand.

"OK, so are you going to tell us what this is about?" asked Fitz.

"What time is it now?"

The four with watches glanced down at them, while Howey leaned backward a little to peer into the little kitchenette to check the clock on the wall.

Nancy Fitz announced that it was 10:40 p.m. Lewis asserted that his read 10:30, which Sam concurred with. Then Sam asked Melinda. She indicated her watch said 11:30. Everyone looked at Howey who announced that Melinda was correct, according to the clock on the wall.

Fitz was getting a little miffed with what she thought was a game.

"Let's not beat around the bush. Tell us what this is all about."

Sam paused and then proceeded.

"Nancy, you and Howey were in the craft for about fifty minutes. I know because I counted the minutes until I could go in. Marvin and I were in there a full hour, and Melinda and that clock were not. What do you think that might mean?"

Howey joked, "That you guys need new watches or at the very least, new batteries."

No sooner had he finished saying that, than Fitz seemed to experience a light bulb moment, then Lewis and finally Howey. Only Melinda seemed immune.

Lewis spoke slowly and hesitantly, his eyes growing larger, "Are you saying what I think you're saying?"

There now was a huge smile on Sam's face.

"Yes, I am. We were wrong. . . . The EGG isn't a spaceship at all. It's a time machine!"

Part Two

Chapter 23

Still standing in their nightwear, the scientists and Melinda were in shock at Sam's assertion.

It was Lewis who first responded.

"That would explain so much," he said.

Touching Sam on his right arm, as though to try to communicate a concern, or that he was beginning to understand the implications, he continued, "If not a spaceship, then we aren't dealing with extraterrestrial beings, are we?"

Sam shook his head.

Howey's and Fitz' eyes opened wide at the realization of what this might mean.

"That could provide an answer to our questions about the propulsion issue," he said.

Fitz injected her thoughts, "And that could solve the problem of something alive, assuming you are correct, coming through the earth's atmosphere and not being destroyed."

Sam smiled with satisfaction, and in agreement as each of his team members' conclusions seemed to fall in line with the conclusions he had come to.

Even for Melinda, the profound ramification of Sam's theory was beginning to sink in.

"You're trying to tell me that the EGG isn't a vehicle built by creatures from outer space, but rather from some time in the future?"

Sam turned to her and calmly asserted, "That's right. If I'm correct, and that has yet to be tested, we are dealing with humans who, I assume, came from the future. The DNA testing has been puzzling, leading us and the previous investigators in different directions. I suspect the bones I analysed are indeed human, but from another time."

"Holy cow!" exclaimed Howey. "We have to start our experiments all over again, but with this new perspective in mind."

Melinda put her hand to her mouth, realizing she now had to disclose this information to the President and then consider how she would need to proceed in order to keep it under wraps until the big guy decided if he would make the information public.

"Do we inform the military brass about this now?" Fitz said soberly.

Sam looked at each one briefly.

"I don't know that we should quite yet. Do we investigate a little more with this new tangent or do we bring the generals into the fold?"

They all looked at each other quizzically, and it was Howey who spoke first.

"I don't know about you, but if I was one of the two generals, I would be royally pissed off not being informed. Besides, we will need their backing to continue to perform our experiments based on this new light."

Everyone seemed to decide this argument reflected the reality of their situation. They were used to working on their own, individually, free of general scrutiny. Nevertheless, they were charged in this case, by the President, to come up with answers, and they were in a military setting. It was incumbent upon them to share this information.

Melinda spoke up.

"I agree with Howey, but I think we should wait until morning at the briefing. I will, at any rate, call the President. He needs to know now. He may then want to notify the generals himself and may have some directives to give them."

There seemed to be agreement with her suggestion, but Lewis added his concern.

"Let's hope the generals understand why we didn't let them know tonight."

Sam felt it was time to end the impromptu meeting, suggesting they each return to their quarters and try to find avenues of thought relevant to the matter, and bring any argument, for or against the theory, to the briefing in the morning.

Then he added, "Remember, we still don't have proof of my assertion but rather only evidence which could support it. I think, true to the scientific approach, we now try to tear it apart."

And with the exaggerated tone of a pompous orator, he concluded by saying, "To quote the great Vulcan of the Starship *Enterprise*, 'Once you have eliminated the impossible, whatever remains, however improbable, must be the truth.'"

There was a round of laughter and a moment of relief as they headed back to their rooms, each in sober, thoughtful silence.

Chapter 24

About an hour and a half later, Melinda was returning to their quarters after having gone to the communications room in order to call the President.

Alexander and his wife had been awakened by the night guard who stated there was an urgent call from Under Secretary Gordon.

"Yes, I'll take it in the library."

He leaned over to kiss Ashley and told her to go back to sleep. Like Melinda had said earlier when Sam had awakened her, he too muttered that this had better be good.

He donned his housecoat, quickly tying the belt and followed the guard to the library next to their bedroom on the upper floor of the White House. He quietly closed the door behind him and took the telephone receiver from the guard who was handing it to him.

"Melinda . . ." He looked at the guard and made a gesture for him to leave, ". . . for you to call at this time, you must have something important."

Melinda began to explain what Sam and the other team members were now considering. The President's jaw literally dropped, and he went silent until the end of Melinda's description of the events.

"And that's it, in a nutshell, sir."

His head was swimming. This came as a total surprise to him, shocking him even more than the initial revelation of the EGG's existence.

Finally, after a long pause on his part, he asked, "How sure are they of this?"

"They are trying to keep an objective mind on the matter, wanting to redo their research in light of this new lead. In any event, they believe all the evidence from the past and from their own investigation seems to lead logically to this conclusion."

"Has the base commander been advised?"

"No, sir, they plan to do so at the briefing in the morning. They want to think this through on their own tonight, to see if they still uphold their findings tomorrow. I thought I needed to inform you, sir, in order to keep you apprised of the situation and to see if you had any instructions for me or the others."

After another pause, Alexander responded, "No, nothing for the moment. Please inform the team that I'm astounded at the news and congratulate them in how far they have come in trying to solve this riddle. Now, I have some thinking to do myself. Thank you, Melinda. I'll be in touch. Good night."

He hung up and slowly walked over to one of the oversized leather chairs next to the desk the phone was on and let himself fall into it, eliciting a *pffft* sound from the seat cushion.

He sat pensively for almost five minutes. He then reached over to the phone and picked up the receiver.

"Yes, can you ring generals Hanson and Baxter for me. And then, call Captain Jones and tell him to get Air Force One fired up."

Just then, the door linking the library and the bedroom opened and Ashley peeked in.

"Is everything OK, darling?"

Alexander put his hand over the mouthpiece of the phone and gestured to her that everything was fine.

"I'll be there shortly."

****

When Melinda walked into the living room, she found Sam sitting on one of the high counter stools along the breakfast bar in the small kitchen.

There he was, feverishly writing on a notepad.

He looked up and over to Melinda.

"Oh, hi. How did he take it?" he asked.

"What do you think? Over sixty years of conjecture shot down by a theory which is as astounding in itself as the original mystery."

She walked over to Sam and wrapped her arms around his shoulders giving him a much needed hug.

"What are you up to?" she asked.

"Just going over everything and putting down the key points for the briefing in the morning."

Then he turned his head to look into her eyes and hesitantly said, "Tomorrow will either be the most important day of my life," quickly going on to say, "other than the day we were married, that is . . ."

Melinda smiled and added, "Good recovery."

Sam chuckled but then became serious again.

". . . or, it will be the day my career goes down the tubes. It's one thing to express a scientific theory to other scientists. They understand the position it puts one in, and they know the next steps are to verify the contention. That being said, it's quite another thing to present these ideas to military men who deal with black and white issues on a daily basis. It's really risky since doubt and uncertainty don't sit well with them. My reputation could take a huge hit, especially if the others come up with flaws in my thinking."

Melinda squeezed him once more.

"Judging by their reactions while in the hallway, I have the feeling they will only come up with conclusions that will support yours."

"I hope you're right. I need to check and double-check all my assertions. It will be a while before I finish this. I'd suggest you get some sleep. I'll sneak into bed quietly when I'm done."

Melinda leaned down and gently kissed his forehead.

"You do what you need to do, but try to get some sleep yourself. That eight a.m. meeting will come quickly for you."

She leaned down once more but this time he turned up to kiss her on the lips.

Chapter 25

The next morning, Sam and Melinda walked out of their quarters and were met by Lewis, who was also heading to the cafeteria. As they rode their scooters down the hallway, they compared notes on the issue, and Sam was relieved to hear that Lewis had not changed his mind. On the contrary, he was more certain than ever that Sam's theory was the most valid one available.

Sam still seemed a little uneasy, checking behind them and looking ahead in the long corridor.

"What's the matter?" asked Melinda.

"I don't know. Nothing I guess, although things seem rather quiet, don't they?"

As they entered the large canteen area, they were surprised to see it empty, and only one cook was visible in the kitchen section, rather than the four or five they were used to seeing.

Now the three of them looked puzzled, but they shrugged it off as a possible base drill.

When they asked the cook what was up, he replied by saying he had been told to hold the fort for the day.

He served them, as well as Howey and Fitz when they arrived.

They ate their breakfast while they talked about the upcoming briefing. They were all united in the belief that the EGG was indeed a time vehicle or machine, which proved to be a welcome relief for Sam.

When done, they all rose together and headed to the boardroom.

It was time!

One by one they entered the room and stopped dead in their tracks as they realized that there, sitting at the head of the table and flanked by the two generals, was President Alexander.

"Ladies and gentlemen, welcome and grab a seat. I understand you have incredible news for me."

****

95

Sam was startled. He leaned toward Melinda and whispered, "Did he tell you he was coming?"

"No," she replied under her breath. "He didn't say a word of his plans. He obviously decided to inform the generals."

Alexander had, in fact, decided he wanted to come himself, in order to get the details about the conclusions the scientists had reached. In order to do so, he knew he needed to bring the generals into the fold. In any case, they were to be briefed and he wasn't about to hear the information from a third party.

"I need to thank Under Secretary Gordon who informed me last night about what I would consider to be the most important scientific discovery in human history."

The President continued, looking at each member on the team. "I'm sure I don't need to impress on you what this will mean if you find your theory to be correct. I'm anxious to hear how you came to this conclusion. So, who's first?"

Normally, Howey would have been the spokesperson for the group. This time, though, considering that the discoveries resulted from Sam's research, he announced, "I believe Dr. Buckner should explain how he arrived at his conclusions."

Sam was ready, but still turned to Howey and said, "Thanks. No pressure, right?"

The others chuckled but quickly quieted to let Sam take the lead.

For the next two hours, he methodically laid out each step he took to obtain each result, from the idea that he believed the EGG to be plantlike, and therefore, alive, to the DNA results on the bone artifacts he had had analysed and finally, to the episode which led to his reasoning that the vehicle was a time machine.

During the presentation, Alexander asked a series of questions in his effort to comprehend fully how Sam had developed his theories.

The next hour was handed over to the other members of the team, in order to inform the President on the reasons why they believed Sam to be correct, based on each one of their areas of expertise.

Throughout, the two generals remained silent, but took copious notes.

Once the briefing was over, Alexander rose and approached the scientists. He continued to quiz each one of them in a more intimate one-on-one manner, impressing the group with insightful and pertinent questions.

This allowed Melinda to draw nearer to General Hanson.

"Sir, if I may. We noticed the absence of soldiers in the hallways and cafeteria. Was that on your orders?"

Hanson anticipated the question.

"Yes, it was. I didn't mean to supersede your authority, Madam Under Secretary. When the President requested that we minimize potential leaks, he felt and suggested that we needed to reduce the number of personnel in the pod to a minimum. We thought you would be asking us to do so this morning."

"Actually, yes, I was," she responded, "and I think it was wise of you to send troops and personnel out when you did. Thank you.

"So, how many troops are still on this level?" she asked.

"There are but three of our most trusted soldiers: one in the kitchen and two still guarding the EGG. All the others were sent on furlough this morning at 0500 hrs, without explanation."

"And what of the other research pods. Have they been sent home as well?"

The general shook his head, "No. Of course, should you order us to do so, it will be done," responded Hanson.

Melinda thought for a moment.

"No, I think the rest of the base should continue operations as usual since the potential for a leak seems to be well controlled. Thank you, General."

Just then, the alert sirens began to blare throughout the pod and three of Alexander's security detail burst into the room and approached the President, surprising everyone in the room.

One walked briskly to the President and whispered into his ear, "Sir, we need to remove you from the facility immediately."

And with that, the three surrounded Alexander and ushered him toward the door.

General Baxter stepped in front of the four, slowing them down enough for him to ask what the alert was about. The lead agent told him he didn't know the reason behind the evacuation-- only that he was following orders from his supervisor.

The telephone in the corner across the room rang out.

Hanson picked it up and bellowed, "What's happening?"

He listened for a moment, and his face became ashen.

He put the receiver down and called Baxter over to him. They spoke in a hushed but animated fashion.

The team members were bewildered, waiting to be told what was wrong.

Melinda spoke up and asked, "Sirs, are we at risk?"

Hanson looked at Baxter and then at Melinda.

"I don't know."

He turned to the scientists and said, "For the moment, you will be safe here. I'm asking that you trust us and remain where you are until we send for you."

He then faced Baxter and uttered, "General, I believe you need to come with me."

The two exited the room without a word, leaving the others dumbfounded, wondering what could possibly be happening.

Chapter 26

The group must have sat for an hour or so, speculating on the latest goings-on. No one seemed to be interested in letting them know the reason for the alarm. Thank God the siren had been turned off, although the silence was equally oppressive.

At one point, Howey impatiently got up and made his way to the door. When he opened it, he found the same soldier that had fed them breakfast that morning standing opposite the boardroom. He had dispensed with his cook's white garb and was donned in full military attire, sporting a deadly looking assault rifle.

He remained silent, needing to say nothing. Howey immediately understood that he should just go back inside and wait with the others.

About two hours later, General Hanson finally made an appearance.

"I apologize for the wait. We needed to ensure there was no danger to you and that the situation had been contained. Protocol demanded the President be evacuated, but, based on the initial report, I felt you might want to remain here until we determined it was safe. We've been in constant contact with the President and he does want to return to the base. Air Force One has been circling the premises at a distance of fifty miles and he's anxious to rejoin the team, if we feel it is safe for him to do so."

That simply confused the group all the more.

Howey spoke up, "Sir, can you tell us what happened exactly?"

Hanson looked at him and said, "I can do better than that. I can show you. Please follow me. We've brought in additional troops to assist us."

They made their way to the cafeteria and down the hallway leading to the main road in the pod. Several golf carts and their drivers were parked there at the ready, waiting to take them somewhere. They all assumed it was back to the EGG.

Something must have happened to it, but what?

****

As they were whisked silently down the road under the large vaulted ceiling, they saw that the former was lined with armed soldiers, positioned ten metres apart, on either side of the tunnel.

When they were approaching the hallway leading to the laboratory where the EGG was housed, Melinda observed that there were no soldiers standing against the wall opposite that corridor and none in the hallway itself.

She leaned over to Sam and said, "Did you notice there aren't any soldiers in the sightline of the lab?"

Sam shook his head indicating he hadn't noticed.

"Don't worry, it's a good thing. Hanson is most efficient. He doesn't want them to see," she responded with satisfaction.

As they veered into the parking bay adjacent to the lab, the carts slowed to a stop. The team jumped off their vehicles and before they could head to the large door blocking their way to the EGG, General Hanson held up his right arm to tell them to halt. He then ordered the carts away. Only when the area was completely deserted did he invite the group to proceed.

The team members' heart rates had increased dramatically in anticipation. Hanson punched in his security pass code and the large door began to rise.

From where they stood, nothing seemed to be out of the ordinary. But given this context, what was ordinary?

The EGG was still there, held down by the cables and surrounded by the array of scientific instruments. The ramp leading into the craft was still deployed.

Sam noticed the guards weren't in their usual positions next to the EGG, but rather had their backs to it and were facing something on the further side of the large room.

As the team advanced to get a better look, they let out a collective gasp.

There rested, about ten metres from the first, a second EGG.

****

General Hanson was standing next to his colleague, sporting a large grin.

"Please, ladies and gentlemen, come forward."

Howey questioned the generals, "You must feel it's safe to be here?"

Baxter turned to him and explained, "Yes, we feel it is. The second EGG has been here for several hours now, showing no signs of movement or hostile action. Based on what we have found out about the first one, we don't believe we have to worry. But, for the moment, I would suggest we continue to watch it from a distance."

Lewis then commented, "This one is different from the first."

Turning to Sam, he continued, "Do you see the shifting of the sheen or colour on the exterior? It's as if there are ebbs and tides of energy moving in all directions along the surface."

He then remarked, "Holy crap, Sam, you nailed it. It seems alive, as if pulsating or channelling energy of some type."

Sam was mesmerized by the new EGG. Smiling at Melinda and then at the group, he said with astonishment, "You know what this means? More than likely, this craft is manned!"

That comment struck Fitz hard.

"My God, you're right."

She looked at Hanson and asked when they might be able to approach or investigate the thing?

General Hanson was serious now.

"To be honest, we are not sure. We were hoping your team might be able to help us determine what we should do next. Needless to say, there are no operational manuals to cover this situation."

The scientists looked at each other with bewilderment. How *should* they proceed? Then they gravitated toward one another and began questioning and brainstorming, trying to develop an approach to the experiments they might perform.

They had little to go on other than what had happened when Sam, and then both he and Melinda had touched the EGG. Plus, there was the hypnotizing motion of the mottling green on the surface of the ship. The original EGG had none of that.

While they were deliberating, the two generals asked Melinda to approach them.

"What do you think? Should we suggest to the President that he return, as he wants to do?"

Melinda shook her head.

"No, I don't believe it would be wise."

She shifted her gaze to the group discussing options and then back to the generals.

"They aren't certain where to start yet and coming to see the new ship would add nothing to the President's knowledge of it. I would suggest we let them do their *thing* and keep the President informed at every step."

She then looked at Hanson and commented, "I assume the only soldiers who know of the new EGG are the two here guarding it?"

Hanson nodded.

"That's good," said Melinda, "it will make my work easier. Can they be segregated from the rest of the troops?"

"Yes, they will be, but we will have to replace them for the rotating shifts."

"May I have an opportunity to interview these two and those you would like to use as replacements?" Melinda asked.

Again, the general nodded.

She turned to glimpse at the new craft and spoke in a low whisper, "I need to get a handle on all and anyone who could become aware of the second EGG."

Facing the generals again, she carried on, "It was one thing to find the first. The conspiracy theories that came out of that proved to be difficult to manage. This one raises the bar considerably.

"My gut tells me we will be meeting whoever or whatever is inside that one. Perhaps when we do and we determine they aren't a danger, the President could then return."

Hanson mulled this over and added, "I tend to concur with your suggestion. Still, if we see any sign of hostility, it will be my responsibility to respond. If they are friendly, then it will be up to the politicians to deal with them."

Melinda looked at General Baxter and proposed, "Sir, you might want to head to Washington to be with the President. If things should take a turn for the worse here, it would be important for someone with up-to-date information there with him to help coordinate a response."

Baxter thought for a moment.

"I hate to admit it, only because I would prefer staying here, but you are right. Jonathan, do you think you could get me a plane to head back to DC?"

Hanson nodded, yes.

Then they went silent with the all-encompassing awareness that they were the only people on the planet dealing with this subject of discussion, the scope of which was just now beginning to sink in.

Chapter 27

The team spent the next several hours analyzing the new ship, but from afar, only using instruments that would not send out the wrong message. The results were no more conclusive than when they had applied the experiments to the original EGG.

Then they discussed the only real difference which they perceived: that of the shifting green colour. Based on Sam's theory that it could be alive, they wondered what would constitute the difference between the two. If it was plantlike, then would it be possible that it might need extra light?

They agreed to have more of the floodlights brought to the lab in order to see if exposing the first EGG to them would elicit a reaction to the change.

It took about forty-five minutes for the additional lights to be delivered to the lab, and to be brought in and then installed by the team. Inasmuch as the room was bright before, it was now almost blinding.

They guessed it would be a while before the lights produced an effect, if they did at all. So, they decided to take a short lunch break and get some relief from the glare.

When they returned an hour later, they were riveted to the spot.

Fitz grabbed Lewis' arm and exclaimed, "Do you see that? The colour is moving."

Turning to Sam, she added, "Looks like your hunch could be correct."

Everyone was smiling over the thought that they were actually beginning to lift the shroud of mystery surrounding the Roswell event. Even so, there were so many questions yet to be answered.

They moved toward the EGG, anxious to get a better look at it up close. They crossed the invisible boundary they had previously set up for themselves, no longer worried about the possible dangers. They were drawn to it, as though they were hypnotized. Even Melinda threw caution to the wind and approached the craft.

She looked at Sam and asked, "Do you think it would be safe to touch it?"

He shrugged and answered, "It would probably be OK. We all felt it before, and none of us was harmed."

Howey interjected with a thought of his own, "Right, but it did respond to you and Melinda. And, maybe it was too weak to do more than resonate and give off a pulse of light."

"True," said Lewis, "but even the new one hasn't made a hostile move."

They all glanced over to the second EGG, having almost forgotten it was there.

"Well, I guess I should be the first to have a go at it," Sam chimed in, "since my contact with it seemed to have created its initial response."

The others approved but instinctively stepped back a few paces.

Only Melinda stayed next to Sam.

As Sam tentatively raised his hand to touch it, he simply said, "Well, let's have another go at this."

Just as his hand was about to touch the skin of the vehicle, Melinda winced a little apparently preparing herself for some reaction or other.

He stroked the surface and, nothing.

He smiled with relief as he turned toward the others, still moving his hand over it.

"No reaction, but I do feel a slight tingle," he said.

He put his other hand out to Melinda and added, "Do you want to try again?"

Without hesitation, she placed her hand in his and let him pull it up to the ship.

Again, nothing other than the lighter shade of green seemingly surrounding the areas where they touched the surface.

The others all shed their concerns and approached the EGG. They began to feel it as well, also experiencing the tingle Sam had spoken of.

Lewis was amazed.

"It's as if it's interacting with our touch."

"Or our aura," added Fitz.

Sam turned to her with a questioning smile.

"Do you mean the electric field our nervous system creates?"

Fitz quipped back, "That's one way of wording it. But, yes."

Sam looked at Melinda and winked.

"Does that bring back some thoughts about one of our discussions just prior to the fundraising dinner for the President in New Orleans, about the body being a sort of radio transmitter and receiver?"

Melinda stared back and in a moment of insight, remarked, "Do you think this is related in some way?"

Howey asked, "What?"

Sam turned to him and said, "Just another hunch. We'll discuss it later over a pitcher of beer."

"You're on," Howey responded with a smile.

Just then and from the corner of their eyes, they all noticed the two soldiers back up several feet, their guns aimed at the new EGG.

"Step away from the craft!" exclaimed one of them.

Surprised at the command, they instinctively followed the orders.

As they did, they saw what provoked the soldiers' reaction.

Unseen from their previous positions, but now clearly visible, was a ramp and set of stairs similar to the one on the original EGG, protruding down from the new one.

They congregated about ten paces away in silence, trying to catch their breath in anticipation of what they all assumed would happen next.

Sam slowly reached over to take Melinda's hand and held it expectantly.

The soldiers had already communicated with General Hanson, but unlike the previous times something had occurred with the EGGs, there were no loud sirens or alarms.

Sam turned to Melinda and whispered, "This is it. We get to meet them."

"Who?" she absent-mindedly responded.

Pointing to the two small legs that had appeared on the steps leading down from inside the craft, he said, "Them!"

Chapter 28

Sure enough, there were now, below the ship, two sets of legs coming down the ramp.

General Hanson arrived in the lab at that very moment and seeing the pair of guards with their rifles up in a firing position, snapped the orders to stand down.

"If they had wanted to inflict harm, they probably would have done so before now," he said.

The soldiers complied, but kept their guns at the ready.

Hanson then turned to the group and suggested they move back a little more, closer to the exit, saying, "Better safe than sorry."

By then, the first creature had emerged from the ship, closely followed by the second who was just stepping off the ramp onto the ground and easily walked under the craft. In any event, the two seemed to be holding their heads down, hands covering their eyes, as though shielding them from the brightness.

Sam looked at the general and said, "Sir, it's the floodlights. They seem to be hurting them."

Pointing to the lights and gesturing with a slicing motion across his neck, Hanson quickly gave the orders to cut the new ones that had been brought in. A few seconds later, they went out and the light intensity dropped dramatically.

It took a moment or two for everyone's eyes to adjust, but when they did, they were dumbfounded by the sight before them.

The two one-metre-tall beings before them were smiling.

Howey made the first comment.

"We have munchkins!" he said.

Both Melinda and Fitz had covered their mouths with their hands, astonished and overwhelmed by what they were seeing.

Whatever everyone had imagined they would look like, this wasn't it.

Standing before them were not Hollywood-stylized, naked and grey-skinned creatures with large black and foreboding eyes. These were two diminutive human-looking . . . well . . . *humans*.

Melinda leaned into Sam and whispered, "They look like anime characters."

Sam nodded back in agreement.

The two were similar in many ways: very small with thin delicate arms and legs. As Sam had speculated when he was inspecting the skulls of the artifacts, they indeed had very large eyes: not black, but clear light-blue, bordered by long dark eyelashes. They also had small but cute noses and button-style mouths. It was obvious that their skulls were large, relative to their size, but the chin-length, somewhat dishevelled black hair, seemed to camouflage the oddity.

The one standing to the left was without a doubt a female. Her face was delicate, with a small pointed chin. And she had breasts showing beneath her outfit. The other was more male looking, with a squarer chin and a slightly more muscular physique than the first.

The only throwback to the Hollywood aliens was what they were wearing. They each had on a white one-piece, full-body, form-fitting leotard, made from a material that moulded to their bodies, both at rest and while on the move.

If their appearance was a shock to the onlookers, what came next literally blew their minds.

Sam and everyone heard them say, "Hello. Do not worry. We mean you no harm."

"My God," said Fitz, "they speak German."

"No," said Sam, "that was French."

The others looked at each other, puzzled.

"No way," argued Melinda, "they spoke English."

The two visitors turned to look at one another and then back to the group.

"We will adjust to communicate in English, since it seems to be your common language."

Only then did it dawn on the 'welcoming committee' that they hadn't seen either of the little people mouth the words.

"I'll be damned," exclaimed Sam, "they're telepaths."

Chapter 29

As they all stood there, dumbfounded by the events, Lewis felt something on his upper lip. He took out his handkerchief and wiped his nose, only to see a smear of blood on it.

Melinda happened to look at Sam, and a small amount of blood was dripping from his nostril as well. She quickly took out a tissue and dabbed the blood off.

"What happened?" she whispered.

"I don't know. I just got flashes of images," Sam responded.

Hanson saw the commotion and signalled to the soldiers to stand at the ready.

A look of fear replaced the smile on the visitors' faces.

The male raised his hand to *wait.*

"I am sorry. We hadn't anticipated the effect of that on you."

This time, he was clearly speaking the words but in a voice that seemed as though he had inhaled helium, altering his voice to sound cartoon-like.

"It would seem that some of you are hypersensitive to that type of communication. We will endeavour to speak aloud rather than *comthink.*

The soldiers looked to the general who waived them down.

Hanson then turned to the visitors.

"I am General Hanson, the commander of this facility. You are welcome and we too mean you no harm. May I ask how we may address you?"

The smile returned to the small ones' faces.

The male responded, "You may call me Tong and my partner is Voot."

By then, everyone was smiling and eager to ask the hundreds of questions that had just crowded their minds.

Surprisingly, Tong winced and said, "Please, not so many at once. We will be able to answer all of your questions in time."

Sam perked up and asked, "You can read our minds?"

"Yes," said Tong, "but we will try to tune you out in order to give you some mental privacy. We apologize for the intrusion."

Hanson picked up where he had left off.

"Thank you, Tong. I am authorized by my president to show you every courtesy in welcoming you. This is probably the most momentous event in human history and I, and I am sure all my colleagues present here," he motioned to the group behind him, "feel so privileged to be present to witness it. I know my president will be anxious to meet with you as well."

He smiled and added, "And yes, we have so many questions to ask you."

He glanced toward the others behind him, all nodding their heads in acknowledgement and in anticipation of what they felt would be the beginning of a marathon question and answer session.

The general introduced the scientists, one at a time and each in turn eagerly shook hands with the visitors. They in turn smiled and seemed genuinely pleased at meeting them. Be that as it may, when meeting Sam and Melinda, they took extra time before releasing their grip, as though to indicate favour of some kind. The gesture wasn't lost on the married couple, and Sam made a mental note to pursue a line of questioning to try to figure out why.

Hanson then suggested the group move to more appropriate quarters in order to allow them comfortable surroundings for their discussions. He checked with Melinda to see how she would like to deal with the issue of security while the *guests* were with them.

She had anticipated the question and suggested that all personnel should again vacate the entire level, all but a security detail at the main blast doors by the elevator.

"I think we have to reduce the possibility of exposure to zero until the President can determine how he would want this to be handled."

Hanson agreed and ordered one of the guards to set off to find First Lieutenant James in the main corridor outside the lab and relay the orders to evacuate the whole research level.

Returning to the group, he interrupted the scientists who had already begun asking questions of the visitors.

"For security reasons, we are sending all personnel out of the area. This will allow us to navigate freely and head to the living quarter pod. There, we will be able to more comfortably begin our talks."

Addressing the two munchkins as Howey had called them, "We will also be able to provide you with sustenance and any comfort you require."

Within five minutes, the guard had returned and informed General Hanson that everyone had left as ordered.

Emulating the moves of a master of ceremonies, the general raised both arms in a welcome pose, inviting the group to follow him out of the laboratory.

Everyone followed his lead and began to move toward the exit door.

Voot stopped, turned to look at the original EGG and said, "Please, would it be possible to turn the lights on once more. He needs it to gain his strength."

The comment took everyone aback. *He*?

Tong saw the stunned look on everyone's face and simply said, "I expect I will have to explain that as well."

Hanson gave a hand signal to the guards, pointing to the lights and then put up his five fingers, indicating when to turn them on, giving the group time to leave so as not to affect the visitors negatively.

The rest of the ensemble hesitantly followed the general, all the while looking back over their shoulders in wonder. Again, they were proven so wrong about the nature of the craft. No, machine. No, it. No, *he*!

Melinda looked at Sam. She saw the same look of awe upon his face that she felt within, but something more: that boyish glint in his eyes revealing what she knew to be his mind whirling at a thousand kilometres per hour.

She then made her way to the general and they spoke in private for about two minutes. Sam saw Hanson nod several times, seemingly agreeing to what Melinda was saying to him and realized she was probably directing what was to happen next.

They split up, with Melinda joining Sam and the scientists, while the general waved everyone to follow him. They made their way to the empty corridor and to the waiting carts. Tong and Voot were directed to the first and climbed up onto the rear seats, while General Hanson assumed the driver's position.

Sam and Melinda chuckled at the sight of the two visitors having to pull themselves up onto the cart, while everyone else simply plopped into their seats. It was difficult to comprehend that these two small creatures resembling Japanese comic characters were surely more intelligent and advanced than any of them.

They all rode to their destination in silence, each almost in shock from what they had witnessed. Well, all in silence but the general.

Much as he had done when he had first driven with the scientists to the hangar and down to the research pod, he gave the new visitors the same description of the base and the facilities they were riding through.

As the carts came into the hallway leading to the living quarters, Sam looked down the main road, to the area that housed the laboratory and the remains of the first visitors. His heart sank, and a deep sadness filled him. Suddenly, he felt guilt pangs at the thought of their deaths, now seeing them as living beings and not simply bone artifacts to be studied. He turned to Melinda, tears beginning to well in his eyes.

She saw the emotions on his face and asked, "What's wrong, sweetheart?"

He cleared his throat and whispered back, "Can we talk about it later?"

Melinda knew him well enough to realize that something personal had affected him. She would wait until the right moment to press the issue.

He reached down for her hand and brought it to his lips. He cleared his throat once more and then smiled at her.

By then, the carts had come to a halt and they all disembarked.

They walked through the sliding glass door, allowing the visitors to accompany the general, while the rest followed from behind, all thinking the same thing.

Seeing the size of the general, walking next to what seemed to be children, struck them as strange. Here were two beings, they assumed from the future, and most likely the two most unique and important people on the planet.

That was a concept they were all having problems wrapping their heads around. If Sam was correct, they *were* people, just not quite like regular people.

Melinda had recommended the initial sit-down be in a room with a casual atmosphere and Hanson had proposed they use the stall lounge. It had a games section with table tennis, card tables and an eighty-inch flat-screen, 3-D TV and beverage and snack dispensers. As well, there were several areas with groupings of sofas, loveseats and upholstered chairs which would allow all of them to sit back, relax and ask the pertinent questions that were burning in their minds.

She tapped Sam's arm and whispered that she needed to leave the group for a moment, in order to inform the President. She would join them as soon as her phone call was over.

As the rest continued on toward the lounge, she exited through one of the tangent hallways heading to the communications room, in order to give the President the news he was so anxious to receive.

Chapter 30

General Hanson entered the staffroom, closely followed by Tong and Voot and the scientists. He asked everyone to sit in whatever seat they preferred. The visitors strangely chose two padded leather office-type chairs, which they rolled close to the other seats occupied by the team members.

When they had all taken their places, it became evident that the seats were positioned to accommodate normal-sized people, making Tong and Voot look even smaller.

Contemplating the possible embarrassment she would feel in such a situation, Dr. Fitz quickly got up and went to them, leaning over to make adjustments to the height of the seats in order to raise the couple to almost the same eye level as the rest of the group.

Voot smiled and said to her, "Thank you for your thoughtfulness, but though very much appreciated, it was not necessary. Both of us are very comfortable with our size, even in your presence. Actually, it is we who feel fortunate not to have to carry such weight and require the resources you must expend to maintain your stature."

No one expected a comment such as that. It truly began to dawn on them that they indeed were dealing with very special beings and not just childlike creatures.

General Hanson seemed to be taken aback a little, not quite sure how to proceed from this point. He decided that what was to follow should be best handled by the scientists. After all, there was no question of danger and so, military control was not called for. The President wasn't there yet; therefore, the political issues could not be dealt with. All that was important for the moment, were the questions everyone had in mind and the answers the guests would provide. This was the realm of the scientists.

"Before we begin with the questions whose answers we have yearned to find for over sixty years, is there anything I could provide you with in the way of refreshments such as food or beverages?" Hanson asked diplomatically.

The two simply shook their heads, and Tong said, "No, thank you. We were able to eat and drink just after we arrived and during the time we were assessing your interactions with our vehicles."

Hanson quickly responded with some suspicion, "You were watching us?"

"Please do not be alarmed," responded Voot, "we needed to see what your intentions were. Since we had to invest some time to do so, we used some of it to take sustenance."

"And what conclusions did you reach?" asked Hanson.

Tong looked at the general and very calmly answered, "We were pleased to see the care you took to look after *Traveller One*. That is when we decided we could trust you and came out to meet with you."

Howey had been uncharacteristically quiet since the visitors had first stepped out of the craft. He needed to ask the one question everyone involved, including the President, desperately wanted answered.

"Can you tell us where you came from?"

Tong smiled once more and responded with, "Perhaps the better question to ask is when we came from."

All the scientists turned and stared at Sam with that 'you were right look'.

They turned back toward Howey who re-posed his question, "OK, when did you come from?"

Voot answered with, "Using your calendar, we are from the year four thousand six hundred and thirty."

The expression of disbelief on everyone's faces was most evident.

Lewis blurted out, "You're kidding us, aren't you?"

Tong and Voot looked at each other for a moment before responding.

"No, we are being truthful. We have come to you from a time far into the future."

Fitz was next to ask, "Why?"

Once more, the two visitors glanced at each other. This time, Voot seemed to shake her head slightly before looking at Dr. Fitz.

"We have come to retrieve Traveller One."

General Hanson became agitated.

"You mean you are taking the ship back with you into the future? Do we have any say on the matter?"

Sam recognized that the general was worried about losing a piece of equipment which could revolutionize the world and which the visitors, according to Hanson, were stealing back to their time. He thought this could get out of hand if the general resumed his military role.

"I can understand why you would want to do that," Sam interjected, "but does this have to be done before we have a chance to talk with you and ask our questions?"

Tong saw what Sam was getting at.

"No, there is no hurry. We are ready to answer any and all of your questions, to the best of our ability."

Sam noticed the general's demeanour change from displaying apprehension to becoming somewhat calmer.

"Good," said Sam.

"Then I think we should begin getting answers to questions which have been filling our heads since we have arrived.

"May I ask why you have come now and not at some other time since the craft you call Traveller One crashed here in 1947?"

Tong was the one who responded.

"The reason why we have not returned before now to bring him back, is that we simply did not know where he was. Traveller One is the first of our time crafts, and when he was sent back to 1947, we lost track of his position and of the people who were with him.

"Normally, his tracking beacon would have triggered a call through time to us, but we now believe, because he was brought here underground, there wasn't enough solar or light energy to maintain his power levels. You seem to have realized he needed more light to replenish his level of energy. Something triggered his beacon, and we were able to locate the position the signal originated from. It was then that we were asked to board Traveller Two to come retrieve him."

All eyes turned to Sam, who now comprehended the reason for the flash of light and the deep resonating sound, when both he and Melinda had touched the craft.

Tong continued.

"On another issue, because there has been a lapse of sixty-seven years in your timeline, we assume our friends are no longer alive. Are we correct?"

Sam's heart sank, but it was Hanson who answered that question.

"You are correct. We did find remains not far from the craft back in '47. Your friends must have abandoned it shortly after they crashed. We have kept their remains and will be willing to hand them over to you if you wish. However, I need to advise you that due to circumstances around the time we found them and which I will explain to you later, the bodies are not complete. I will ask Dr. Lee to prepare the remains for you."

Tong and Voot both nodded in agreement, as did Sam.

Lewis was chomping at the bit to ask his first question.

"My area of specialization is the molecular composition of materials. I'm very confused, though. We have been perplexed by the surface of the craft and its composition. Dr. Buckner here," pointing to Sam, "has postulated that the craft is alive and possibly a plant. Yet, you keep calling it a *he*. If I may ask, what is the craft?"

Tong raised his hand toward Voot, indicating she should take that one.

She began, "That is a good question. Traveller One is many things, and you might find it difficult to understand. It actually took our scientists over five hundred years to create him . . ."

She turned to Sam and continued, ". . . and to some extent, we need to . . .", then she stopped.

Voot looked back at Tong, and then nodded. They were obviously communicating telepathically.

Carrying on with her explanation, she said, "We need to thank scientists from this era for giving us the initial concept which led to the creation of Traveller One and Two. They are many things. And yes, they are alive, but not alive in the sense you consider life.

"Dr. Buckner is partially correct in thinking Traveller One is plantlike. We learned hundreds of years ago, in our timeline, that we could borrow from plant DNA and combine or grow these characteristics with what you call molecular memory."

That provoked a reaction from all the scientists except for Howey.

"I see some of you are familiar with the science," Voot suggested.

Lewis responded, "I can't speak for the others, but I have heard of it."

Sam added, "I know of some studies in Israel dealing with research in molecular charge storage, photochromism, and changes in capacitance."

Voot nodded and went on, "Our scientists found documents on the topic and decided to pursue it further. They discovered that they could grow a plant and attach a charge to each of its molecules, essentially making the plant a storage unit which could be retrieved and manipulated, something like the data or information stored in human DNA."

"So what you are inferring," Fitz interjected, "is that they could create a computer from a plant."

"Yes," Voot responded.

"It wasn't long after that, that our scientists applied the concept at the atomic
level."

Lewis interrupted the explanation.

"You're saying the EGG is a computer?"

Voot stopped for a moment and then pursued her description.

"Precisely. Traveller One has characteristics of a plant . . ."

Sam interjected, "A cactus, perhaps."

"Yes, Dr. Buckner, a cactus, because of its ability to survive harsh climates and droughts. Our scientists have been able to grow a computer with some of the characteristics of a cactus, in which every quark within its atoms is a bit of data that can be programmed. In fact, it is what you call a quantum computer."

The reaction to this information was the same and simultaneous with everyone in the room, except for General Hanson. They all drew in a deep breath and sat back in their chairs.

Sam spoke first.

"What you are saying is mind blowing. If that is the case, the computing power of the EGG, sorry, Traveller One, is almost beyond comprehension."

"You are correct. Traveller One is the most powerful computer ever created."

General Hanson was in above his head on the topic.

"Could someone explain what this means?"

Astounded, Lewis picked up the ball and tried to make sense of it to the general.

"Sir, if you could attach one bit of information to each molecule of, say a cube of sugar, you would have the storage or computational power equivalent to anyone of our supercomputers. Now, if you could do the same with each of the quarks, which make up each component of the atoms that make up the sugar molecule, you multiply the power of that supercomputer by a factor of hundreds of billions. And, if I understand what a quantum computer can do and how it should work theoretically, these bits of information, or *qubits*, can each represent any number from 0 to 255, simultaneously. "

Looking at Tong, he asked, "Did that make sense?"

Tong nodded his head and added, "You are right other than the fact that it isn't theoretical in our time. He uses extremely powerful quantum algorithms in order to run all the required programs he has access to."

Listening quietly, Hanson's mind was now working overtime. He was thinking that the visitors were going to steal the most important invention in human history, and on his watch. Its military applications could forever put the US in the position of dominance in the world. Already, he was deliberating where he might move the EGG, preferably to a dark area, to weaken it, so as not to allow it to be located. There were many places this could be accomplished.

"You say it is plantlike in some ways and a computer in others," asked Fitz, "so why refer to Traveller One as *he.*"

"That is because his computing powers are so great, he has become self-aware; thus, we found it difficult to call him an it. He's even developed a sort of personality. He sees himself as a bit of a swashbuckling pirate of ancient times."

The group broke into laughter at that comment.

"So you can communicate with it," asked Sam.

"Yes, we can, by using comthink. That is how we are able to direct him in our time travels."

"Amazing!" responded Sam.

"He was particularly moved by the care you seemed to give him and the tenderness you demonstrated while you touched him," continued Voot.

Howey needed to address the pair regarding an issue which had been on his mind since he had met them.

"May I ask, if you are saying you are us in the future, why would you be so small?"

"I should think that would be obvious. We learned a long time ago that with the excesses of your time period and the depletion of the world's natural resources, we needed to do something to reduce our, I think you call it footprint, on the world. Our scientists began to experiment on accelerating our evolution to be smaller in stature, thereby reducing our need for food and water by at least half of what you need to survive. They also helped us evolve a larger frontal lobe, allowing us to more fully use our brains. Hence our ability to comthink, the ability to communicate telepathically, for one."

Sam was sitting there with a large grin on his face. He was amazed at what he was hearing. Never in his wildest dreams had he thought he would ever be so privileged as to be part of and privy to such a life-altering event.

Just then, Melinda came into the room. She sat next to Sam and whispered to him, "What did I miss?"

"You won't believe what they have revealed. I'll fill you in later. In any event, is the President coming?"

She answered, still in a lowered voice, "No, not yet. He's decided to let you all do the job he brought you on board for. He expects complete and detailed reports twice a day. He does plan to come in a few days; furthermore, he's working with his national science advisers on how to deal with this situation. As anxious as he is to meet with the visitors, he is also quite aware of the ramifications of what is happening here, on the world."

Fitz was next to pose a question.

"I can't believe that my colleagues," as she looked at Howey, "haven't asked how time travel works. Some of the greatest scientists of our time have speculated, and most have concluded that it could not be possible. And yet, you are living proof that it is. Can you describe how it's done?"

Howey gave her a thumbs-up.

Voot took on the question.

"The principle is simple in nature, but extremely complex in its execution. As we have explained, Traveller One and Two have been programmed to use every single component of their atomic structure to be not just part of the matter that they are constructed of, but simultaneously, a qubit of their programming. When fully charged, by absorbing light from any source, they can energize each particle and force them to separate ever so slightly . . ."

Sam's body language changed, and he reached over to cover Melinda's hand which was resting on the table.

"What?" Melinda whispered.

He didn't answer but simply put his finger up to ask her to wait a moment.

". . . and then they emit a pulse of energy which moves them forward a micron. Because quarks, or strings as you call them in your timeline, are the smallest components of matter and energy, they can pass through the minuscule portals into other dimensions or places. Depending which direction in time they want to go into, they use a different mathematical formula."

Sam interjected, "M-Theory?" and then squeezed Melinda's hand.

She looked at him and then whispered, "The cubes with which you tried to describe your hunch about the universe."

Sam nodded.

Voot smiled and continued, "That is what you call it now. We have a different term for it, since it is no longer a theory, but a fact."

Sam couldn't believe what he was hearing. Before he and Melinda were married, he had once tried to explain to her a hunch he had concerning his perception of the theory, which requires at least ten dimensions: nine physical and one time dimension. He had fashioned a series of articulated cubes to show how the three physical dimensions could be connected to the other six. Now he was being told that the M-Theory also held the secret to time travel as well.

Howey, also very familiar with the theory, couldn't help but jump in.

"OK, let me get this straight. You are saying that time travel is possible if, whatever is to do so, is extremely small, in order for it to travel into another dimension."

"Yes," confirmed Voot. "Our universe exists using one of the five mathematical equations you have theorized. It requires our timeline and yours to follow a forward direction in time. The formula which is the exact negative or opposite of ours, has a backward direction in time. The other three formulae are the timelines we need to follow to get back to the timeline we want to go to. The longer we travel in one of these three, the farther we go back or forward in time."

"How small are these portals you speak of?" Howey asked.

"I believe you call them Planck lengths, which are the smallest divisible units possible. They exist at every point in the space of our universe."

"So," Howey continued, "Traveller One and Two basically puff themselves up in order to allow everyone of their sub-particles to pass through these portals you speak of."

"Not only do they 'puff' themselves up, as you say, but also anything within them, such as we, the pilots," Voot added.

When she stopped speaking, the room went silent. No one seemed capable of expressing their astonishment at the information they were being provided.

After a pregnant pause, Hanson spoke up.

"Your answers have definitely given us much to ponder. I would suggest we resume our discussions tomorrow morning. It is presently eighteen hundred hours, and by now I would imagine everyone is hungry and perhaps exhausted."

He turned to the visitors and asked, "Do you require any special type of food?"

Tong indicated that they were vegan and would appreciate a meal with some balance between plant protein and carbohydrates.

Hanson then suggested they make use of the base's accommodations. What he didn't say was why: He didn't want them to return to the Travellers, in case they decided to leave to return to their time.

The meeting broke up after Hanson got everyone's orders, which were prepared in one of the other research pods' kitchen and delivered to Level S

even.

After their meal, they all retreated to their quarters, with Tong and Voot in tow, having accepted to stay in one of the apartments. They had revealed during the discussions at supper, that they were not only travelling partners, but also life partners, much to the delight of the group who simply found them to be adorable.

After having been brought up to speed on all that the visitors had revealed, Melinda headed off to the communications room to call the President, leaving Sam alone in their quarters, assessing what it all meant.

Chapter 31

On her return, Melinda found Sam sitting on the sofa, along with Voot and Tong.

Sam looked up at her and said, "Hi sweetheart, we have company."

Melinda had been caught by surprise, but tried not to show it.

"I'm so pleased you're here. I have to admit I wasn't expecting to see you until tomorrow morning."

Voot tried to reassure her.

"We are sorry for imposing on you. Nonetheless, Tong and I needed to speak to the two of you, in private."

Melinda sat in the upholstered chair opposite them, still wondering what this was all about.

Sam stepped in, explaining that they had arrived at their door about five minutes prior to Melinda's return and that they had requested to speak to the two of them in order to give them information that could not be revealed in the meeting with the rest of the team.

If one was to step back to take in the scene before them, they would swear they were looking at two parents having a discussion with their children in their living room. Tong and Voot sat on the sofa, their feet not touching the floor, their hands clasped together on their laps, in a sheepish pose, waiting for their parents to speak.

"Is this information that I can share with the President?" asked Melinda.

Tong responded with, "I will leave that to your discretion once we have finished explaining why we are here."

Sam looked at Melinda with a puzzled expression and turned back to the visitors.

"I'm curious about what you have to say and honoured, to some extent, that you feel you can trust us with the information."

"We hope that is how you will feel once we are done," responded Voot.

"Now, I'm truly intrigued," Sam quipped.

Tong began what would be a two-hour-long discussion.

"First of all, we are from the time we said during the meeting today. And, we are back to retrieve Traveller One. That was not a lie. By the same token, we do come from a world which has been through a great calamity."

Hearing that, both Sam and Melinda leaned forward, supporting themselves with their elbows, bracing themselves for whatever they were about to learn.

Tong continued.

"Six hundred and fifty years from now, the earth will be struck by a primordial black hole. Do you know what that is?"

Sam shook his head but added, "I know what a black hole is, but I've never heard of a primordial one."

"That is understandable. They were considered theoretical during your time, but proved to be real.

"These entities were created at the birth of our universe and were dispersed by the Big Bang. They have been travelling through space, rarely encountering any other star or planet. As small as they are, which is about the size of an atom, they have one tenth the mass of earth."

Both Sam's and Melinda's jaws dropped in awe.

"One of these will crash into the earth, or rather pass through the earth as though it is not there. It will take only six minutes for it to penetrate and then emerge on the other side, to continue its journey back into space. Because of its mass, the gravitational pull will create colossal shockwaves in the earth's mantle. Estimates will put the effect as being equivalent to one hundred thousand fifty megaton atomic bombs exploding at once."

Melinda picked up on the tenses of the verbs Tong was using.

"You are predicting this will happen in our future. How sure are you?"

"This is *your* future, since it is *our* past."

"Did the world explode?" she prodded Tong further.

"No, that is not how it affected the world."

"What will, or did happen?" Sam asked hesitantly.

"The energy released into the core and mantle first affected the tectonic plates the surface of our planet is composed of. All around the world, a series of devastating earthquakes flattened many of the major cities close to what was called in your time, the Ring of

Fire. In addition, every continent was shaken: Some were hit by tremors that registered as high as 10.2 on the Richter scale."

Melinda put her hand to her mouth and Sam sat back into the sofa.

"That would mean cities such as Los Angeles and San Francisco?" he asked.

"Not just those cities, but Seattle, Vancouver and Tokyo, to mention but a few," admitted Voot.

"My God," Melinda said in horror.

"Millions were killed: in Tokyo alone, seven million died, crushed by collapsing buildings and explosions. Many more were displaced.

"The tsunamis that were triggered by the rolling and upheaval of the continents wiped out most of the coastal cities around the world. The waves generated by the multiple earthquakes travelled at speeds as high as five hundred kilometres per hour and some reached two hundred metres high. Not only was Florida almost totally flooded, but it also sank anywhere from twenty to fifty metres, drowning most of the population.

"It was estimated that within the first week of the shifting of the plates, the number of people who had lost their lives probably amounted to five hundred million."

By now, Melinda was crying. Sam got up and walked over to her to give her as reassuring a hug as he could muster.

He turned to Voot and asked, "Is there anything we can do to prevent this?"

She merely shook her head.

"As tragic as that was," Tong resumed but now spoke in the past tense, "all these cities could have been rebuilt in time and the population could have regenerated. Though in chaos, world governments tried to combine what rescue resources they had left, in an attempt to help any survivor, regardless of origin. They might have been successful."

"You're saying there was more?" Sam fearfully asked.

Tong nodded in the affirmative.

"Next, the shockwaves affected the volcanoes of the earth, in particular the supervolcanoes."

The blood in Sam's face began to drain and he almost felt faint, realizing what he knew Tong was about to explain.

126

"The first to erupt without warning was Campi Flegrei, beneath Naples, in Italy."

"Oh, no," uttered Sam. "How many died?"

"Records show that, of those who had not been killed by the earthquakes and flooding, about one hundred thousand died instantly, with another half million dying of exposure to the fallout and pyroclastic clouds . . ."

Tong paused a moment and then continued, ". . . and an additional seven hundred thousand in the vicinity, due to buildings collapsing under the weight of the ash."

"Any more eruptions elsewhere?" Melinda asked.

"Yes. The next was the one beneath Yellowstone Park. It erupted with a magnitude 8, making it ten thousand times the strength of Mount St. Helens. Hundreds of thousands of square kilometres were covered with ash within the first three days, spreading to cover about one third of the United States within one week. Countless thousands died of ash inhalation, even while trying to evacuate to other areas of your country."

Melinda's arms collapsed at her sides.

"Finally, the supervolcano at Lake Toba became unstable and erupted as well. With these three volcanoes all erupting within four days of one another, millions of cubic kilometres of ash were thrown up into the atmosphere, quickly spreading around the world.

"Soon after, the global economy, travel, law and government, as it was known, broke down. In your United States, by Day 33 after the black hole passed through the earth, there were over four million dead. By Day 172, this number had risen to forty million, mainly due to starvation or the effects of riots everywhere. The situation around the world was similar."

Melinda repeated her comment, "My God. That can't be possible!"

Voot could see the feeling of desperation which was overcoming the two before them. She would have loved to be able to give them some hope, but knew they had to know the entire story.

"I'm afraid it gets much worse. In short, thirty years later, the world's population had dropped to a little over four hundred thousand, surviving on what food, water and shelter they could find, on what was left of the surface world."

Sam was shocked.

"You can't mean that almost eight billion people died?"

"No," Tong stated, "I'm saying that because the world population at the time was closer to twelve billion, that is how many died."

Sam's legs almost buckled underneath him. He sat on the arm of the chair, next to Melinda.

Both were in a state of deep despair over what they had been told. But then a puzzled look came over Sam and he cocked his head slightly.

"Wait a moment, please. The two of you are here, and you say you are from a future beyond the calamity. And, you said 'surface world'. Can you explain what you meant by that?"

For the first time during his description of events, Tong smiled.

"Yes, we are, and yes, I did. You have perhaps guessed the answers to your own question."

He turned to Voot and nodded.

She took over, trying to explain the events that were to happen in the future.

"You are correct in questioning the fact that Tong said 'surface world'. The population there essentially disappeared, as did animal life and vegetation, due to the cold and ice which formed across the surface of the planet."

Melinda appeared to be incredulous.

"So, if you are indicating that the planet died and everyone on it, how is it you survived?"

"What you call nuclear winter, and which gripped the world, lasted about one thousand five hundred years, but the surface temperature rose rapidly during the past five hundred years, our time. The ice has since retreated and life has returned, with our help."

"How is it that you have survived when every one else didn't?" Sam repeated.

"About three hundred years before the black hole struck the earth, the nations of the world began to secretly expand their underground facilities, much like this one, thereby creating what would become underground cities . . ."

Sam and Melinda fixed their gaze on each other in astonishment.

". . . where a select group of people were chosen to move into after the calamity."

Sam had to ask, "How many people are we talking about and how were they selected?"

"The process of selection had been worked on over a great number of years and each generation was screened to find the correct ratio of scientists, engineers, artists and so on. When the black hole struck, the operation to move people below ground began in earnest."

Melinda asked, "Didn't people realize what was happening with the 'chosen' people disappearing around them?"

Voot shook her head, "No, the chaos everywhere was used as a cover for the operation. Additionally, many who had first been selected had been killed, so alternates were designated to replace them.

"As for how many, a quota of fifty thousand people per city had been identified as the required number to help maintain the population over the period of time needed to survive the winter."

"And how many cities were there around the world?" Sam asked.

"There was a total of two hundred and fifty cities. Several were destroyed because of their proximity to the volcanoes, but most survived," continued Voot.

Sam did a quick calculation.

"Which would mean that, in the end, only about twelve million people survived?"

Tong nodded.

"Yes, that is correct."

"What about the people on the surface? Wasn't there any effort to help them?" Sam questioned.

Tong responded, "Difficult decisions had to be made for the survival of the human race. Nothing could be done to reverse the devastation caused by the earthquakes and the nuclear winter. The people on the surface survived as best they could, for as long as they could. Of course, when the numbers dropped to the point where, if they were brought below, they would not overwhelm our resources, we did go to the surface to find them and invite them down."

Melinda understood the logic. It was so bureaucratic in nature, that at first, it seemed inhumane; but, the goal was nothing short of assuring the survival of humanity and civilization.

Sam needed answers to other questions--so many questions, his head was spinning.

"How did they produce the food required to survive?"

Tong explained, "Each city has large growing domes, where all the food required is produced. Part of the planning for the underground facilities was the storing of millions of seeds to produce the plants we would need to live."

Melinda finally regained some of her composure and asked, "What about the animals? Did they bring any down with them, as a source of food?"

"No," responded Voot, "not only would they eat much of the crops needed for the population, but for disease-preventing measures it was not considered a viable option."

Sam remembered that when Hanson had asked them what they would like to eat, they had said they were vegan. It made sense now.

"Can you tell us how it is that you," Sam asked, "became the size you are presently?"

Voot took on the question.

"That is an interesting topic," she said.

"Thirty-five years into the sequestering, as we call it, we realized that our resources were slowly dwindling. Our population was increasing at a faster rate than the projections had anticipated, and the food supplies were being stressed. It was decided we needed to do one of two things: increase the food production or reduce the need for it. For about one hundred years, efforts were made to create space for growing more food. Larger and larger caverns were dug to provide for the required space and that seemed to help alleviate the problem.

"However, as the population grew, it became clear that increasing the food source also helped increase the size of the population. That is when our scientists researched methods to try to reduce the size of the average human, in order to reduce the need for food and water."

He smiled and looked at Voot. They nodded to each other and then he turned to Sam.

"During the research, they found an obscure document in the archives, written by a Dr. Samuel Buckner, that described the concept of gravitational impact on evolution and DNA."

Sam stiffened when he heard that. Melinda's eyes grew large and she exclaimed, "What?"

Tong looked like the cat who had just swallowed the canary.

Now smiling, he continued, "Yes, they studied your work and found the inspiration to develop a method to alter our DNA through the use of magnetism, emulating the gravitational pull of stars."

Sam was reeling from the revelation.

"My research was useful in your survival?"

"Yes, indeed," said Voot. "The name Samuel Buckner is held in high esteem by all in our time, and for more reasons than the theory on gravitational effects on evolution."

The look of surprise and pride shared by Melinda and Sam was apparent to the visitors.

"You mean to say you know of me?" a baffled Sam questioned.

"We have access to all the DNA records of your time and up to the calamity," Voot answered.

"We found both of your sequencing data and they were included as part of Traveller One and Two's programming. So when you first touched him, a beacon signal was sent into the future to let us know he was still alive and where he could be found. Moreover, when the two of you touched him, we were told that you were together in the same location. This, in part, was why we were sent back."

Melinda perked up and followed up on the last comment.

"Because we touched the EGG, sorry, Traveller One, you came back into the past?"

Again, Tong and Voot looked at each other, comthinking.

Tong simply skirted the issue by answering, "Yes. Now, you mentioned you had many more questions, Dr. Buckner. What is your next?"

Sam took the bait.

"You said there were more reasons why my name is important for the future. Can you tell me what those are?"

Melinda was about to put a finger up to get them back to her question, but Voot immediately began addressing Sam's query.

"If you will remember our explanation about how time travel works, well, a paper will be published in six years concerning the angles between the connected dimensions in our universe. This paper earned the author, a Dr. Leonard Wasik, a Nobel Peace Prize in Physics."

Sam interrupted Voot.

"That's my friend."

Looking at Melinda, he clarified, "Remember the friend I spoke about and my hunch theory? the cubes?"

"I remember," she responded.

"He actually won the Nobel Prize?" exclaimed Sam.

Voot continued, smiling, "Yes, and while he gave his acceptance speech, he praised a colleague of his for the inspiration: a Dr. Samuel Buckner."

Sam was blown away.

"I'll be darned," was all he could say.

Tong continued the discussion.

"There is one other area in which you have been greatly influential in our civilization. Our ability to comthink is in part due to you."

Sam looked puzzled.

"But I haven't done any work in that field. How is it possible for me to have helped you develop that ability?"

"It was your research in the different levels of telepathic communication. Once our scientists were able to help us evolve with a large frontal lobe, it became apparent to us that telepathy was possible. It was your research in differentiating the levels of communication down from words or language, to the symbolic level and again down to the fundamental level of being, that precipitated our understanding of how it could work.

"Let me explain why each one of you *heard* us speak in your different mother tongues. It wasn't that we were speaking the words. We were only reaching down to the fundamental conceptual levels of your thoughts and reflecting the ideas back to you. You, yourselves, translated the thoughts into words."

Sam sat back in amazement.

"That is something else. Still, I haven't done any research in that area."

"But, you will," responded Voot, "you will."

****

At that point, Tong interrupted the direction of the discussion.

"I need to explain one more thing, before all of this can make sense to you."

Sam and Melinda glanced at each other.

"Please do," said Sam, "but I don't think anything you are going to say could possibly top everything you've just described to us."

Tong took a moment to ponder how he was going to present the rest.

"Let me summarize the situation in our time. In spite of all the precautions we have taken to ensure the survival of the human race, we are losing the battle, as you would say."

Sam and Melinda looked on with an expression of bewilderment and concern.

"We have all the technology required to house and feed us, to allow us to pursue scientific and artistic advances. What we do not have enough of is the variety of DNA to allow us to continue to procreate and produce viable and different human beings. In short, we are running out of DNA."

Sam was astonished.

"You can't be serious? With the numbers your ancestors protected underground, you should have had enough unrelated individuals to ensure a strong human strain."

Tong seemed sad.

"You are correct. We should have. Regardless, when we began to introduce your concepts of modifying our DNA to enable us to become smaller and capable of living with fewer light levels, we only factored in one direction, effectively cancelling out all the permutations and combinations our DNA could have produced."

He looked at Voot.

"If you think we two look alike, then you might have an idea of what our total population looks like."

Sam was confused.

"If you said there were several hundred underground cities around the world, surely you must have access to all the variables of our DNA."

"You are again correct. We did. About six hundred years after we descended, there were signs. So we contacted the other cities and a combined effort was set in motion to connect as many as possible through a series of tunnels. The ability to intermingle helped stem the flow of the problem with our recessing genes, but only for a while.

"Not long after that, we began to investigate the possibility of time travel to allow us to return to the past, and hopefully find enough DNA to help us not only survive, but prosper as a race.

"We carried out many community-based comthink mind conferences and . . ."

Sam blurted out, "Wait. You can have telepathic conferences?"

Tong wasn't disturbed by the interjection.

"Yes, we can and we do. Actually, it is the manner in which we vote on most of the issues which affect us, including the election of the officials who serve as our leaders."

Sam chuckled and shook his head. He looked at Melinda and commented that it was too bad US and Canadian elections couldn't be conducted in the same way. What a savings that could warrant for the economy.

"Sorry, I didn't mean to interrupt. It's just that it is such a natural application to a marvellous ability," Sam tried to explain.

"I can imagine we are dispensing a tremendous amount of information on you. Nevertheless, there is, how do you say it, method to our madness," admitted Tong.

He continued.

"Our dilemma has divided our population into two camps. One is of the opinion that with our ability to travel back in time, we should return to find the necessary DNA to allow us to continue to live below ground, and allow the surface world to evolve on its own, without the influence of humankind. They believe humans had their chance once and that they failed miserably.

"The other camp asserts that we owe it to humanity to help repopulate the surface world with humans from different times or eras of the past, who, along with help from us, could finally be able to create a new earth above. Indirectly, we too, the people below, would have access to DNA which would allow those who want to remain there, to continue as we have for over a millennium and others to move to the surface world."

Melinda is the one who asked the obvious question.

"Which camp do you represent?"

Voot answered, "We are of the second persuasion. We feel that one of the fundamental strengths and defining qualities of humankind is the proficiency to make choices. The others want to impose one set future, while we believe we have the ability to give all a chance to choose their future."

Sam chirped in.

"This raises the issue of all the sightings and alleged alien abductions and experimentation. Are they real or fictitious?"

"They are probably real, but they have not happened yet in our timeline," Voot admitted.

"Pardon? I'm not sure I understand," responded Sam.

"It would seem they could be the result of the other camp winning the argument in our future."

Tong looked at Voot yet again. He nodded once, she shook her head, paused and then nodded as well.

Their interaction did not go by unnoticed and when Tong returned his gaze on him, Sam asked, "Can you tell us what that was all about?"

"Yes, indeed. It may be by chance that we are here with you. On the other hand, it isn't by chance that we have been sent back to meet with you."

After a short lull, he then continued, "We have been sent back to help direct our future."

Melinda was starting to understand the argument that the time travellers had been trying to build.

"What does that have to do with us?" she asked.

"We . . ." Tong reached over to hold Voot's hand, ". . . we are here to plead for you to come back to our present with us."

Part Three

Chapter 32

There was a long pause while Sam and Melinda tried to process what Tong had just asked of them. The two sat in a stupor, not quite sure if the request was a joke.

Sam finally broke the silence.

"You are kidding us, aren't you?"

Voot calmly replied, "No, we are absolutely sincere in our request."

Melinda spoke up.

"We simply can't pick up and leave everything behind. We have family, jobs, commitments . . ."

"We know what it is we are asking of you. If it wasn't important for your future," a moment passed before Voot continued, ". . . our future, we would not entreat you to sacrifice this way."

Sam was still sitting on the arm of the chair, above Melinda.

He turned to look down at her, and with a questioning tone in his voice, almost whispered, "What do you think? Is it something we could consider?"

Melinda's eyes grew larger with the realization that Sam was actually subscribing to the idea.

She turned her gaze to the visitors and asked, "Why us?"

"For one, the two of you carry the DNA of generations from three continents, "Voot responded. "This could help us immensely in bolstering our genetic pool. And, we could not think of a better person to invite, but the one which is to a large extent responsible for our survival, based on the contributions we spoke about."

That answer caught Melinda by surprise and prompted her to acknowledge the possibility of going.

"Why exactly is it so important that we go with you into the future, and, could we come back to our time if we chose to do so?"

"The answer to the second question is easier to give you. Yes, you could come back to your time, but not one in which you have already lived. It could be moments after we leave this time, but not before. Two of the same person cannot exist at the same time."

"So we could go into the future," Sam queried, "and then return before anyone here, now, would know?"

"Essentially, yes," Voot confirmed.

Melinda seemed to relax a little.

"Would we remember anything from the future if we came back?" she asked.

"Everything," Tong answered.

Again, a long moment of silence in the room.

Sam turned to Melinda and a huge smile appeared on his face.

"Do you understand what an incredible experience we've been offered? Think of it. To actually go to the future and see it first-hand. The advances, the technology!"

Melinda could see Sam was ready to go. Even so, she had a feeling of apprehension, but the fact they could return to a few minutes after their departure was consoling and made the opportunity that more palatable. That being said, so much could happen while in the future which could jeopardize their return.

They needed to talk this over, and in private.

Melinda put her hand on Sam's thigh and squeezed it to get his attention. He looked down at her. She simply wrinkled her brow, cocked her head slightly and looked at him with large eyes.

He caught on.

Sam turned to Tong and said, "This is an incredible opportunity and we are so grateful for the chance you are giving us, but, we need to discuss this more before we can give you an answer."

Tong nodded and responded, "That is understandable. We fully agree. However, we believe you should decide in as little time as possible."

Melinda picked up on the urgency in Tong's tone.

"Why so?" she questioned.

He continued, "While I was explaining why we had come back into our past, Voot was probing the thoughts of the people there, including you, I'm sorry to say."

Sam cut in.

"Why didn't anyone's nose bleed as it did when we first met?"

Voot explained, "That is because I did a very shallow read, only trying to get an impression of your mood or state of mind. All but the general were processing the information with a positive approach. He, on the other hand, was in a different mood: it was one of reserve and of fear of loss. I had the impression, and still do, that he plans to move Traveller One in order to hide him from us."

Melinda spoke up.

"If true, that would not surprise me. I can understand why he would resist losing the gem of the base. And, I wouldn't put it past him to move it sooner rather than later."

She looked at Sam and added, "I think we need to discuss the issue now."

Sam rose slowly from the chair's arm, followed by Tong and Voot, who had to hop down from the sofa.

Tong turned to Voot and said, "I believe we should leave them alone in order to discuss our request."

Then addressing Sam and Melinda, he added, "When you have decided, please come to our quarters and inform us of the verdict, so to speak. We will wait for your visit."

On that note, he ushered Voot toward the door.

Sam reached it before they did, cracked it open a little and peaked out to see if anyone was in the hallway. There was no one, so he opened it completely to allow the two to leave.

"Do you want one of us to escort you to your room?" Sam asked.

Tong smiled and shook his head.

"No, that will not be necessary. If we could find you from over two thousand years away, it won't be difficult to find our room just a few metres from here."

And off they went down the empty hallway.

As Sam closed the door behind him, he leaned up against it and exhaled with a loud *whew*.

"I don't know exactly what to say at this moment."

Melinda was still sitting in her chair and responded with a whispered yes, me too.

Sam walked to the sofa and took his seat once more and asked, "Are we really contemplating going with them?"

They spent the next hour discussing the request. By the end, they had agreed they could not *not* accept.

Another hour was taken up deliberating upon how they would circumvent the security at the base, in order to get to the EGG without being noticed.

Then, Melinda left to make the difficult call to the President, while Sam headed in the other direction, stating simply that there was something he had to do.

Chapter 33

"Harry, I'm telling you, I'm not ready to let it go." Hanson was speaking loudly to General Baxter in Washington, from the communications room.

"I'm responsible for the craft as long as it is here at the base. I need you to authorize me to do what I've suggested."

"Look, Jonathan, I don't disagree with you. But, what type of message do you think we would be sending to the, how did you call them, the visitors?"

"Damn the message!" Hanson yelled back. "We've had possession of it for over sixty years--hell! almost seventy--and possession is nine tenths of the law. We need to ensure they will negotiate with us for as much of the technology as they can reveal to us, starting with the EGG. This is more than we ever dreamed of."

"You are correct on that count," replied Baxter.

"But, I'll need to inform the President and he'll be the one to decide."

He looked at his watch.

"It's presently 2300 hrs. I'm not about to disturb the President now. I'll contact him first thing in the morning and see what direction he will give us. What I do suggest though, is that you secure the craft first thing in the morning. We can then implement whatever the President wants us to do."

"Good," responded Hanson, "I think that's a good idea. Will do. Thanks Harry. I'm just acting on my gut feeling about this. Good of you to have my back."

They hung up and General Hanson left the room. On his way to the surface and his home on the base, he decided to stop into the lab where the time vehicles were.

As he walked in, the lone guard snapped to attention.

"Sir, is there anything I can do for you?" he asked.

"No, soldier. I'm just looking in on the two crafts."

Peering up at them in the brightly lit room, he noticed that Traveller One and Two now resembled each other in colour, with the movement of the green hues similar on both.

Without meaning to, he found himself speaking to no one in particular.

"Wonderful, aren't they?"

"What, sir?" the guard called out.

Catching himself before saying too much, Hanson quickly responded with, "Nothing. Just thinking out loud."

He turned to leave, but then stopped and addressed the soldier.

"Keep your eyes open. I'll have new instructions for you soon."

Then, he gave the soldier a quick salute and left.

As he did, General Baxter in Washington was picking up the phone.

Chapter 34

Melinda sat at the table with the secure telephone on it. By now it was past midnight and she dreaded disturbing the President. But she knew she had no choice. She needed to convince him that it was best to allow them to go with Tong and Voot into the future.

She dialled the number for the White House and got the receptionist to transfer her to Alexander's library. She was stunned that he picked up the call almost immediately.

"Yes, Melinda. What is happening?" was his first response.

"Sir, there have been major developments here that you need to be aware of," she blurted out.

"I hear you," he said, "just start from the beginning."

She summarized that part of the story concerning the primordial black hole and its effects on the earth and on mankind. She suggested that Tong and Voot could be believed, in part because they were without a doubt from the future and that all they had told them about the issues of their survival would seem reasonable, if only based on their physical attributes.

Then she relayed the fact that both herself and Sam had been asked to go into the future with them. This took the President by surprise.

"Why do you think they did that?" he asked.

Sam and I aren't a hundred percent certain, but it would seem it may have something to do with our DNA and the fact that Sam has had, or rather, will have something to do with their survival."

"How is that?" Alexander queried.

"Apparently, some of his research will have been instrumental in key advancements they will make."

"Well, I'll be damned," Alexander said. "Maybe there really is something to his theories. I wonder what impact his thoughts on Homo symbolicus might have had."

"Nothing on that concept, sir. But we feel we should go for the ride."

The President paused for a moment.

"You might not know, but General Baxter called, not more than half an hour ago."

That stunned Melinda.

"Why, sir?"

"He has authorized General Hanson to move the EGG in the morning and I've agreed with him. We can't lose the craft. There is too much at stake here."

"But, sir," pleaded Melinda, "there's more to consider."

"And, what would that be, Melinda?"

Melinda told the President about the fact that if the two of them did indeed go into the future, there could be more to gain by learning everything they could and bring it back to the present. The EGG itself was quite the prize, but its technology was so far advanced that it could take centuries before it could truly be understood, let alone used. What she and Sam could learn, though, could possibly be implemented more readily in the present.

Once again, the President took time to consider what Melinda had suggested.

"And you say you could actually return to our time, minutes after you would have left, but actually be in the future for a much longer period of time?"

"It's what we've been told, sir," Melinda responded in anticipation.

"Give me a minute to take this all in, will you please," requested Alexander.

Then he broke the long silence.

"OK, you need to go, but I haven't been informed about this."

Melinda's eyes grew wide but she kept her cool.

"Understood, sir," she said with resignation.

Alexander explained, "I think you are right. Either way, the EGG has served its purpose. I, however, can't be linked with its disappearance. And, whatever information you come back with could be extremely useful--*a bird in the hand* so to speak."

By then, Melinda was smiling.

"Yes, sir. I'll let Sam know and we'll make this happen. Is there anything else, sir?"

"Just one thing: Know that I'm not rescinding Baxter's orders. If you don't make it out, I want the EGG."

"A bird in the hand issue?" Melinda commented.

Alexander laughed.

"You're learning. But, no, Melinda, there is nothing more other than to wish you two good luck. I truly envy you. I can just imagine what adventures await you there, or then, should I say.

"Though I have not met them, please convey my regards to Tong and Voot. I would have had so many questions of my own to ask them. Perhaps the information you return with will fill in the blanks. Just a few more items."

He spent the next several minutes giving Melinda further instructions and when done, he hung up.

He sat back in his chair, trying to assimilate everything Melinda had told him. Though he could not put his finger on it, something was not quite right. His political experience told him there were gaps in the narrative. It wasn't that he didn't trust Sam and Melinda. On the contrary, he did so implicitly. So that wasn't it.

His doubts were less about them and more about the unknown. What if they didn't return when they thought they would? Or worse, what if they didn't return at all? What dangers would they face?

He was beginning to overthink the situation, feeling more and more helpless by the minute.

Then it hit him: It was all about his need to control any situation and be able to solve any problem, while protecting the ones he loved.

He had to do something, but what? He sat for quite a while pondering over all his options. That's when he realized he only had one.

He turned to face the desk he was at, pulled open the centre drawer, removed a sheet of paper and began to write.

Chapter 35

Melinda walked back to their quarters, down empty hallways and through an empty cafeteria. She thought how eerie it appeared. For the first time, she also sensed the sheer physical depth of the level they had called home for the past while. Until now, it was as though they had been on the surface, with only a roof and walls to protect them. Now, she felt as though she was a miner, somewhere down deep inside the crust of the earth.

Or was the feeling one of weight concerning the decision she and Sam had made to go into the future. Even though they were to return soon, as she had stated before, there were so many things that could go wrong. They could become ill, or worse, they could die. Or the EGGs might not work with them on board. Or there would be a mistake in the time they returned. Or, how would their families be told about any of it?

No! She forced herself to think reasonably.

She wasn't going to double-guess their decision. They would do their part in this incredible . . . what did the President call it? . . . adventure.

When she arrived at the room, she found Sam waiting.

"And?" he asked.

She nodded and said, "It's a go. The President approved it. But we only have until early morning."

"Why is that?" Sam asked.

"Hanson has been ordered to move the EGG to somewhere secure."

She checked her watch.

"That's in three hours, give or take," she added.

"That should be plenty of time," responded Sam, "but we'd better not delay. We know what we have to pack, so let's hop to it."

Melinda looked over to the right of the sofa and saw something bundled up in a white lab coat.

"What's that?" she asked.

Sam looked sad when he explained he had gone for the remains of the time travellers who had died those sixty plus years before. He had to bring them back to the future, if only as a sign of respect to the families they must have left behind.

147

Melinda was touched that Sam would think of that. She approached him and hugged him tightly and then gave him a kiss on the cheek.

"I know why I married you," she whispered in his ear.

"But, I think we need to get this show on the road, don't you?"

The two went into the bedroom and began packing some of their personal effects: mainly changes of underwear and light clothing, which they put in a small carry-on with wheels and a handle.

Sam pulled out a knapsack from the closet and went into the living room, only to return with it on his back. Melinda understood that he had placed the remains in it.

She went to the night stand on her side of the bed, pulled the drawer open and reached for the Ammolite pendant Sam had given her the previous Christmas. She then carefully placed it around her neck. Seeing her do it brought a smile to Sam's face.

They then walked to the door, opening it slightly and peeking out to see if anyone might be in the hall. Seeing no one, they quietly slipped out and headed to Tong and Voot's quarters.

They reached their door and before knocking, checked again to see if they were being followed. Still safe.

Voot answered the knock and smiled as she stepped back to allow them in.

As they entered, Tong suddenly appeared from behind the kitchen bar counter, barely visible due to his height.

"Welcome," he said, "and have you decided?"

Sam answered firmly, "Yes, we have. We are accepting your invitation and will go with you."

This time it was Tong's turn to smile.

"We are pleased you have chosen to do so. We promise you will not regret your decision. When do you suggest we leave and how do we get to the Travellers?"

Towering over the two visitors, Sam and Melinda explained their strategy and why they had to move quickly.

They also told them what he had in the knapsack. Voot was moved to tears and thanked Sam profusely.

Within ten minutes, the four were sneaking from the door into the corridor. Sam and Melinda walked side by side, trying to camouflage the other two behind them. All was quiet in the bedroom wing and as they approached the cafeteria, they slowed to see if anyone might happen to be there.

Unfortunately, one of the two guards was taking his break, enjoying a cup of coffee and a doughnut. Also, who else was there but Howey. Luckily, both had their backs to the hallway entrance and did not see the group.

The four reversed direction just far enough to get out of their line of sight.

Melinda glanced at Sam with a concerned look on her face. "What do we do now?"

Sam thought a moment and said, "This could be to our advantage. One of the two guards is here, leaving only one in the lab. All I have to do is distract these two long enough for you to get Tong and Voot out of the cafeteria and into the hallway leading to the main road. I'll find a way to join you there and we'll continue on to the lab."

They slowly walked to where they could just barely see what was happening in the cafeteria. Sam pulled the knapsack off his back and handed it to Melinda, who carefully slipped it on.

Sam then walked into the cafeteria, trying to stay as quiet as possible until he was about to overtake the two sitting at the table.

"Hi, guys," he said, quickly taking a chair opposite them.

"Couldn't sleep either?" he asked.

Howey just nodded.

"Funny, sir," said the guard. Then he added, "Just on my break. I have another twenty minutes."

Sam tried to act nonchalantly.

"I couldn't sleep, thinking about some of the results of one of my experiments. So I decided I'd just check on the data."

Howey looked a little puzzled and was about to ask which experiment Sam was referring to. Realizing he could be in trouble, Sam tried to remain as expressionless as possible but wrinkled his forehead and shook his head ever so slightly.

Howey caught on and stifled his question.

The guard hadn't detected the communication between the two, too busy chomping on his jelly doughnut.

Sam looked at Howey again and said, "Guess I'll head over to the lab. I'll fill you in tomorrow morning."

"OK. See you then," Howey responded, still unsure what had just transpired.

Sam took a quick look toward the exit hallway and just got the tail view of Melinda silently ushering Tong and Voot ahead of her, out of the cafeteria.

Before leaving, he turned to the soldier and added, "I'll see you later as well. Take your time. I'll let the other guard know you'll be a minute or two longer. Then he can tack on a few extra minutes to his break. What do you think?"

The guard looked up, stopped munching and with a morsel still in his mouth, responded, "Not regulation, but if you don't tell, I won't either."

"You're on," Sam answered and then left.

He so wanted to run but knew he needed to act casually. He might have gained a bit of time, but he understood they barely had twenty or so minutes.

As soon as he was out of sight, he looked back to make sure he was alone, and as such, ran as fast as he could to reach Melinda and the other two.

He did so at the golf cart bay. Everyone was already sitting, with Melinda in the driver's seat, waiting for Sam.

Hopping in next to her, he said, "Let's move. We don't have a lot of time. I'll have to improvise when we get to the lab."

The cart was already moving quickly toward its destination. On the way, Sam gave Melinda instructions to drop him off and to move just beyond the curve in the road, so that they could remain unseen from the entrance to the lab. He was going to try to convince the guard to take an early break while assuring him that he would look after the EGGs while he checked on his instruments.

Melinda barely stopped, dropping Sam off before scooting away to the spot Sam had recommended. She got out of the cart and, pressing her back against the wall, slowly crept up just enough to see the entrance to the lab, but not be seen herself. Her heart was beating rapidly.

Sam slowly walked into the lab, waving to the second guard and yelled, "Hi. How goes the battle?"

The soldier responded with, "Same old, same old. Nothing different from all the other nights I've spent here. Boring, but easy to take."

"I suppose so," said Sam.

"I couldn't sleep so I thought I'd make myself productive."

He sat in front of his instruments, pulled the long ticket tape to look at the squiggles and pretended to analyse the data. He checked his Emopulse watch and saw that he only had minutes to get the guard to leave and let the others in. Otherwise, he would somehow have to surprise and overtake the guard. He really didn't relish the thought of that option.

Looking over to him, he said, "Hey, aren't you due for a break?"

"Yes, as soon as my partner returns," he responded.

"I just left him and one of my team. They're having a good time in the cafeteria. Too bad he has to leave so soon."

He paused a moment.

"Hey, I'm going to be here at least an hour working on this. I can look after things if you want to head off early for you break. I don't mind, actually."

The guard pondered on the offer.

"I honestly shouldn't, but a longer break would be nice. I could get into real trouble if anyone found out."

Sam smiled and added, "If you won't tell, I won't either."

A big grin crossed the guard's face and he said, "Thanks, that would be great. OK, we'll see you in about an hour. I really appreciate this."

Sam knew he had lied to both guards and that they truly could get into trouble over this.

"Not a problem. Enjoy."

With some luck, Sam thought, they would have gone to and been back from the future before the two soldiers returned. They would find Sam sitting there in the same spot. He made a mental note to remember what he was wearing, so as not to raise questions when they found him then.

The soldier left the lab and headed down the hall toward the cafeteria. It would take him about ten minutes to get there, in time to stop the other guard from leaving.

Melinda saw the guard exit. She waited thirty seconds, got back onto the cart and drove it around to get to the lab.

Everyone scurried to join Sam.

"OK, how long will this take?" he asked the two visitors.

Tong said that from start to departure, it would take about fifteen minutes. There was much he would like to explain to them about what would happen in order to prepare them and what they would experience on the way. But Sam asked that they summarize it for the sake of their safety.

Tong asked them to board the Travellers, Melinda with Voot and himself with Sam. That way, the energy drain of the Travellers would be roughly minimized and equal. Then he explained that once inside, the Travellers would seal the entrances and begin channelling the energy through their programming. As well, once seated, Sam and Melinda should lean back into their chairs and not worry about what would happen.

"I'll explain to Sam the rest once the process has begun, as will Voot to Melinda."

"OK," said Sam.

He reached over to Melinda and drew her into his arms. Looking deeply into her eyes, he said, "You good, sweetheart?"

She nodded yes.

"You know I love you and everything will be alright."

Then they kissed and held each other tightly.

Halfway through their embrace, they were all startled by the alarm siren.

The howl was deafening.

Sam and Melinda looked at each other somewhat like deer in headlights, not quite knowing how to react.

That's when Sam said, "They must have figured out that the details of my story didn't quite configure and that I'm up to something."

Tong had to yell over the alarm, "Hurry. We'll be safe inside the Travellers."

Turning to Voot, he comthought for her to take Melinda and get inside Traveller One. She nodded and grabbed Melinda's hand and pulled her toward the ramp beneath the craft.

Both Sam and Melinda had to crawl up behind each of the two visitors, Melinda with the carry-on, Sam with the knapsack.

On her way into the craft, Melinda thought to herself that she was happy she was wearing slacks.

This was her first time inside the vehicle and she marvelled at the interior, much as had the other scientists.

No sooner had they entered, than both ramps melded back into their original positions as part of the outer skin of the Travellers.

By then, the two guards had arrived by cart and had run into the lab, closely followed by Howey. They saw that the ramps had retracted and were amazed at what was transpiring.

The patches of lighter and darker green were now moving in every which direction around the skins of the crafts, shifting faster and faster, to the point that the surface of the two Travellers was now fairly uniform in colour. The lights in the lab, including the additional ones that had been requested by the team, were also beginning to glow more brightly.

The guards weren't sure what they could do. They knew bullets would have no effect on the crafts, but they also knew the alarm would bring a large contingent of soldiers down to the research pod level. They would have hell to pay for this!

As the three of them watched, the rest of the scientists appeared at the door, all in their nightwear, dishevelled and bewildered.

"What's happening?" yelled Fitz.

Howey turned to her and simply said, "It's Sam."

Lewis looked around and realized Melinda was not there either.

"No, I think it's both Sam and Melinda," he yelled back. "She's not here, either."

Howey turned to look at the two Travellers and said in total confusion, "What have they done?"

****

Inside the crafts, similar routines were being performed.

Both Voot and Tong had entered first and once everyone was inside, they told the Travellers to close the entrances and the noise from the alarm subsided completely. They then asked their two guests to sit on one of the three small seats in the crafts.

As Tong was doing, so was Voot, mentally connected to each other and acting in unison to prepare Sam and Melinda for their journey.

"Please relax and sit there in that seat. I have a few things I need to tell you in order to make your time travel easier to understand," she said.

"Do we have enough time for that?" asked Melinda.

"Have no fear. Nothing the soldiers can do will harm Traveller. We need only to wait long enough for the Travellers to program themselves with our instructions and prepare the energy flow which will make it happen."

The same scenes repeated themselves from craft to craft.

"When you sit back into your seat," Voot spoke to Melinda, "it will mould itself to you". . ."and encase you," Tong completed the thought to Sam.

"Once cocooned inside, Traveller will scan you," Tong added, "and will incorporate all that is you into its programming, which will make it possible for you to travel with it."

"Will I be awake?" asked Sam.

"You will be in a dreamlike state, but you will be aware," answered Voot to Melinda.

"We need to let you know that you will find the trip to the future very pleasurable and perhaps shocking," said Tong, "but you will gain an understanding of one of the great questions in life," completed Voot.

"Now, please relax and lean back into the seat," both Tong and Voot requested of their guests.

As Sam and Melinda complied, they found the fabric of the vehicle slowly shift and change. First, the seat lengthened to accommodate their size. Then, it slowly began to mould itself around their bodies, beginning with their legs and arms. The sensation was that of being wrapped tightly in warm jello.

A thought crossed Sam's mind and he had to ask, "Tong, before this process is complete, could you tell me where the controls are? Howey was killing himself to figure it out."

Tong smile and simply raised his arm and pointed to his head with his finger.

Sam gave a good laugh and said, "I should have guessed. You control him through telepathy."

Tong nodded, just as the fabric of the craft wrapped around Sam's torso and then his head.

In Traveller One, Melinda was going through the same procedure, but just before her head was covered, to Voot's amusement, she took a deep breath, as though it would be her last.

Then the two drifted off into a gentle sleep.

Tong and Voot comthought one last time and sat down in their own seats, waiting for the craft to meld with them.

****

Twelve minutes after the alarm sounded, General Hanson came rushing into the laboratory, followed by some fifty or more soldiers.

Approaching one of the two guards, he yelled, "Soldier, what is happening here?" Not waiting for an answer, he addressed his second-in-command and hissed, "Turn that goddamn alarm off! I can't hear myself think."

Focusing again on the soldier, "I asked you what, in the hell, is going . . ." the alarm stopped and in the absence of the interference, the general's voice sounded that much louder . . . ON!"

At a complete loss for words, the soldier blurted out, "Sorry, sir, but, sorry, sir. I, we were on break. Doctor Buckner . . ."

Just then, several of the lights grew in intensity and blew simultaneously with a loud bang causing a stream of sparks and shards of glass to fly everywhere.

Everyone in the room instinctively ducked and looked up at the source. Then another blew and another, and yet another.

Howey tapped Fitz on the shoulder and pointed to the Travellers.

The colour of the skin had now gone from the mixed level of a few minutes before, to a bright, glowing green.

Hanson finally understood.

"They are leaving!" he yelled.

Turning to the scientists, he barked orders to take cover.

Then he ordered all the soldiers to assume positions around the crafts and prepare to fire. The troops rushed around the two ships and raised their rifles to shoot at the general's command.

Hanson made a quick reconnaissance of everyone's position and began to utter the order to fire.

155

At that moment, the two crafts disappeared.

Chapter 36

The Travellers were functioning perfectly. As described by Tong and Voot to the team, every quark within the EGGs had been mapped and sufficient energy was streamed to each quark to weaken the strong force keeping them together. This would cause them to separate ever so slightly, allowing them to be bumped through the small Planck-length openings connecting the two dimensions. Every particle flowed through these portals, much as water flows through a sieve.

As they drifted sideways into this other space and time, the travellers dreamt the whole time although they weren't actually sleeping. They weren't quite in a REM dream state either, but rather in a state of reverie where one seems to have some control over what is happening, or, at least is able to control the reaction to events in the dream.

Sam and Melinda felt as though they were floating in a void. They could hear sounds and voices. Some were familiar and others not. It was difficult to pinpoint, but during the voyage, Sam was under the impression he heard his name called and the voice seemed to be that of Melinda.

Furthermore, Sam thought about his father and mother and he felt as though they were speaking to him, asking how he was and what he had been up to. He relived many moments of his childhood with them and described what he had accomplished. He felt their pride in him, not quite knowing how he could possibly feel the emotion.

He then thought he heard the bark of a dog. The sound was familiar to him and he immediately recalled his favourite pet, Arthur. He spent time playing with his pet, seemingly throwing his ball and having the dog retrieve it.

On her ship, Melinda was encountering some of the same types of thoughts and feelings. In her case, she felt as though she was spending time playing with her nephew, Troy. She had loved him dearly, but he had drowned in her sister's pool when he was only seven. She was thrilled to talk to him and reminisce about all the fun times they had had. It was then that she had experienced some of the best moments of her life.

Then, both Sam and Melinda seemed to be in the same dream, interacting with each other as though at a family get-together.

All the while, they were feeling bliss and love all around them.

Tong and Voot had been correct. This experience would be a pleasant one.

Then, everything went black and the two slept.

Chapter 37

Sam awoke from his sleep and tried to focus on his surroundings. He still felt a little woozy, but he was quickly coming to.

He blinked a few times and looked down at his body which was under a blanket. He lifted it, only to find he was lying in a bed, wearing what seemed to be a hospital nightgown.

Glancing next to him, he found Melinda, wearing the same type of garb. Just beside her, close to her head, he saw a pole from which a drip-bag was hanging and a tube snaking down to her right arm. Only then did he realize that he too was connected to the same type of medical bag, and also had a needle stuck in his left arm.

He started to panic a little, but took comfort in the fact that Melinda was there with him.

Looking a little more closely at the room they were in, he realized it looked much like the one in their quarters in the research pod at Area 51: same layout with closet, night tables and a similar headboard.

Damn, he thought. We didn't make it into the future. How could General Hanson have stopped us?

Melinda was beginning to stir and wake up.

Sam grabbed her by the arm closest to him and shook it, saying, "Melinda, come on, wake up."

"Uh, what?" was all she could manage to mumble.

He shook her arm a little more and added, "We're back in Area 51. We never made it out."

Then he looked around and realized they were alone, without a guard at hand.

Melinda was now almost fully awake. She too cast her gaze around the room only to be as shocked as he was.

"How is this possible?" she asked.

"I don't know, but I think we're in a heap of trouble," Sam admitted.

A knock was heard at the door of their bedroom, and their heart almost burst out of their chest.

The opening became wider and a head peeked in.

They fully expected to see a soldier walk through, but to their surprise, it was Voot.

"Voot!" the two screamed out.

"Are we glad to see you. But we're back . . . or still . . . in Area 51. How is it you're walking about freely? Shouldn't we all be in jail or something?" Sam asked.

Voot smiled broadly.

"Yes, we are in Area 51, but not the one you know. We are in the year 4666, according to your calendar.

Sam and Melinda were stunned and speechless.

Voot entered farther into the room and was followed by Tong, who was holding a tray of food and drinks. Having discarded the one-piece jumpsuit they had on when they first met, Voot had donned a brightly coloured blouse and loose-fitting slack-like pants. Tong had on a long-sleeve sweater made of the same material as the original travel outfit he had worn while at Area 51 along with black pants.

"Welcome back to the world of the living," Tong said as he set the tray down on the night stand next to Melinda.

Sam hesitantly asked, "We made it into the future?"

Voot nodded.

"So, how is it we are also in our quarters, or similar quarters?" he added.

"We replicated the room you had in the past in Area 51, if only to try to make your surroundings a little more familiar. We were hoping to be here when you roused, but it seems we were a little late. We apologize for that and any concerns you might have had."

Melinda finally spoke.

"I have to admit, we almost panicked."

Looking at the IV tube, she asked, "Do we really need these?"

Voot answered her, "Yes, for a short time. The medication is to help you get over your time trip more quickly. Otherwise, you could be incapacitated for several more days."

"How long have we been out?" Sam asked.

"It has been about ten hours. But don't worry, you are doing well," Voot responded, "and we thought you might be hungry and thirsty."

She reached onto the tray and took two glasses of what seemed to be orange juice.

"Have a sip of this," she urged.

Melinda took one of the glasses and then handed the second to Sam. They sipped on the liquid and realized it was indeed orange juice.

Sam was surprised and said, "You grow orange trees?"

"That and much more," Tong said, "but, enough for now. There will be time to show you all we have."

Melinda sipped on her juice but noticed one more glass on the tray with a clear liquid in it.

She looked at Voot and asked, "What is that and who is it for?"

Again a large smile appeared on Voot's face. She turned to Tong and it was obvious they were comthinking.

Both then turned to gaze at Melinda.

"When we arrived in our time, Traveller One informed us of an unexpected event," Voot resumed.

Sam and Melinda both appeared a little worried.

"No, no. Do not fret. Traveller One told us that we two, Melinda and I, were not alone on the trip here."

Now, that set off alarm bells in both Sam and Melinda.

Voot continued, "As Traveller One mapped out everyone's molecular and nuclear makeup, he realized there were three of us."

She picked up the glass containing the clear liquid and handed it to Melinda.

"This is for your baby."

Chapter 38

Tong and Voot stood there, still smiling, looking at the other two, once more speechless with jaws dropped to the floor.

Finally, Sam was able to utter, "You are kidding, aren't you?"

With an expression of confusion on his face, Tong answered, "No. We are not in the habit of kidding. Melinda, you are pregnant."

Spontaneously, both Sam and Melinda broke out in a wide grin of their own. Melinda turned to Sam, just in time for him to embrace her as best he could, being held back by the IV tube in his arm.

They kissed for a long time, ignoring Tong and Voot.

When they finally let go of each other, Sam pulled back a little and still not acknowledging the presence of Tong and Voot, asked Melinda if she was OK and feeling well.

Melinda chuckled and half sarcastically said, "Certainly. I'm pregnant, not ill."

That's when it hit Sam that he was now not only a husband, but a father-to-be.

"Incredible!" he said, "Did you know?"

"Not at all," responded Melinda.

She turned to Voot and asked, "Would you know how long?"

"Traveller One estimated, based on the molecular count, that you would be about two weeks along."

Melinda turned to Sam, "That would make it sometime around our romp in the shower back in the apartment."

She turned to Voot once more and asked, "Do you know if it's a boy or a girl?"

"Do you really want to know?"

Melinda looked at Sam and he nodded yes.

"I'm pleased to tell you," began Voot, "that you will be the proud parents of a boy."

The thought of a baby boy brought a swelling of joy and pride in the two new parents.

At that moment, Tong stepped in and indicated he and Voot would leave for an hour or so, in order to allow Sam and Melinda to take in this announcement privately.

As they turned to leave, Sam stopped them.

"Wait. I think I speak for the two of us when I say thank you, not only for the wonderful news of our baby, but also for having invited us on the greatest adventure of our lives. We couldn't be happier."

With that, Tong and Voot left, prompting the parents-to-be to once more lovingly hug each other.

Chapter 39

Tong and Voot left the couple alone for two hours before returning, this time with a doctor. She was as tall, or rather, as short as the other two and indeed had many of the same features.

Sam and Melinda were still sitting in bed, still connected to the IV tubes. They had eaten the food and beverages on the tray, including the special liquid for their baby.

"We see that you are fully awake and I am sure, ready to see our world," said Tong.

"But first, please let the doctor have a look at you," he added.

As the doctor approached, Sam could see that she was somewhat hesitant.

"Is there a problem, Doctor?" Sam asked with a smile on his face.

She stopped just short of the bedside and blinked her large blue eyes.

"None whatsoever, Dr. Buckner. It's just that you are the first ancient I've ever seen face to face. I've studied your anatomy and thousands of pictures of your time. Although it seems strange, it is truly wonderful to see you in the flesh, so to speak."

Although Sam was taken aback by being called an ancient, he laughed and Melinda giggled.

"I can fully understand your reaction. We experienced something similar when we first met Tong and Voot. What would you like us to call you?"

The doctor smiled in return and answered, "I'm Doctor Peters."

Sam cracked up but quickly added, "Sorry, I'm not laughing at you because of your name. I was just surprised that you would have a name I would be familiar with."

Sam turned to Tong and Voot and asked, "It never crossed my mind, but do you have a surname as well?"

Voot responded with a wink, "Yes, we do. You may address us as Mr. and Mrs. Belvedere."

"I'll be damned," Sam responded, "I should have asked sooner."

The doctor then proceeded to remove the needle from both arms, checked their eyes and ran the hand-held scanner over their bodies. She then spent most of the next few minutes examining Melinda more closely.

Addressing Voot, "I think they are healthy and weathered the *slip* perfectly."

"As for you, Mr. and Mrs. Buckner, I'll be available to you anytime, day and night," and then she left the room.

"Heavens," Melinda commented, "you've re-introduced home visits by doctors. A definite improvement."

Sam was eager to start asking the multitude of questions he had.

"Tong, I have so many questions to ask already. When could we sit to discuss them?"

Tong gestured for a little patience.

"We'll answer any and all questions. I think you should dress and meet us in your quarters' living space. We've taken the liberty to clean your belongings. You should feel more at home wearing your own clothing and sitting in familiar surroundings."

Voot touched Tong's arm to get his attention. They comthought a moment and Tong nodded.

Voot turned to Sam and Melinda and added, "We would like you to know that we will not be alone to answer some of your questions."

Melinda looked puzzled.

"Who else will be with us?" she asked.

"Our Zone Leader has expressed an interest in meeting with you, to welcome you officially to our time and city."

Until that moment, everything had seemed both normal and weird all at once. Their surroundings and being with Tong and Voot had put them at ease. Then came the news about Melinda's pregnancy, also comforting and exciting, but learning about it in the way they had, was a surreal experience. Now, they were going to meet an official of the future, much as President Alexander had wanted to do with the two visitors. Their new reality was beginning to sink in.

Melinda spoke first, "Please tell your Zone Leader that we would be pleased and honoured to meet with him."

Voot smiled and corrected Melinda, saying, "The Zone Leader is female."

Melinda quickly apologized for the mistake and turned to Sam.

"There's so much we will need to learn about the future."

Sam added, "I agree and we'll have to shelve all our presumptions and biases."

Voot chuckled and gestured with her hand for Melinda not to worry.

They left the room, leaving Sam and Melinda to dress and prepare for their first sit down in the future.

Chapter 40

The two walked out from the bedroom and stepped into the living room area. Again, it was almost an exact duplicate of the one they had left in the past.

One of Tong's comments about them still being in Area 51 now struck Sam like a sledge hammer and made him dizzy: same place, slightly over two thousand years from when they left! This was going to be more difficult to absorb than he had originally thought.

He took Melinda's hand and led her to the sofa where Tong and Voot were waiting.

Seeing only the two, Sam asked, "Is your Zone Leader not coming?"

"Yes, she should be here very shortly. She had a distance to cover in order to get here. She is travelling by *VacTube* from the eastern zone," Voot explained.

"VacTube?" Melinda questioned.

"Yes," responded Voot. "All twelve North American zones are connected by a network of communication tunnels through which, what you would call trains, travel. The trans-zone shuttles are long tubular vehicles which float on electromagnetic cushions and are propelled at very high speeds from one zone to another. They can reach speeds of eight hundred kilometres per hour."

"Amazing!" exclaimed Sam.

"How are they and your cities powered?" he added.

Voot responded, "We are getting far ahead in the sequence of information we need to provide you. At any rate, to give you a short answer, all our power is generated by fusion reactors. We essentially have all the energy we need."

Sam leaned back in his seat and whispered to himself, "Fusion power. Incredible."

Tong stepped in and said, "Let us get underway by answering some of your other questions while we wait for her arrival."

Sam was eager to begin, as was Melinda.

"OK, let's start with you confirming the fact that we are actually some two thousand six hundred and fifty years from when we left?"

"Precisely," responded Tong.

"And, we are still on Level Seven of Area 51 in the quarters' wing of the research pod?"

"No, that is not quite correct," answered Tong, "we are actually on Level Twenty-seven, but the Travellers are indeed on Level Seven."

That took Sam and Melinda by surprise.

"Let me explain," Tong said.

"Back in your time, Area 51 was one of the first underground military facilities. It was well built and hardened, allowing it to survive any nuclear war or severe earthquake. It was eventually expanded by tunnelling deeper and farther from the central core. The original structures were maintained and have survived to this day.

"When we received the signal from Traveller One, we were both shocked and pleased that it was actually coming from one of the rooms within the complex. It was a simple thing to move Traveller Two into the same space and then slip back in time to the moment you saw us appear."

"So, until then, you had no idea where it was?" Sam asked.

"No, not really. Originally, Traveller One had been grown in one of our underground laboratories not far from what was your city of Roswell. He was moved to the surface and the three pilots took it back to 1947 as a first full test of the time travel concept. Unfortunately, our scientists had not factored in the elevation of the ground on the surface. They had not realized that during the great cataclysm, the crust had heaved about two hundred metres in that location."

"So when it materialized," Sam jumped in, "it was in mid-air."

"Yes, exactly. The Traveller follows the gravitational orbit about a little more than a metre above the surface of the ground beneath it. It had to have fallen until it hit its orbit line, seriously injuring the pilots. We assumed one or more of them might have survived. They probably exited the craft and then disappeared, leaving the Traveller by itself. Now we know what happened to them."

Sam thought a little and then added, "So, that's when the military found the Traveller and moved it the several hundred miles to Area 51, and the rest, as they say, is history."

Tong nodded in the affirmative.

"That explains a lot about the myth of Roswell," interjected Melinda, "but I have a question for you."

"Please, feel free to ask," said Voot.

"I remember you saying something about time travel being a pleasant experience. I had the most vivid dream about my nephew and then Sam."

Sam looked at her with wide eyes.

"You too? I dreamt about my parents and then you, as well," he admitted.

Melinda turned to Voot and continued, "Is that what you were talking about?"

Voot was about to speak, when a knock was heard on the door.

Tong stood up and said, "Ah, that must be the Primus."

Turning to Melinda and Sam, he added, "Don't forget your question. I think you'll find the answer quite fascinating."

He walked to the door and opened it allowing the Primus to enter.

A diminutive woman walked in, dressed in a full-length multi-coloured slip. She looked much like Tong and Voot, with her large blue eyes and button nose and mouth. Her hair was long, straight and pure white, and was pulled over her left shoulder resting over her breast.

Sam and Melinda rose to meet her.

In a voice sounding similar to Tong's and Voot's, she spoke as though she had inhaled helium.

She raised her hand to give Melinda a handshake and said, "Welcome. I am Primus Lee. You must be Melinda?"

She turned to Sam and repeated the gesture to shake his hand.

"And you must be Samuel?"

He hadn't been called that in a very long time and in spite of the slightly comical difference in their heights, Sam put on his most formal front and instinctively bent over to reach for her hand.

"Yes, Madam Primus," he said hesitantly.

She laughed and corrected him, "Please, call me Lucy. I prefer keeping things as informal as possible."

Sam gestured for her to make her way to the sofa. Once she was seated, Tong and Voot took their places on either side of the Primus. Melinda sat in one of the upholstered chairs while Sam went and retrieved one of the chairs from the table in the kitchenette.

When they were all sorted out and comfortable, Primus Lee began.

"This is indeed a momentous day for us and all of humanity. I am so pleased to welcome you and I hope you will find your time here pleasant and productive."

Melinda spoke up, "Thank you. I've been asked by our President to offer you his greetings and best wishes. He has authorized us to come on this fact-finding mission, in the hope that you will share as much information as you can with us."

The Primus looked at Tong and obviously comthought with him.

She then turned back to Melinda and Sam, and continued with her message.

"Thank you for that. I am as amazed as, I would think, you are about the fact that we are exchanging civilities across more than two thousand years. This is beyond what we had originally conceived when we began our time travel project."

She looked at Sam with a sad smile.

"May I also express my gratitude for the kind gesture you extended to us, in returning the remains of our people. You have no idea how much this means to all of the citizens of this sector."

She then took on a more business-like pose.

"Now, I understand you are interested in getting as much information as you can. Rest assured, no question will go unanswered and there is nowhere you may not go, in your quest to find answers to your queries."

"Thank you," Melinda responded, "we are thankful for the opportunity to be able to learn as much as possible. I am at a loss to describe how important it is to my President."

Primus Lee interrupted her.

"Of course, there is one item you need to be made aware of."

Sam's heart sank. He had kept quiet, leaving the diplomatic protocols to Melinda. But now, he felt uneasy about what information they might be receiving.

"I believe," Primus Lee continued, "that you have been told about the difference in opinion our citizens have concerning the use of the surface world."

She looked at Voot who simply blinked and nodded.

"I must impress upon you that the debate is a very serious one. I, personally, am of the same persuasion as Tong and Voot. We believe we need to assist in repopulating the surface world. The fact that you are here means it is possible to bring ancients to the present.

"Your being here," she continued, "means our faction now has the proof that it would be possible to bring more of you to our present. We are worried about what lengths our opposition would go to in order to prevent this from happening."

Sam quickly responded, "Do you mean they would try to kill us?"

"No, not at all," Primus Lee said, "we are a world without murders. We are a peaceful race. But there are many ways of preventing more of you from coming to the present. I simply offer the information for you to be aware of the controversy this has created. Know that your presence has been made public around the globe, a fact that is politically charged for many."

Melinda was the one to speak up.

"Thank you for revealing that to us. We feel terrible that we might have created a problem by coming to your time. Moreover, we do plan to return to our time and perhaps our departure will contribute to the resolution of your problem."

"That would be something to hope for, but I fear the cat is out of the bag," Primus Lee said.

"This issue is one we will have to deal with. It is not one of the problems you need to concern yourselves with," she added.

"But now, I must tend to more matters which require my attention."

Lee rose, followed by the others. However, before reaching the door, she turned and added, "No matter what the conclusion of the controversy will be, I am so pleased you have come and that I have had the opportunity to meet you."

Melinda extended her hand to the Primus.

"It is we who are honoured to have met with you. Rest assured, we will bring back nothing but good news about your time."

Sam also shook hands with and bid farewell to the dignitary.

Chapter 41

Sam and Melinda stood there, speechless, for several moments. It was Tong who broke the silence.

"Well, may I say that went well. Why don't we sit for a moment to discuss a few issues and then we can take you for your first tour of our world."

This time, Sam and Melinda sat close to each other on the sofa, next to Voot and across from Tong. Melinda reached over and intertwined her right arm with his left, grasping his hand firmly. She was having more difficulty than she had originally thought, in accepting the fact that they were really there, twenty-five hundred years in the future, pregnant with their son and just about to walk out into a whole new world. The grip Sam responded with let her know he was feeling the same.

"Do you have any concerns about some of the information the Primus shared with you?" Tong asked.

Sam caught Melinda's eye and the two turned to Tong, shaking their heads.

"No," Sam responded, "I can only imagine the furor the knowledge of your presence would create if it was made public in our time. So, the controversy which ours is creating is more than understandable."

Tong glanced at Voot and both smiled slightly, nodding their agreement.

"That is true. We appreciate your approach to the problem and believe it will be important to remember it as we walk among our people. Now, are there other issues you would like to discuss before we leave on our tour?"

Again Sam and Melinda looked at each other in a quizzical manner.

Melinda shook her head to indicate she had none, but Sam hesitated and turned to Tong.

"I have one question relating to a topic Melinda brought up just before the Primus' arrival."

"Please, what would you like to know?" Tong responded.

"Ever since I woke up, I too haven't been able to shake some of the feelings I sensed as we travelled to your time."

"Yes, we were wondering how long it would take you to ask about that," Voot replied with a smile.

"Well, the dream was so real. You had told us that the trip would be a pleasurable one. Is the dream I experienced something the Traveller was programmed to make me see or just something I subconsciously wanted to feel?"

Melinda reacted excitedly to this comment by claiming that she was hoping they'd be able to explain this phenomenon.

After taking a moment to organize her thoughts, Voot began to speak.

"The answer to your question raises profound issues for us. Firstly, I can say that the Traveller was not programmed to have you live those thoughts. When we first began to slip through time, we too experienced similar moments. It took us many trips in *SlipTime* to be able to come to some conclusions and to understand what they were."

Sam's eyes were fixed on Voot, as were Melinda's, waiting to hear the rest of the explanation.

"The answers we reached intensely affected our beliefs and values. We realized that when we would travel forward in time, each passenger would have the same types of visions: those of people we had lived with and loved, as well as those of a host of other *minds* with which we could communicate. We began asking questions of these entities and analysed the answers which were received."

Sam's eyes grew large.

"Are you saying you could consciously ask questions and get answers other than those you might expect to get in a dream?"

"That and much more," Tong interjected.

"May I ask," he went on, "Who did you dream about?"

Sam responded, "I dreamt I was meeting my parents and even played with my favourite dog. Melinda was in the dream as well, and in it, she introduced me to her nephew . . ."

Melinda was dumbfounded at what she was hearing.

"You dreamt of Troy?"

Confused about her reaction, Sam simply answered, "Yes. In the dream we all had a wonderful time getting to know each other."

Melinda sat open-mouthed.

"I had the same dream!"

She turned to Tong.

"How can that be?"

Calmly, Tong continued.

"We had the same type of experiences in our travels and when we accumulated enough data, we realized that we were indeed communicating with these entities."

The blood was draining from Sam's face. Both he and Melinda were trying to wrap their mind around the revelation they were being made privy to.

"Are you saying I was actually communicating with my parents, along with Melinda and Troy?"

Tong simply nodded.

"My God," whispered Sam.

Hesitantly, he added, "How is that possible? Are you saying there's an afterlife?"

"Of sorts," answered Voot.

She went on, "After many SlipTimes, we concluded we were in fact communicating with the actual people, or their thoughts and feelings. Without going too deeply into all the comthought conferences we have had and the science behind the phenomenon, let me give you the short explanation of the conclusion we have arrived at.

"We now know that every thought and feeling anyone has throughout their lifetime emanates from their body as radio waves . . ."

Sam tensed up, remembering a discussion he had had with Melinda about the very theory he had developed and how he thought it applied to telepathy and things such as mediums and psychics.

". . . and these waves not only travel out into space, but also through inner space. If you'll remember how we described the Travellers' work and how we can travel through side dimensions and bump our way back to the timeline we want to get to . . ."

Sam interrupted, "My friend's Nobel Prize."

". . . Yes, precisely. Those thoughts and feelings also travel in those other dimensions we use to slip through time. Because we are telepaths, we believed that was why we could interact with these radio waves. But now, because you have interacted with them as well, we have concluded it is probably not our telepathic abilities, but simply our life force that excites or energizes these radio waves. This alone has been a revelation to us."

As had happened so many times in the recent past, both Sam's and Melinda's minds were reeling.

"So we were actually interacting with the people we were dreaming about and with each other?" Sam asked.

"Yes, and no." Voot paused and then resumed, "You were interacting with who they were. They were actually alive, in thought, because of your life force, without which they would be in what you would call limbo. They cannot formulate new thoughts, only fall back on those they had while they were alive. Nevertheless, your link to Melinda was real because her life force is real and present."

A hundred questions of *how* this worked, almost short-circuited Sam's mind.

Melinda dared a question.

"Because the occurrence was so wonderful, would you call that Heaven?"

"It is interesting that you should ask," Voot responded.

"We, too, have had many comthought conferences over the topic and we are still debating the issue. What complicates it even more is that, when we travel back into time, we again undergo sessions of communication with these entities. The difference, conversely, is that we experience fear, regret and anxiety. Some of our philosophers have suggested this would be similar to what you, in your day, call Hell."

Melinda wasn't quite sure how to react to that. It would seem this confirmed the old religious idea of Heaven and Hell, but also presented a possibility to describe a new state of being for the departed, allowing them to be in both places at once.

Sam was still trying to understand what Tong and Voot had described. He was struggling to find a plausible explanation to solve the problem.

"Is it possible that our thoughts and ideas, say the good ideas, as they emanate from our bodies as radio waves, do so at different frequencies from the bad, moving more easily in one dimension of inner space than the other?"

"We've considered that as a possibility," said Tong.

"OK," Sam added, "So, what if . . ."

Before he could complete his sentence, Melinda squeezed his hand.

He stopped in mid-sentence and looked at her, only to see an expression on her face which he understood to mean this might be a good time to stop the questioning.

"Oh, OK," he said. "There will be plenty of time to discuss this later."

Looking at Melinda, he added, "It would seem we might both be right about all those issues we spoke of regarding psychics, life after death and the meaning of life. I feel so close to understanding all of it."

Melinda kissed him on the cheek.

"This is truly an adventure like no other, isn't it?" she said with a smile.

Chapter 42

Sam and Melinda walked holding hands, following Tong and Voot along a familiar-looking hallway leading away from the quarters they had been in. After about twenty metres, they reached a dead end. To their left stood what seemed to be an elevator, but the doors were only about a metre and a half tall.

Voot turned to Sam and said, "We will be heading up to the tenth level. We apologize for the height of some of the doors you will be using on the way. We created the rooms you first found yourselves in to meet your usual height restrictions."

"It was considerate of you to do that for us. Still, we'll just have to be a little more careful walking in and out of rooms," Sam responded.

Then he added, "I do have another question which has been on my mind since we first met you. Being a biogeneticist, I am curious about your species. I understand you are our descendants and are human. But obviously, you have evolved. What do you call yourselves?"

Tong answered the query.

"We call our species *Homo gnoman*. Once we reached our present state through our engineered evolution, one of our scientists was asked to label the species. He had a bit of a sense of humour and thought a variation--taken from your time-- of the word gnome, the small garden variety, would be appropriate. So, we adopted the term *gnoman* to describe us."

Sam and Melinda smiled at the obvious tongue-in-cheek reference.

Tong gestured to Voot to call for the elevator.

She turned and passed her hand between a small slit in the door frame, interrupting a beam of light which Sam realized was the way for someone here to call for an elevator.

The doors suddenly and quietly swished open, revealing a very feng shui-like interior. The whole area seemed to be one moulded off-white unit, with no sharp corners, reminiscent of the inside of the Travellers. Unlike present-day elevators, this one had a bench which ran around the three interior walls, just at the correct height for Tong and Voot to sit comfortably, but not their guests.

Sam and Melinda had to duck as they entered the elevator cavity and even had to crouch a little when standing inside because of the low ceiling.

"Though the seats are low for you, I would suggest you sit down as best you can. The ride will be more comfortable that way," Tong added.

Once more, Melinda was thankful she was wearing slacks and a blouse. She had to sit with her legs bent to the side, trying to look stylish, resting her thighs on the bench for stability.

Sam had a less polished look. He sat with his arms propped on his parted, bent knees, which almost reached his chest level. If ever he had felt his height, this was the time.

The doors closed silently and the elevator cage moved upward gradually at first and then sped up. A soft, female voice sounded out the levels as they rose. At Level Fifteen, the elevator slowed down and suddenly veered to the right, to begin travelling horizontally.

"Wow," exclaimed Sam, "this thing also goes sideways?"

"Yes," Tong answered, "our connecting network forms a large tubular grid which not only allows us to move up or down, but also laterally in order to let us reach any area on each of the levels. If you wish, I can take you to the pod depot to see the wheel and stability mechanisms, as well as the tub system we utilize."

Sam felt like a kid with a new toy at Christmas.

He grinned and said, "That's a date."

Melinda chuckled when she realized that the look between Tong and Voot indicated they didn't understand the meaning of *a date*.

A few minutes later, the elevator shifted back into a vertical direction and finally toward Level Ten.

Before they reached their destination, Voot felt she should try to prepare the two for what they were to see.

"When we reach Level Ten, we will be stepping out into our main city area. People will be milling around, shopping and going about their business. Your arrival there will not surprise them.

We've had a city-wide comthought conference to prepare them; therefore, if anyone is surprised, it will be you."

Melinda thanked the two for being so considerate. She too was giddy with anticipation, but tried to look cool.

The pod slowed down and the passengers rose to their feet. The doors swished open once more and they all stepped out into the short alcove which opened to the main street.

Sam and Melinda followed their guides out. One look, and both stared open-mouthed at what they were seeing.

They were . . . outside!

Chapter 43

They stepped out of the alcove into a space that resembled Times Square: tall buildings with video billboards, shops and theatres, and hundreds of people wandering around. True, they were all short, but nevertheless, the place was busy and resembled the New York they both knew.

Sam's and Melinda were spinning around, trying to take it all in. They were so surprised at what they were looking at that they were oblivious to the hundreds of eyes focused on them.

Sam turned to Tong, with a stupefied look.

"How . . . how is this possible? Aren't we below ground?"

He looked up and actually saw the sun dipping quickly behind one of the buildings.

Melinda squeezed Sam's hand to get his attention and pointed down to the main roadway.

"Look how far this goes."

"I know," Sam responded, "I don't get it. This isn't possible. Either that, or we're still in the dream state we were in while getting here."

He looked down at Tong and asked, "How is this all possible?"

Tong smiled and pointed to a small outside patio with tables and chairs.

"May I suggest we take a seat there and I can explain what you are seeing. It will all make sense to you."

Sam took Melinda's hand and followed Tong and Voot to the patio. As they walked in the direction of the restaurant, they were now very much aware of everyone's eyes on them. It was reassuring to also see the smiles and the private reactions of glee on their faces.

Unfortunately, the tables and chairs weren't of normal size, much like the bench in the elevator, but the two giants didn't seem to care.

They all sat at a table for four, and while still looking and trying to absorb what they were seeing, Sam said, "OK, explain how all of this is possible."

Tong began his explanation.

"Obviously, what you have before you is not the real Times Square. That is long gone. What we have created is the closest facsimile we were able to reproduce, based on images and videos of your time. Similar to the streets in old Las Vegas which had images represented on the ceiling covering the road, we have created holographic representations of the scenes we are looking at."

"Holograms?" Sam quizzed.

"Yes. A few years after our ancestors descended into the underground cities, they realized that the functional, but nonetheless dreary environment they lived in, would create a great deal of stress on the population, leading to strife and conflict. Finding a solution to the potential problem became one of their priorities. Our best engineers were able to propose building on the rudimentary science of your time concerning imagery, or more specifically, holograms. They realized that if the feeling of being in a more natural setting, whether that of a city or the countryside, while being below ground, would probably be the single most important element to a stable and happy society."

"And the level of sunlight? Sam asked. "I assume that is to compensate for your large eyes and pupils."

"Correct," responded Voot. "Our ancestors engineered us to need less light, therefore allowing us to keep our energy usage here below ground at a much lower level."

Tong paused and then asked Sam a simple question: "You have lived for a short while in Area 51. Do you believe you could have done so for a lifetime?"

Sam gave Melinda a quick look.

"No. Though it felt comfortable, that sensation was only due to the fact that we understood the stay was temporary. I see your point."

Sam quickly added another question.

"How is all of this powered?"

"We use fusion generators. The larger ones are for the basic infrastructure of each city and the intercity transportation systems. Much smaller ones on each level meet the needs of the local consumption of power. We are totally self-sustaining," Tong stated with delight.

"You've mastered fusion power?" Sam said with amazement.

"Actually, your descendants did, not long after your time. We simply miniaturized the equipment," Voot added.

Melinda suddenly grabbed Sam's arm to draw his attention to her. She looked frightened. At the same moment, Tong and Voot turned to look at the crowd passing by, only to centre their gaze on three individuals who had stopped to look at the visitors.

Sam asked, "What? What's wrong?"

She quickly reached into her pocket and retrieved a tissue and then dabbed Sam just below his left nostril.

Sam took the tissue and realized there was blood on it. He continued to wipe his nose, while looking curiously at Tong and Voot.

The two were now standing, staring into the crowd with a scowl on their faces. They were silent but it was obvious they were communicating telepathically with someone or some of the people there. They were obviously furious at an occurrence of sorts.

"Is there something wrong?" Sam asked.

Voot turned to look at him while Tong continued to stare down three individuals.

"You were just attacked," she explained.

"How can that be?" Sam exclaimed.

"They were deeply probing your mind to get information. They are of the other equation in our discussion about our future and your possible role in it."

Sam turned to look for the people Voot was referring to, only to notice that every other spectator was now also staring at the three.

Voot continued.

"Our Primus explained that there were many ways of posing a danger to you. One is probing. The fact that you have bled from your nose is an indicator that not only do you have some ability to communicate telepathically, but that subconsciously, you tried to fight them off. That is a good thing."

Sam turned to Melinda and rose his eyebrows, recalling his nose having bled during their first encounter with the gnomans.

"I got a bunch of images," he said, "although none I could focus on. Mostly, I sensed anger or fear."

Turning to Voot, "Does this mean Melinda is in danger as well?" Sam asked, concerned.

"Everyone from your time has the potential, but at a rudimentary level, and each of you, to a different degree. It was our genetic manipulation which enhanced our abilities to communicate our thoughts this way and to reach our level."

"We can all do it?" Melinda asked Voot.

"Yes. It's a matter of concentrating on the concept or idea of the thing or feeling you want to send or receive. Any effort in formulating the word itself prevents you from reaching the fundamental level of the thought you want to project."

At that point, Tong turned back to his guests, but not without a quick, second look at the three, who had moved on and away.

"I am sorry for what has just happened. Had I been able to react more quickly, I could possibly have prevented the incident."

He put his hand on Sam's shoulder.

"Are you feeling well?"

"Yes, I am. It's only a nosebleed. Nothing serious," Sam answered.

"It could be," Tong responded. "Rest assured that I will be on my guard from now on. This cannot be allowed to happen anymore."

Sam looked at Melinda and then back to Voot.

"Does this mean we have to stop our tour? Please say that isn't so?"

Tong fixed his gaze on Voot and they comthought.

"No. You have travelled twenty-five hundred years to get information. We will continue, as long as you are up to it."

Sam dabbed his nose once more and saw that it had stopped bleeding.

"Absolutely. Our mission is too important and there's so much to learn. I think I speak for Melinda when I say that we are eager to continue."

Melinda simply nodded yes and rose from her chair.

"Shall we go?" she asked.

Tong and Voot appreciated the courage the two were demonstrating and felt they had chosen well.

****

The remainder of the day was spent touring the rest of Level Ten, strolling into the little shops along the way. Though Sam and Melinda knew they were but walking along semi-circular roadways, much like, yet larger than, the ones in Area 51, the images they were seeing were somehow projected on the walls, making them feel as though they were actually sauntering along the streets of New York.

The following two days, they visited several more of the levels, some of which housed the residential areas, with holographic projections of small subdivisions. Others were more utilitarian, much deeper in the complex and devoid of the projections of the other levels.

The ones which housed the agricultural and the manufacturing units were huge and cavernous, equivalent to the Sarawak Chamber on the island of Borneo. These, of which Tong and Voot stated there were many more, bore resemblance to the cafeteria back at Area 51: circular but much, much larger. Measuring six hundred metres in diameter and one hundred and fifty high, they were filled with hydroponics or manufacturing robotics, producing all the food the gnomans consumed or the goods which stocked the shelves of the stores they had visited. The grow-op caverns were brightly lit, while those housing the robots required little or no light, since everything was automated.

Both Sam and Melinda never seemed to run out of questions and Tong and Voot never tired of answering them. When they had no answer for a particular question, they simply comthought to an individual who did.

Tong and Voot were to finish the tour planned for the couple on the following day, by taking them up to the surface world. They were also promised a special treat, after a final meeting with the Primus.

****

Later, after having supper, Sam and Melinda were exhausted and requested returning to their quarters on the twenty-seventh level. They needed some alone time and a chance to mull over everything they had seen.

They showered and then retired to their bedroom. Sam was propped up in his PJ bottoms, leaning against several pillows, while Melinda, in a soft cotton nightie, sat hugging her knees with her chin propped on them, facing him.

"I can't believe what Tong and Voot have shown us," Sam commented.

"No kidding. It's incredible that a whole society, or rather civilization, has been able to exist and even prosper below ground for so long," Melinda responded.

Both went into a bit of a mental trance, reliving everything they had experienced.

Melinda broke the silence by asking a totally unrelated question.

"What are we going to name our baby?"

Sam was shaken out of his reverie and grinned.

"We haven't had or taken much time to discuss that have we?"

Melinda instinctively put both hands over her stomach, prompting Sam to reach over and place his over hers.

"Believe it or not, I've been thinking about that very issue for the past few days" he said.

"So, what would you like to call him?" Melinda asked.

"Well, I fancy Jacob and we could call him Jake, for short."

Melinda chuckled and shook her head.

"You fancy, do you?" she said.

Sam responded with, "What?" feigning hurt at the comment.

"I love the name," she said. "Could we also give him a second name?"

"Sure. Which one?"

Melinda teared up a little.

I'd like to call him Troy, after my nephew.

Sam's dream of Troy while travelling to the future flooded his memory.

"I think that would be a fantastic middle name. Jacob T. Buckner has a great ring to it."

Melinda looked into his eyes and smiled.

"I love you."

Sam simply pulled her over to him and kissed her.

As tired as they were, their lovemaking was intense.

****

About the same time, but deep in the city complex, the three individuals who had scowled at Sam and Melinda were meeting in one of the large caverns housing the machinery which controlled the VacTubes in this zone. The noise from the huge fans was deafening but the group didn't seem to mind.

They had, in fact, selected the place because of the noise level: It would prevent anyone who might by chance come down to the site from overhearing their discussion. As well, the noise would be distracting enough to hamper anyone's ability to comthink who might happen upon them trying to probe their minds in order to understand what they were talking about.

In spite of the volume of noise around them, the three were concentrating sufficiently to block out the interference.

". . . So, the question is when? When will we send them to?" one asked.

The leader of the group comthought back, "We need to send them to a time when they cannot influence our timeline."

A variety of images were shared in response to the question.

One was the image of a large inland ocean and young mountain range, the beginnings of the Rockies, in the distance. Large dinosaurs could be seen roaming between the lush forest and the beach.

"No!" comthought the leader. "We cannot send them to a time when they could not survive. That is against our code."

Another image was shared among them, projected by the third conspirator.

This one was obviously millions of years in the future of the first scene. The inland sea was gone, as were the dinosaurs. There was a lake, though, but this one was the product of melting ice from the kilometre-high glacier which could be observed on the horizon far to the north. People could be seen there and according to their clothing of fur and animal skins, it was evident that the time period was about ten to fifteen thousand years in the past, at the end of the last Ice Age.

"Hmm," the leader mused out loud.

"Better, but even if they were to have no way of influencing the future, their chances of survival would still be slim."

"What about this time period?" the leader asked.

They all experienced the image of a desert landscape, with mountains, much like the terrain Sam and Melinda would know from their time at Area 51. To complete the picture, a stagecoach, pulled by four horses could be made out forging its way along a narrow dirt path, kicking up dust in its passing.

"Perhaps this would be better," added the leader.

"It would be a time when they could find ways to survive. They could communicate with the other humans of that era, and no matter what they said to them about us and the future, no one would ever believe them. As well, there is no technology available then for them to create inventions which could affect our timeline."

The others nodded and comthought their approval.

One of them questioned the leader about the procedure he intended to follow to send Sam and Melinda back to that time.

"I've contacted several sympathizers who are willing to help. Among them are two of the maintenance crew on the pod level where the couple have their quarters. They have already installed the equipment which will render them unconscious. It will be a matter of getting them up to the Traveller level, along with provisions to help get them by until they can forage for food on their own."

"When will we put the plan into action?"

"Tomorrow night, after they have returned to their rooms. Our sources tell us that the Primus intends to meet with them later tomorrow. We fear she will ask them to join her faction and work with her. We need to make sure they have no time to become part of their movement."

They paused for a moment, allowing the noise to fully envelop them.

One of the three looked at the leader and comthought, "You do understand what you are asking of us? Whether or not we succeed and/or are found out, we will be banished from this zone and from our families and friends, forever."

The leader glared back at him with a stern look on his face.

"A small price to pay when you consider what we will be doing for the world. It must be allowed to evolve naturally, without

188

the influence of humans. If our species dies out below ground, that will be retribution for what we have done to the planet. Who knows: Another intelligent species might evolve. They might be able to work with Nature as opposed to trying to rape and exploit her as our ancestors have done."

There was silence between them.

After a moment, the leader placed his hands on the shoulders of the two accomplices.

"It's time to go. There is still much to do. Just trust that this is the only course of action available to us and the right one to follow."

They nodded and all turned to head to the elevator which would take them to their tasks.

Chapter 44

The next morning, Sam and Melinda met Tong and Voot and were taken up to the seventeenth level for breakfast. Much to their surprise, the hologram was a replication of the Montmartre district in Paris, with its boutiques and quaint cafés.

Melinda had the quiche and knew from their tour of the food production areas that there were no chickens or other animals anywhere underground, due to the issues of hygiene, food supplies and emissions. Although the piece of pie she had was meatless, it was quite savoury. Sam opted for the chocolate croissants which satisfied his sweet tooth. As for coffee, both found that what was touted as a latte, was far from the rich-looking beverage which was advertised. They joked that when they returned to their time, it would be nice to actually go to Paris and savour the real thing with real milk.

While they ate, the four spoke about what they would see on the surface world.

" . . . and what type of flora and fauna can we expect to encounter?" Melinda asked.

"Unfortunately, most of the animals you are used to seeing in your time disappeared during the cataclysm."

"No," responded Melinda. "So all the horses and deer, elephants, dogs and cats are gone?"

"Yes and no," answered Tong.

"In their wisdom preparing for the future . . ."

Voot turned to Tong quickly and they were obviously comthinking, a little to Sam's consternation.

Tong blinked his large eyes signalling he agreed with Voot and continued.

" . . . our ancestors harvested DNA from every known genus of animal and vegetation, much as scientists in your time, and had it stored in underground repositories buried deep beneath the permafrost in several countries around the world.

"The plan was to wait until the surface world was warm again and reintroduce these seeds and the animal DNA in the wild. This is something we have been doing for the past one hundred and fifty years.

"Once the debate over whether or not to bring past humans into our time to repopulate the surface is resolved, we will either leave the surface to itself or allow these humans to work with plants and animals they would be familiar with."

Knowing what was on Melinda's mind as well as his, Sam interrupted Tong by asking, "Where would you fit into this plan, assuming your side of the argument won?"

"Obviously, we would be compromised if we tried to live on the surface. Our sensitivity to light, our skin colour and our physical size would not lend themselves to being able to fully cope with the world above or with the tasks that would need to be accomplished. In spite of that, we would work with the surface people to assist them with some of the technology we possess and negotiate a share in the abundance the surface could offer."

Tong got up from his seat and suggested, "Should we go show you what we are talking about?"

Sam and Melinda couldn't hide their eagerness to see what the world above looked like now. They quickly rose and followed Tong and Voot toward what seemed to be an opening in the side of one of the buildings lining the street. Above the opening was a sign which read *Métro*.

No sooner had they entered the hallway, than the Parisian skyline disappeared and they were in a plain utilitarian corridor. They reached a bank of elevator doors. Selecting one, Tong summoned the transportation pod and ran the back of his hand over a sensor on the left side of the door saying, "Seven, Traveller bay."

When they had all taken a seat, as uncomfortable as that was for Sam and Melinda, the pod glided upward, laterally and then upward again. When it stopped and the doors opened, the four walked out into a large space Sam could have sworn was the laboratory room where they had worked on the Travellers back at Area 51.

"Traveller One conveys his pleasure in sensing you," Voot said.

Sam looked at Melinda in amazement and simply replied, "Please tell him we do too," not quite knowing which of the two was actually Traveller One.

Voot quickly led them to a large six-metre square door off to the right of where they stood. Again, passing her hand through a slit on the left of it, the door dropped down into the floor, revealing a slightly larger empty chamber.

"This is the elevator we use to move the Travellers to the surface," she said.

"Actually, it is the only access to the surface in our zone," she added.

They walked in and turned to the opening. Voot once again ran her hand over a sensor and said, "Surface". The large door slid up and an accordion-style safety gate closed behind it. The elevator moved very quickly, but smoothly, upward.

****

It took them very little time to get to the surface. The elevator stopped at ground level, lodged in a concrete cubicle.

Sam and Melinda stood hand in hand in anticipation of seeing the new world, not knowing what to expect.

The safety gate slid open, followed by the large door which dropped out of the way allowing for the passengers to go through.

Visible from inside the elevator was a large prairie-like field, covered in tall grasses.

As they walked out into the warmth of the sunlight, Tong and Voot fitted their goggles, while both Sam and Melinda shielded their eyes from the bright sunlight trying to adjust their vision after being underground at low light levels for several days.

Looking up at the sky, Sam was struck by how clear it was. He commented he had only seen such a clear sky once, on the day after 9/11 when every plane in North America had been grounded. In this sky, there were no signs of haze from the plane contrails they were used to.

Looking as far as they could, they noticed the hills around what had been Area 51 in their time, but which now were bare of trees and somewhat lower due to all the erosion they had experienced since.

Sam quizzed his guides about the fact that the desert he knew to have been there, no longer existed. Tong's explanation was that the world's climate had altered drastically due to the tectonic shifts and the changes in the ocean currents, effectively affecting most of the weather the world now experienced, as seen with the increase in moisture where they were presently and its effect on the vegetation.

Besides the grasses, they did see insects such as ants which had somehow survived and seemed to have reclaimed their place in this early period of the earth's rejuvenation.

As they walked through the fields before them, Tong described how some of the small vegetation had managed to subsist and regenerate as well. The larger species would take more time and would be helped by the people below. As for the fauna, again, the smaller species would be reintroduced to the new world, following a strict code or balance between prey and predator. Due to human intervention, the undertaking would only take centuries rather than eons if left to natural evolution and selection. They also discussed the process which was planned to select and reintroduce past humans to the future.

After roaming for about two hours, the four returned reluctantly to the elevator to be whisked below ground.

Chapter 45

Upon their entrance to the underground city, they were taken for lunch to a restaurant on Level Twenty. Sam was stunned by the holographic scenery which had been recreated for them. It was the lakeside view of Toronto, with the skyline behind them and Lake Ontario to their left.

Sam knew that what they were looking at was actually an image on a wall just ten metres away, but it was so realistic, he felt as though he had never left his city.

"How do you do it?" he asked Tong.

"I'm not sure of the engineering behind it," he admitted, "but they take some of the millions of images that were digitized and saved prior to the calamity. These are synthesized somehow and the electronics in the walls simply reproduce them in a three-dimensional format."

Melinda pointed to the CN Tower and commented that she still had weak knees remembering when Sam had taken her to the top and they had walked on the glass floor which overhung the edge of the tower.

After their lunch, they were escorted back down to their quarters to freshen up and change into the outfits which had been made for them.

Sam's was a stylish tan-coloured, collarless cotton shirt and brown cotton slacks, whereas Melinda's was a simple but vibrant full-length silk dress, with swirls of reds, greens and blues, matching those of the Ammolite pendant she wore around her neck.

Tong and Voot had promised them a surprise and they seemed excited about the prospect when they returned to retrieve their guests.

Both Sam and Melinda wondered about what they were going to witness. The bar had been set high when Voot had indicated that they were going to enjoy one of the highest artistic experiences their society had created.

They reached Level Fifteen and upon exiting the elevator, found themselves among hundreds of others, all heading in the same direction.

Now, Sam and Melinda were truly curious.

"OK, when can you tell us what this surprise is all about?" Sam asked.

Melinda squeezed his hand and said, "Don't be so impatient. It's obvious they want to really prolong the anticipation. I think it's fun just to see the eagerness on their faces."

They walked for about a quarter of a kilometre along a holographically created street that Melinda seemed to remember seeing on one of her trips to Greece.

She turned to Tong and asked, "Is this the Dionysiou Areopagitou in Athens?"

He broke out into a huge smile and replied, "Yes, it is. You know it? And, how accurate is the reproduction?"

"Very. I've strolled this pedestrianized street several times. Just up ahead and on the right should be the Theatre of Dionysus."

Sure enough, after they had passed some of the buildings obstructing the view, there it was, just below the cliffs of the Acropolis, with the ruins of the Parthenon upon it.

Still smiling, Tong continued.

"As much as we all love the feeling of being back in ancient Athens, we also used this projection to enhance the ambiance for what you are about to witness."

Turning to look at the two and blinking his eyes a few times, he added, "We wanted you to experience our music."

Sam and Melinda glanced at each other, pleasantly stunned at the prospect of attending a concert.

As they continued to walk, Sam asked where exactly the concert would take place.

"We've constructed one of our auditoriums to mimic that of the Odeon of Herodes Atticus, which was also situated below the Parthenon."

"Oh, I remember seeing a concert on TV held there and put on by Yanni," Sam responded.

"Yanni who?" questioned Voot.

"Oh, he's an artist back in our time," Melinda answered, while slapping Sam gently on the arm because she knew damn well that they would never have heard of Yanni.

By then, the number of people moving in the same direction had increased dramatically and many of them had overtaken the four. Some would politely turn toward the visitors to get a better look at them, some would simply smile and bow their heads in silent salutation.

Just ahead, the crowd was streaming into what seemed to be two entrances to the theatre. In the real Athens, they would have walked up a series of steps onto a wide stoop, spanning the full width of the stone facade, with the multiple arches which originally framed the front of the Odeon.

Here, on the contrary, they were plain off-white corridors, devoid of the holographic images which adorned the large public hallways. Sam and Melinda were stunned at the contrast and felt a little claustrophobic. Luckily, it was but a twenty-metre walk to the underground theatre. While it was mid-afternoon, they made their way into the area which was lit as though it was just after sundown, and before them emerged one of the most spectacular sights they had ever seen: There, above them and beneath the moon and the stars, stood the brightly lit Acropolis and Parthenon.

To their left was a large stage, filled with musicians preparing for the concert. In the foreground, cut into the rock, were the graduated seats, precisely constructed in a semi-circular pattern and angled upward and back, to create perfect acoustics.

The five thousand-seat theatre was almost full and the buzz from the crowd increased when they saw Sam and Melinda enter. A moment later, several of the people in the audience began to applaud, followed by everyone else, and then, they all rose to give the visitors a standing ovation.

Sam and Melinda were taken aback by the welcome and actually stopped in their tracks. Seeing their hesitation, Tong reached for Melinda's hand, while Voot did the same to Sam. They nudged them forward and toward the centre of the theatre, where their reserved seats were awaiting them in the first row.

The crowd was still applauding when they reached their seats and instinctively, but atypically, both Sam and Melinda turned to the audience and waved, much like movie stars.

As they sat, hoping the applause would stop, Sam leaned over to Melinda and whispered, "Now that was awkward."

She responded with, "And that's an understatement. Did you expect anything of the sort?"

"Not at all. All the time we've been here, they did their best to pretend we weren't present. Tomorrow, I'm going to ask Tong to allow me to speak to as many of them as possible, in order to get their impressions of our presence. I have to admit, up until now, I've felt a little isolated and protected."

"I feel the same way," Melinda replied.

The applause soon diminished and the cacophony from the orchestra was silenced as well. The lights dimmed and everyone sat back to enjoy the concert. Sam was finally able to direct his attention to the members of the orchestra.

Somewhat similar to the orchestras he was familiar with, the musicians wore black. Not tuxedos, but body-clinging outfits resembling the ones Tong and Voot had first worn back in Area 51. Although the familiar sounds he had heard when entering the theatre were those of winds, brass, strings and percussion, the instruments played by the orchestra members producing those sounds were very different in shape and size, quite unlike those he knew. This could prove to be interesting, he thought.

The conductor came out from a side entrance, once more to the applause of the audience. He, too, was wearing black, but sporting a chin-length pageboy hairstyle, popular in the 1950s and 60s and whose bounciness made him look mischievous. By the same token, the silver-grey colour of his hair gave him an air of distinction.

He took a bow and looked toward Sam and Melinda, and said with a smile, "This first piece is in honour of our visitors. Welcome."

He then turned toward the orchestra and put his hands up at the ready. He gestured toward the group of musicians and on cue the music began. Four notes into the song, both Sam and Melinda recognized *The Blue Danube*, by Johan Strauss II. The next piece was *La primavera*, Antonio Vivaldi's musical evocation of spring.

The music was exquisite and superbly interpreted while the ambiance created by seemingly sitting in the most remarkable of theatres under the stars was magical. Melinda wrapped her right arm around Sam's left and leaned into him, taking it all in, completely forgetting where and when they actually were.

Though he was enjoying the concert, Sam looked around at the audience. Other than seeing thousands of "almost clones" of Tong and Voot, he noticed something else as well. Most of them had their eyes closed and were swaying gently to the music.

Looking over to Tong next to him, he saw him doing the same. He happened to glance once more at the orchestra and realized that they too had their eyes closed as they played.

He hesitated but then decided to get Tong's attention.

He leaned over to get closer and whispered, "Tong, why are everyone's eyes closed?"

"I apologize for not informing you before. They are comlinked to the musicians and the maestro."

Sam's eyes grew large.

"They're actually in touch with the musicians?"

"Yes," responded Tong.

"When we come to a concert, we comthink with the artists. That way, we are not only able to hear the music they are playing, but we are also able to feel the emotions, pleasure and apprehension they might have while they are playing. As well, the maestro and musicians are able to feel the emotions of the audience and this helps them to play off those emotions and enhance their performance. It is quite the experience."

Sam was astonished at the revelation and couldn't believe he hadn't thought of the possibility earlier.

Before he could comment, Tong added, "If you allow me, I would like to try something with you."

"Sure, what?" Sam replied.

"You have shown some signs of being able to communicate telepathically, even if only at a basic level. No offence is intended."

"None taken," Sam responded. "What are you suggesting?"

"I would like to comthink with you to the point of allowing you to feel what we are feeling."

"You can do that?" Sam said in amazement.

"Yes, I believe I can. I will, however, keep it light so as not to cause you to bleed by the nose."

Sam turned to Melinda and whispered in her ear what Tong had offered to do.

"Is it safe?" she asked.

"I trust Tong. I would love to try it. It could be a rush!"

He turned back to Tong and nodded yes.

Tong closed his eyes and said, "Clear you mind of words. Try to float as though on water in your mind. If you see images or feel sensations, don't discount them. Allow them in."

Imitating Tong, Sam closed his eyes and said, "OK. Let's do this."

The music was still playing and Melinda was watching Sam intently. She saw him jerk slightly and his left cheek quivered a little, but then a smile lit up his face.

Sam had done what Tong had suggested. He didn't know what to expect, but slowly, images--no, sensations, began to creep into his mind. It was as though he was a feather floating on the wind. He sensed feelings of joy, rhythm, and even bliss. Then the impressions started to become a little more focused. The thought of minor disappointment which coincided with a particular bar in the music rose to the surface in his mind. No sooner did that happen, than the thoughts of someone else, which seemed to come from somewhere in the orchestra, apologized and an upsurge of effort followed. As this was going through Sam's mind, he could hear the effects of the music being played and the sense of a job well done well up in him. Sam assumed it must have come from the maestro. By then, Sam was swaying to the music, mirroring what the rest of the audience was doing. Then, it all went black.

Startled, Sam looked at Tong with an air of puzzlement on his face.

"I am sorry," said Tong, "but I did not think it wise to continue for too much longer. Still, I felt it was enough for you to understand."

He looked briefly at Melinda and then again at Tong.

"That was absolutely amazing!" he said. "Thank you so much for granting me such a privilege."

Tong smiled and slowly nodded his head, then turned to the orchestra and continued to listen to the music.

Sam, who was getting teary-eyed, grabbed Melinda's hand.

"I can't describe what that was like."

She smiled and said, "Don't try now. There will be time later. Let's just enjoy this while we can."

Sam marvelled at her ability to put things into perspective with just a few words.

The orchestra played for another hour and a half. Sam and Melinda recognized some of the pieces, but there were also several which were of the time and foreign to them. They wondered at the amazing sounds which were generated by the strange instruments.

Some of the scores were deep and brooding, while others could only be described as angelic.

Chapter 46

The concert at an end, the thousands of spectators who poured out of their seats, heading toward the exits, made a point of allowing Tong and his guests to leave first and not in the sea of gnomans. It crossed Sam's mind that his hosts might have had something to do with it telepathically.

When they were again out in the main corridor which still mimicked the outdoor pedestrianized street leading to Leof. Andrea Siggrou, one of Athens' main streets and which was just across the road from the great Temple of Zeus. Sam and Melinda could not get over how real it all felt, right down to the breeze. What was missing, of course, were the cars and buses, the smell of exhaust fumes and the heat.

Tong had set up a meeting with the Primus after the concert. She had requested a get-together to discuss an important matter. So, the group headed back to their quarters where the zone leader was to convene with them once more.

To their surprise, Primus Lee was already waiting for them in their apartment.

"I apologize for intruding into your quarters. My last meeting was shorter than I thought it would be and I hoped you would not mind if I made myself at home."

Melinda assumed her role as political liaison in their mission.

"Not at all Madam Primus . . ."

She then remembered the Primus' request and corrected herself.

". . . Lucie. This is more your home than it is ours and you are always welcomed, invited or not."

Sam reached down to shake her hand.

"Lucie, let me express our thanks for the unique opportunity to visit your city and for everything we have experienced. We feel honoured and by the same token, we owe you a debt of gratitude which we would like to repay somehow."

That startled the Primus and Sam noticed Tong and Voot looking at each other.

"Did I say something wrong?" he asked.

The Primus seemed a little relieved when she answered, "No, certainly not. But that allows me to get immediately to the core of why I needed to speak to you."

Melinda gestured for everyone to find a seat. She sat very close to Sam on the sofa, while the Primus sat on the upholstered chair and Tong and Voot pulled up two chairs from the kitchenette.

Once all were ready, the Primus began.

"I must confess that we had a reason for asking you to come into the future and witness our society."

Melinda nodded and said, "We assumed so, though we can only guess what that might be."

"Please do," responded the Primus.

Melinda looked to Sam, who attempted to explain their assumptions.

"Well, Lucie, at first we thought we were simply helping Tong and Voot get to their ship and return both Travellers to your time. We were told that we could return shortly after our departure and that no one would be the wiser. Melinda received the President's approval for the mission in return for agreeing to share what we saw and learned. He, in the end, was to make the decision to reveal or not reveal the information. At any rate, it became apparent with the number of sites we visited and the depth of information our guides shared with us, that there could be another agenda."

The Primus paused and then said, "Quite perceptive of you."

Sam continued, "We gathered the purpose of our meeting was to unveil this agenda."

"Correct, once more. As you have been told, there is a great debate going on which has divided our citizens. There is a group which wishes to see the surface world repopulated and one that feels it should be left alone to regenerate on its own and take its proper direction.

"It would seem that the large majority sides with the first opinion, as do I and therefore, we are ready to move ahead in our plans. We need you to help us."

Melinda responded, "Do you want us to stay here with you?"

"No, the fact you were able to travel through time safely means our plan is possible."

She hesitated once more.

"We need you to return in time. Just not *your* time."

Melinda instinctively grabbed Sam's knee and the two looked perplexed.

"What do you mean, not our time?" was her response.

"We were always led to believe that we would return to our time within minutes of our departure, though going back now after the way we left, we would have a lot of explaining to do."

Sam intervened.

"So, if not to our time, then when?"

The Primus calmly continued and explained.

"We have analysed the history of your time and beyond, up until the calamity and we have identified a particular moment when there seems to have been a shift in history leading to events which allowed our timeline to exist."

She noticed a look of realization on Sam's face.

"I see you are starting to make sense of what I am getting at."

Sam nodded and added, "I think so, but please continue."

"Our timeline exists only because of major developments in world politics, economics and social movements. We noticed that the indicators for our timeline did not exist during your time. Actually, that timeline was going in an opposite direction. What's more, we saw that the situation about three hundred years after your time was conducive to the required change, and in fact, history shows that this did happen."

Melinda interrupted and asked, "So, if history shows that this will happen, your timeline will come about no matter what."

The Primus shook her head.

"Not quite, I'm afraid. That shift in direction was brought about by a catalyst. That variable in history, we believe, is the two of you."

This time, both Sam and Melinda were speechless.

"I understand fully what we are asking of you. In any event, our society . . . the survival of humanity depends on it."

Accompanied by Tong and Voot, the Primus left the two some ten minutes later, after asking them to consider the request and to let her know of their decision in the morning. She understood they had much to discuss.

Chapter 47

The couple had showered and changed into their nightwear: Sam in his T-shirt and boxer shorts, Melinda in a soft grey, full-length spaghetti-strap nightgown, made of the same material as Tong and Voot's time travel outfits.

They hopped onto their bed and sat cross-legged facing one other. They reached for each other's hands and both took a deep breath.

"Where do we start?" Melinda asked.

"No idea," responded Sam, "but I can honestly say, I didn't see this situation happening. Not in my wildest dreams."

"I don't know if I can do it. Leave my family, my job, our life back in DC," Melinda admitted.

Sam chuckled and teased, "Well, at the very least, you won't have to face the President."

Melinda pretended to be miffed at him and slapped his knees.

"Having to justify our actions would be relatively easy, what with the information we could provide him.

"You haven't told me which way you are leaning."

Sam looked at her pensively.

"I'm not sure either. I know what you are saying about leaving our families. If we don't go back to our time, how . . . what will they be told about our disappearance?"

"I can imagine," Melinda answered, "some elaborate story about an accident while we were on some secret mission and our bodies not being found. Trust me, coming up with a plausible story isn't the issue. It's the effect on our families that most bothers me."

The two went silent for a few moments.

Finally, Sam spoke up.

"You asked me which way I was leaning. As much as I loved my life with you back when, there were a few comments by the Primus which really struck a chord with me."

Melinda remained quiet, but the questioning look on her face beseeched him to continue with his idea.

"I'm trying to understand the effect--on this timeline--of our returning to our time, as opposed to the time they are suggesting."

Melinda nodded but allowed him to continue without a comment.

"If I understand what they were trying to explain, our returning to our time, no matter what problems that could present to us, could change or even make this timeline disappear. They would all *not* exist. Hell, *we* wouldn't be here!"

Melinda shook her head trying to make sense of what Sam was musing about.

"I'm aware," Sam continued, "that it sounds crazy, but I think that's what would happen. We'd simply be back in our time, trying to figure out what the EGG was and probably not getting anywhere. Christ, the EGG probably wouldn't exist either and we would never have been taken to Area 51."

"I think I know which way you're heading with this," was all Melinda said.

There was a twinkle in Sam's eyes and then he smiled.

"If, and only if, we decide to go along with their request, we would have a lifetime of work trying to convince future politicians . . . future, based on our timeline, that, we are not only rational but also the real thing. Think about it: Two individuals come to them to tell them about the end of the world as they know it and that they need to cooperate on a global level to build underground cities."

Melinda squeezed his hands and finally responded.

"I think you've identified the single most difficult issue for us, assuming we agree to go ahead with this. I know how government works and I can assure you it could be next to impossible."

"You're absolutely right. But, think about it. This timeline does exist. Which means that if we are the ones who helped bring it on, we must have succeeded," Sam beamed back.

"And if we don't," Melinda quickly added, "this timeline disappears and we are left some three hundred years in our future, probably considered to be just two more *end-of-the-world* prophesying lunatics."

The smile left Sam's face.

"Yup. That's a possibility. But what chance does the human race have if we don't try. What about Tong and Voot?"

Melinda looked down at their clasped hands and used her thumbs to gently rub the top of his hands, all the while trying to build her courage up for what she knew was their only real choice.

After a moment, she responded with, "I swear, Sam Buckner, I sometimes find you infuriating. But at this moment, I'm reminded of one of the many reasons why I fell in love with you. I agree. I don't think we really have a choice. Let's do it."

Sam leaned forward into her space and kissed her gently.

Then he saddened.

"You know, if we go ahead with this, neither of our families will ever get to know Jake, nor he his relatives."

Tears welled up in Melinda's eyes.

"Very true. That fact alone would almost make it worth not going through with this plan. But then again, you're right about there being too much at stake for us not to, no matter what the effect on our lives."

Melinda slowly closed her eyes and stopped participating in the discussion.

Sam became concerned.

"Sweetheart, are you OK?"

She finally opened them and seemed as though in a stupor.

"Yes, I think I'm fine. Just got a wave of tiredness creep over . . . me."

She seemed to doze off once more, this time with her head dropping and her shoulders slumping forward.

Sam began to panic, but he too felt an incredible urge to close his eyes and sleep.

He forced himself to gaze at his surroundings and tried to catch Melinda as she collapsed onto the bed. His eyes were again closing when he noticed what he thought looked like vapour coming out of the air vent off to the side of the bed. By then, though, it was too late to react as he too rolled over onto his side and began to slip into dreamland.

Through a haze and just before falling into a sound sleep, he thought he saw small creatures in white, wearing what looked like masks over their faces, surrounding the bed in anticipation of something about to happen.

Though he knew this wasn't good, he couldn't help but give in to the slumber.

Chapter 48

Needless to say, it wasn't a dream. In fact, surrounding the bed were eleven gnomans, four of which were wearing the white time-travel outfits. Off to the side was the group leader, shouting muffled orders from behind his mask.

"No, don't move them yet. We need to let them inhale a little more of the gas. We don't want them to wake before we deliver them to their final home."

They stood there about a minute longer before wheeling in the two gurneys they were to use to usher Sam and Melinda up to the Travellers.

It took all of them to lift each of the two victims onto the gurneys. Unfortunately, they were designed to accommodate gnomans and not people of Sam's and Melinda's stature. Both lay there, knees bent, hanging over the ends of the beds.

"Let us move quickly. We must be in the Travellers' launch bay in no more than five minutes to transfer them into the vehicles and then up to the surface world. We cannot take more than thirty minutes to do so, otherwise, we could be found out."

The group worked efficiently, heading into the hallway where they removed their masks. Three of the normally dressed individuals walked well ahead of the others, acting as scouts, with the rest of the troop in tow.

It only took them four minutes to reach the hangar door leading into the large room housing the Travellers, much to the satisfaction of the leader. This was going to go well, he thought.

As they approached the crafts, the group split into two, each moving their respective and most precious cargo to one of the Travellers.

The four clad in travelling outfits walked over to the vehicles and raised their arms to allow them to touch the surfaces. No sooner had they done this than the skin of the crafts moulded downward into the shape of steps.

While all of them were concentrating on the ships, none had noticed that Sam was beginning to stir from his sleep. In fact, the leader had miscalculated the amount of gas needed to put someone of Sam's size out for the hour they might need to complete their mission.

Still in a daze, Sam continued to keep his eyes closed and was trying hard to try to make sense of his last memories and the sounds he was hearing at the moment.

He opened his eyes quickly to try to determine whether or not he was still in his and Melinda's quarters. Even in this semi-conscious condition, he realized where he actually was.

The feeling of panic gripped him anew, but rather than paralyze him further, it seemed to help counter the effects of the gas contributing to the state of stupor he was in.

He again opened his eyes briefly and flicked them to his left. He noticed Melinda on a gurney, approximately ten metres away. She was out cold.

He tried to move his legs slightly, but realized any movement was more imaginary than real. A sense of dread was starting to creep into his mind and all he could do was try to think of means to save the two of them.

Because of the residual effects of the gas, he was having a difficult time focusing on the present and was finding it next to impossible to think clearly. . . but he had to.

He opened his eyes to look to Melinda once more.

Oh, my God, he thought, they're taking her into the Traveller.

Sure enough, the kidnappers were all working feverishly, struggling to carry Melinda to and then up the steps. The clearance between the floor and the entrance to the craft made it difficult for them to position themselves to lift her up and into the time machine.

Only then did Sam realize that they were probably being sent to a time when no one would ever find them.

Don't panic, don't panic, he kept repeating to himself.

He began attempting to organize his thoughts, working hard at calming his heart.

OK, if I can't move, how can I somehow get help? Think. Think!

Then it came to him: Could he possibly comthink to get help? Would anyone hear him? Or, if he was successful in doing so, would he simply be warning his kidnappers that he was awake?

His mind was clearing more rapidly now and he forced himself to remember everything Tong and Voot had said about telepathy and how simple it was. Right, simple. All he knew is that he had to try something.

OK, don't think words. Think the concept of the word. No, think the emotion of the word. But, how do you think or emote the concept of help?

He peeked toward Traveller Two and saw Melinda's legs disappearing into the craft.

That's when it hit him. Not help, but fear. Fear for the one he loved.

He cleared his mind and only concentrated on the stress he was feeling for Melinda. He pictured her away from him, forever. He felt tears well up in his eyes and incredible heartbreak. Words disappeared and a stillness set in. He felt his tears stream down his cheeks. Then he also felt something drip from his nose. Though he couldn't see what it was, he assumed it was a drop or two of blood.

Good, he thought.

He peeked once more toward the other craft, only to see several of their captors rushing down the steps.

No! They know. What did I do? he wondered.

At that moment, something happened that startled all of them. A deep guttural vibration pulsed from Traveller One. Sam noticed the effect it had on the gnomans that were advancing in his direction.

They stopped momentarily to comthink. Then, they resumed their rush toward him. By that time, the rest of the captors had exited Traveller Two and had joined the first group. Sam could feel them lifting him and carrying him toward the steps. He could see they were straining, attempting to jostle him up the steps and into the ship. He saw the three seats in the centre of the cavity and was pained to think of Melinda who was probably enveloped in the membrane, just as they had been on their trip to the future. His heart broke thinking he had failed to protect and save her.

He had a brief moment of compassion for his captors who were working so hard to carry him, exerting themselves not to harm him. As strange as the thought was, he knew they must have been as careful with Melinda. Conversely, what lay ahead of them could be so much different.

He was still unable to move and felt completely helpless as they finally positioned him on one of the seats. It quickly adjusted to his size and reclined in order to prepare him for the trip.

The membrane began to envelop his body and Sam felt everything was lost. He could only hope that he and Melinda would be sent to the same time. Anything less would be totally unbearable. Together, he reasoned, they could face anything the past or the future could throw at them.

The membrane was now wrapping itself around his chest and over his arms and beginning to creep around his neck and head.

This is it, he thought.

He took one last look around him, understanding life would no longer be the same.

What was he thinking? How would he describe the past several days? His life had already changed, even more dramatically than he could ever have dreamt of.

His thoughts then went back to Melinda and how much he loved her.

Chapter 49

The captors had by now left the two crafts and were standing, huddled in a comconference with the four pilots. They had been trained in the art of time travel along with Tong and Voot, plus a small number of others. Unlike Tong and Voot though, the trips they had taken had left them disillusioned with humanity and they had decided to join the side which wanted to leave the surface world to evolve without human intervention.

The green hues on the Travellers were now moving very quickly, indicating they were charged and ready for the time trip.

While three of the pilots reentered the ships, two in Traveller Two with Melinda, and the other in Traveller One, which held Sam, the fourth steered the leader over to what looked like a podium housing the controls for the large elevator which would take the two ships up to the surface. He instructed the leader on the exact sensors over which to wave his hand in order to operate the elevator. Having accomplished this final task, he joined his fellow pilot sitting next to Sam.

The steps on both crafts melded back into the ships, resealing them for the trip. As the leader passed his hand over a red-coloured sensor, it turned green and the doors to the elevator began to open. The other members of the group slowly and carefully began pushing the EGGs toward the opening.

The leader felt satisfied with their mission, secure in the knowledge they were pulling it off and that the opposition's cause would suffer a serious blow.

The first of the crafts was just reaching the opening to the elevator when the leader heard a noise behind him. He turned to see what was happening and was shocked by the arrival of some thirty individuals rushing through the hangar bay door.

Among them were Tong and Voot and the expression on their faces told the leader that they meant business.

His head began to get pummelled with thoughts and ideas coming from the group heading toward him. They were attempting to overpower his mind to stop him from finishing his task. He was transfixed in a thick soup of images which made it next to impossible to distinguish his own thoughts from those of the others.

He took a quick look over at the elevator and saw that the two Travellers were inside, but he couldn't remember what he had to do next.

He could hear Tong in his mind, ordering him to stop, while Voot was striving to get the rest of the group to the elevator in time.

As the other members turned their attention to saving the EGGs, they relaxed their grip on the leader's mind, giving him just enough freedom to recall what he had to do next. He forced himself to concentrate on triggering the doors to close and sending the elevator up.

He looked down at the console and was about to wave his hand over the sensor once more, when another hand grabbed his, pulling it away. It was Tong.

Helped by Voot, Tong was able to drag the leader several steps from the control unit.

In the meantime, the rest of the group managed to overpower the six rebels and started to bring the EGGs back into the chamber.

There was still a danger that the pilots inside could panic and decide to time travel in order to prevent their capture.

Voot called for Tong to go to Traveller Two, while she went to Traveller One. The plan was to apply their hands to the surface of the two crafts to more effectively communicate with them. Moreover, with the help of the others around them reinforcing their thoughts, they would try to override the commands of the four pilots within.

It was an eerie sight to witness. If a stranger had happened upon this scene, he could have thought this was some type of religious ritual in which the faithful were laying hands on a deity of sorts, which happened to look like large eggs.

A moment or two later, the swirling of the colours on the surface of the two Travellers began to lessen and both groups pulled back from the crafts. The steps beneath re-formed and the four pilots within stepped down the length of the ramp to the floor.

The kidnapping had been averted, but what about Sam and Melinda?

Tong and Voot quickly entered the ships to find the two inside, with the crafts' membranes slowly receding off of them.

"How are you feeling?" Voot asked Sam.

Still experiencing some of the effects of the gas, Sam responded with, "I think I'm OK. Although my arms and legs still seem a little numb, I'm pretty sure I can stand. But, what about Melinda? Is she alright?"

Voot raised her hand signalling him to wait a moment, closed her eyes and then smiled.

"She is fine. Tong is with her now. She, too, is having some difficulty moving, but she will recover soon as well."

A wave of relief engulfed Sam as he slowly sat up in the seat.

"How did you know to come?" he asked. "Were you able to hear me? Did I actually comthink?"

"Yes, you did. But we didn't hear it. Traveller One did."

Sam was shocked.

"He did?"

"Yes. He is quite fond of you. You were good to him back in your time and he got to know you, right down to your atoms during the flight here. When he realized you were in distress and that the activity here was not scheduled, he pinged his location, as he did in your time. We all heard the alert and those closest to the hangar bay came to see what the problem was. When we arrived, it was not difficult to realize what was transpiring.

Sam forced himself to get up and although a little shaky, was able to descend from the ship and onto the hangar floor.

As he emerged, hunched over because of the small clearance under the craft, he assessed his surroundings yet again. There, encircled by a large number of gnomans, stood eleven more, whom Sam assumed to be his captors. At the very same time, he detected the Primus walking into the bay, accompanied by her security detail.

He politely but quickly acknowledged her presence and ran to Traveller Two, crawled under it and up the steps to the interior. Melinda was still lying on the seat and in the process of trying to make sense of her surroundings. Next to her, Tong sat holding her hand.

Looking at Sam as he came up through the opening, he said, "Do not worry. She is fine. She will take some time to recuperate fully, but she and the baby will be, as you say, OK."

Sam was grinning with relief.

"Hi, sweetheart. How are you feeling?"

"Still groggy," she mumbled, "and a little woozy, but I'm coming around. What happened?"

Tong explained: "It would seem some of the opposite faction decided to take action to prevent us implementing our strategy. They tried to kidnap you in order to deliver you sometime in the past, where you might never be found. Don't worry, we have them and they will be scanned to divulge the name of any other member of their plot. This will not happen again."

Tong rose to leave the two alone.

"Take what time you need to safely exit the Traveller. We will be waiting for you."

He paused a moment and then added, "And, the Primus would like to speak with you when you are up to it."

He walked out, leaving Sam and Melinda on their own. They said little, mostly relying on unspoken--not telepathic--words, which spoke volumes about the way they were feeling.

Chapter 50

About ten minutes later, Sam and Melinda descended backwards down the steps, still dressed in their nightwear.

Gone were the captors and the large group which had come to save them. Only Tong, Voot and the Primus were there, patiently anticipating the return of the couple.

As soon as they could stand upright next to the Traveller, Sam, followed by Melinda, reached over and gently stroked its surface and whispered a sincere thank you.

They slowly approached the small gathering waiting for them.

Because she was still in a slight daze, Melinda greeted the Primus formally yet again.

"Hello, Primus."

Then she corrected herself, "Lucie. I can't describe how grateful the two of us are to you all for coming to our rescue. How can we make it up to you?"

The Primus smiled and suggested there could be a way.

"Have you decided on whether or not you are willing to help us as we have requested?"

Sam looked at Melinda and nodded.

"Yes, we have decided to accept," answered Melinda.

"I am pleased," the Primus responded.

"We were worried this episode might have deterred you. Good. We will begin the preparations for you to return to the appointed time. How long will you need to prepare?"

Sam spoke up.

"Knowing now what the mission is, I would like to revisit a few of the sights we were shown and others, in order to acquire more of the specifics of each innovation."

Melinda added, "And I would like to meet with some of your philosophers, historians and medical personnel in order to obtain the details of the process the selection committee used to choose the prospective underground candidates. I can foresee some resistance to the concept."

"We will be happy to provide you with all the information you think you will require. Our present and future will depend on your success," the Primus admitted.

Sam asked if there was anything they could bring back with them which would prove they were indeed from the future.

"Unfortunately, no. Please understand. There is a fine line between introducing objects created in the future, and ideas that could change the direction of time. That being said, if ideas are introduced and they are developed or acted upon by the people of that time period, then the change in the direction of time becomes a natural progression."

She added, "They need, as you would say, to buy into and develop the concept themselves. With any luck, that will lead to the creation of the underground cities, and us."

Both Sam and Melinda paused to let sink in what she had just said.

"I think we understand," Melinda said, "which will help us in deciding who we will need to confide in, in order to convince them to believe us and consequently, get them to help us."

****

The two spent the next three days feverishly meeting with as many people as they could find who they felt could teach them what they needed to know about this future and its society.

The time of their departure finally arrived.

Both Sam and Melinda had great misgivings about leaving Tong and Voot, whom they had grown to love as though they had been lifelong friends. They worried about never seeing them again. They worried about not being able to accomplish their mission and affecting the timeline incorrectly. They worried about the sheer magnitude of the mission which had been entrusted to them: It was perhaps the single most important mission ever taken on by two lone individuals in the history of the world.

The momentousness of the mission for the gnomans was not lost on them. Their departure had been talked about for days and when the time finally came, Sam and Melinda were led into the hangar bay once more. This time, however, they were met by hundreds of well-wishers wanting to witness their leaving and give them an appropriate send-off.

Next to Traveller One were the Primus, Tong and Voot, who were again dressed in their travel outfits. They were to be the ones to take them back into the past.

Melinda approached the Primus.

"Madam Primus, how are you?" she asked as she reached for her hand to give her a handshake.

Sam followed suit.

"As you can see," she gestured to the crowd, "this is a significant occasion for all of us. Those who are not here, present in body, are following these individuals in a massive comconference taking place as we speak. I won't make a long speech, but rather, will simply wish you well on your journey and hope you accomplish what you are setting out to do."

Both Sam and Melinda thanked her.

The Primus broke protocol and asked if she could hug the two of them, which Sam and Melinda quickly responded to by leaning down and giving her a heartfelt embrace. Melinda's eyes welled up, but she was able to keep her composure.

Then she approached Voot.

"I would like to thank you and Tong for everything you have done for us and the care you have given us."

She reached up behind her neck and unclasped the necklace which held the Ammolite pendant Sam had given her and held it before Voot.

"Regretfully, I only have one to give. Sorry Tong, but I hope you accept it with Voot as a token of our appreciation for everything you have done for us."

Sam nodded and smiled at the two.

Voot was taken aback and briefly looked at the Primus who nodded as well.

"I don't know what to say, but thank you, from the two of us."

The crowd broke into a loud applause, amplified by the size of the hangar they were in.

"Let me put it on for you," Melinda suggested as she reached down and clasped it behind Voot's neck. She stood back to admire it on Voot.

"It looks perfect on you," she added, grinning broadly.

Sam put his hand on Melinda's shoulder and suggested it was time to go.

Melinda wiped the tear running down her cheek.

"Yes, OK. Let's do this."

Tong and Voot each headed to one of the Travellers, followed by their respective passengers.

Again, there was loud applause from the crowd as it parted to allow the ships to be pushed toward the elevator.

Once the four were inside and in their seats, the steps reattached to the EGGs, effectively sealing them in.

The two crafts were quickly lifted up to the surface toward their destiny.

Part Four

Chapter 51

(The year AD 2366)

"So, what do you think?" asked Doctor Young.

"Do you believe we should have them meet? I do."

The head of psychiatry was still reading the patients' charts which were projected onto the surface of the desk from the small tablet in front of him.

He didn't respond one way or another but instead gave a command to the tablet.

"Compare the common occurrences in the patients' behaviours."

"Do you want me to do so from the time they were admitted?" queried the tablet's disembodied female voice.

"No, just those of the past twelve hours," responded Doctor Lawson.

The voice began her comparative narration of Patient Joe's and Jane's behaviour during the time specified.

"Both patients have come out of their delirious state and are responding more coherently to questions posed to them. The two are much less agitated, and are accepting the food and beverages offered to them. Both have assumed a more meditative state, often displaying signs of recognition of things they are thinking about, as is evident from their eye and hand movements. Finally, both patients have asked if others suffering the same symptoms have been found. As a result of these inquiries, all reactions, from heart rates to iris contractions, would seem to indicate that this issue is very important to them."

Lawson's eyes grew large at the last statement.

He looked up at Doctor Young and said, "I see why you want them to meet. They obviously seem to know of the other's existence and are concerned about them."

He thought a moment and then added, "Didn't you say that both had wedding bands on when they were found?"

"Yes, which is why I now believe they are a couple. That could be confirmed when they meet for the first time," Young concluded. "Moreover, Doctor, were you aware that Patient Jane is pregnant?"

"No!" Lawson said in astonishment.

"All the more reason to get to the bottom of this case."

He then added, "Have you considered the possibility this whole scenario is nothing but a hoax in order to get some type of publicity?"

Young didn't hesitate.

"Yes, I have, but the circumstances are too strange for this to be a simple ruse for publicity. They were wearing clothing that would have been typical of that worn over three hundred years ago. Some of their language, when they did communicate, seemed to match the colloquial expressions of that time. And, we have searched our medical databases to see if we have any evidence of their retinal scans or their fingerprints on record. Nothing. They simply don't exist in our databases."

Lawson frowned and looked up at his colleague.

"You know what you are saying, don't you, Simon?"

"Yes, but I need to hear it from you," Young responded.

"Either this is one of the most elaborate con jobs ever, or they aren't from our time," Lawson admitted.

Young's excitement at the prospect almost overtook his professional demeanour as he continued.

"I'm convinced they are not fake; furthermore, I would like you to relieve me of other cases and allow me to concentrate on these two."

Dr. Lawson pondered on the request and then said, "I'm willing to relinquish both patients' cases and hand them over to you, but I need to be kept informed on each and every aspect, each and every step of the way. If you are proven to be correct, this will have to go up, way up in the system. But for the moment, I want you to implement our security protocols around the two and restrict contact between them and our staff. You are to be their only link to the outside world."

"Understood," Young confirmed.

"I'll make arrangements for the two to meet in the interview room within the hour."

"Fine," said Lawson, "but I would like to witness the reunion from the observation room."

The two parted and an excited Doctor Young hurried to make the preparations for the meeting between Patient Joe and Patient Jane.

As Simon walked down the hallway to his office, he was mesmerized by the thoughts and questions which had plagued him since their arrival. At one point, he had to stop and steady himself slightly, so affected was he by the knowledge he thought he might gain from this odd couple.

Chapter 52

Patient Jane was seated at a table in the middle of a stark room. She was dressed in a hospital gown. It was one thing to wear it in her room, but here, she felt somehow uncomfortable and exposed.

Looking around, there was nothing on the walls but white paint. Except for the large mirror hanging in front of her. She knew it was a two-way mirror and that someone was probably watching her at that very moment.

****

She was right. Behind the glass, Doctor Lawson was scrutinizing every move she made. He had already turned on all the sensors and cameras which would record everything from the size of her irises, to her heart rate, her breathing and even when and how often she blinked. The recorded data would then be analysed and compared with the responses to the questions she would be asked.

****

She needed to mind her Ps and Qs, so as not to give too much away. She was aware that this was a psychiatric institution where she had to look and sound sane, otherwise she could be held indefinitely.

As she sat there, her hands clasped together on the tabletop, she summoned all her will to maintain an appearance of calm and innocence.

She heard the door being unlocked and then saw it open to reveal a man wearing what resembled a white Nehru jacket.

"Hello," he said with a smile, "I'm Doctor Young and I've been assigned to your case."

He walked over to the table and asked, "May I join you?"

She said nothing but nodded yes.

He pulled out the chair and perched on the edge of it opposite her across the table.

"How are you feeling?" he asked with empathy.

"Well," responded Patient Jane.

"You had us worried for a few days, while you were suffering from hallucinations," he continued, "but, you look much better now."

"Thank you. I do feel more myself," she added.

"Speaking of which, can you tell me your name?"

She hesitated for a moment, trying to decide how much she would divulge. Though she had managed to retrieve and connect the few missing parts of her memories the night before, her overriding thoughts since regaining her lucidity were about Sam.

Where was he? Was he here in this time? For that matter, what was this time? Had she made it to the designated moment which had been planned by the gnomans? So many questions. For the moment, though, the task was to extract information without disclosing any, until the time was right.

She looked up at the doctor with her deep blue eyes and said, "My name is Melinda Buckner," then added, "Can you tell me if you have found another person suffering the same symptoms as myself?"

****

Behind the mirror, Lawson quickly ordered the search system to look for a Melinda Buckner and to sift through all of the linked databases. Within moments, a sultry female voice responded with, "Sorry, Doctor Lawson. I could not find any reference for a Melinda Buckner in any of our active databases."

Could the patient be lying, he thought? And why?

****

"May I call you Melinda?" Simon Young asked.

She nodded yes once more.

"Good. And, to answer your question, yes, another person was found exhibiting the same symptoms . . ."

224

Melinda's breath caught in her throat and she exhaled with relief.

"... and was brought to the hospital. Can you tell me who he is?"

"His name is Sam and he's my husband," she answered.

****

Look up the name Samuel Buckner, Lawson requested. The computer voice returned, stating there was no one with that name in the records.

The doctor thought for a moment and then gave another command.

"Check for both names in the archives. Don't limit yourself to our medical archives. Look into the national, as well as the genealogical archives."

It took a little longer for the new search; in spite of that, when the voice did finally respond, it had news.

"I've identified four Samuel Buckners and three Melinda Buckners in the genealogical records. I cross-referenced these with the national database archives and have found both of them mentioned in the same timeline only once."

"What information do the records provide?" Lawson asked earnestly.

"There is a record of a Doctor Samuel Buckner, a researcher at the University of Toronto, while a Melinda Buckner, née Gordon, was Under Secretary of Intelligence at Homeland Security, one of the precursors of our National Security Department."

Lawson's blood drained from his face. Could it be? he wondered.

"What happened to the two of them?"

"Both disappeared from the records after 2016," answered the voice.

John Lawson slowly turned to look at Patient Jane, aka Melinda. His first thought was that the pair could be incredible con artists. And, if they were, indeed, participants in an elaborate hoax, they had picked the perfect people to impersonate.

Yet, what if they weren't?

****

Dr. Young decided he would try to press Melinda for more information, if only to try to confirm his suspicions.

"Can you tell me how it came about that you were found walking along Highway 95?"

Melinda looked at him and, trying to pretend that she was still in a daze, uttered, "I don't know. I still have no recollection whatsoever about that."

"But you are starting to remember things, such as your husband, Sam?"

"Yes," she answered, "he's about all I'm sure of at the moment."

"Do you know what year it is?"

"Like I said," she responded with a hint of annoyance, "I have no memory of where, or when I am. I remember nothing of my past. That's what I hope you might be able to help me with."

He wasn't getting anywhere with this line of questioning, so he thought he would try to make her feel more at ease.

"Would you like to see Sam?"

Her eyes widened and a large smile replaced her scowl.

Young turned his head to the mirror and nodded.

He then returned his gaze to Melinda.

"So, tell me, what is the last thing you do remember?"

Melinda took her time to respond.

"I vaguely remember lights: red, white, flashing. I think that must have been the police vehicle which found me. I don't remember most of the trip here, besides gentle rocking and more lights flashing by. Other than that, not much."

Dr. Young was becoming a little frustrated with the notion that she was giving him very little to work with.

A knock on the door interrupted the session. An orderly, dressed in white, opened the door and peeked in.

"Doctor, Patient Joe is here."

Young stood and headed toward the door as Sam came walking in, conspicuously dressed in the same type of hospital gown Melinda was wearing.

Sam looked at the man standing before him, vaguely remembering noticing him recently. Then he laid eyes on Melinda, sitting at a table, behind the doctor.

Both reacted simultaneously: Melinda rose from her chair and raced toward Sam, while he attempted to get to her, almost bowling over the doctor.

They embraced as though they had not seen each other in a long, long time. Little did the doctors know, and neither could all the sensors detect that they had travelled twenty-five hundred years to meet again.

It was more than obvious that the happiness emanating from this reunion was not an attempt to try to convince whoever was watching, that they were indeed together.

After glancing quickly toward the mirror and back toward the couple, Dr. Young walked to the corner of the room to a lone chair, and brought it over to the table.

All three finally sat down. Sam slid his chair right next to Melinda's and the two reached for each other holding hands on top of the table, waiting for the questions to come.

"Not trying to sound facetious," Young began, a slow smile warming his eyes, "but, I would feel confident in saying the two of you remember one another."

Both Sam and Melinda grinned, still taking in the other's features in silent recognition.

"Samuel, is it?" he asked.

Sam nodded.

On a more excited tone, Dr. Young continued.

"What can you tell me about who you are, where you have been, or how it was you were found on the highway, in the middle of nowhere?"

Sam looked at Melinda and then set eyes on the doctor.

"I honestly wish I could. I know her. I'm positive she is my wife, but don't ask me how I know that. Just a feeling."

A look of disappointment overtook Young's face. He shifted his gaze to the mirror and then said, "I'm confused why you might not have more of your memories back. It is, albeit, a start. I would like to meet with you again this afternoon, if you are up to it?"

The two patients shared a look of agreement and confirmed they were.

"Anything you could do to help us remember would be appreciated," Sam added, convincingly.

"Could we remain together?" Melinda asked.

"For the moment, I would prefer you remain separate, if only to see if you can independently recall anything which could shed light on the situation," Young responded.

Melinda looked sad but added, "I understand. We'll do what it takes to help you help us."

Sam and Melinda had rehearsed similar situations before leaving the future, in the hopes of being able to withstand the scrutiny they knew they would be subjected to.

"Perhaps, after we get together this afternoon, we could make some modifications to your living arrangements?" Young added, counting on the element of hope to help them divulge more information.

Dr. Young rose and went to the door. He opened it and called the two orderlies who were waiting.

"Can you escort the patients to their rooms, please?"

Sam and Melinda were already standing and holding each other tightly.

Sam whispered in her ear, "I think we're good. Hang in there, sweetheart."

The newly reunited couple pulled apart and meekly followed the orderlies, but not before exchanging looks of wonder and gratitude at the thought of being together.

****

"What do you make of them?" Dr. Lawson asked his colleague.

"Aside from the fact that they know each other, they haven't added anything to the equation. Did the sensors detect anything?"

Lawson hesitated for the briefest of moments.

"No, other than the parting words from Buckner."

He shared what Sam had whispered into Melinda's ear, but not what the computer search had revealed.

"I'm still not convinced they aren't attempting to fool us. I have no idea what they are trying to achieve, but we need to get more information. You must get them to lower their guard."

"That's what I'm hoping to do this afternoon. I plan to take them outside in the courtyard, away from the starkness of the interview room."

The two took their leave, with Dr. Lawson heading to his office.

He walked over to and sank into his chair with a bit of a huff.

He drummed the fingers of his right hand on top of his desk, pondering his next move.

Then, he waved his hand over the telecommunication sensor.

"CASS," which was short for Cyber Analytical Search System, "Are you able to locate images of Dr. Buckner and Melinda Gordon in the timeline in which you found both?"

"I will search for you, Doctor."

A moment later, the computer voice resumed.

"I have found four pictures of the two individuals: one of Doctor Buckner alone, and another in the archives of university professors at the University of Toronto. Two of a Melinda Gordon: The first as an inductee in the now defunct CIA Academy and another as she was promoted to Under Secretary of Intelligence and Research of Homeland Security, now our National Security Agency, as I reported to you in our previous conversation."

Lawson frowned as he thought the programmers had introduced a sarcasm algorithm in CASS.

"Bring the images up, please."

The four images appeared on the floating holographic screen.

The psychiatrist's face showed no emotion, but his irises widened, betraying his thoughts.

There, before him, were Sam and Melinda. There could be no mistake. They were indeed who they claimed to be. So, what was his next step? Should he inform Young?

No, he thought. This was far too sensitive a subject to entrust to a junior colleague. Let him continue trying to solve the problem. If he did, which Lawson had no doubt, Young would be brought up to speed. But, by then, the wheels would be turning too quickly to take any other direction than the one Lawson would have set into motion.

"CASS, open a visual chat with Lieutenant Saunders at the NSA."

Chapter 53

New clothing had been delivered to Sam. As he donned the slacks and top, he speculated that dress of this timeline was somewhat stylish.

Every piece, including the sandals, was off white. The pants were similar to his own, other than being made of a type of material which Sam could not identify. The shirt was shaped like a collarless wraparound, with elbow-length sleeves. When tied on the left side, it formed a V-shaped neckline over his chest.

He had no mirror to see the overall effect, but looking down at himself, he remembered the adage of the clothes making the man. Though he hadn't worked out for, well, a few thousand years, this outfit made him look pretty fit.

The door to his room, or rather his cell as far as he was concerned, opened and an orderly stepped in and asked Sam to follow him.

They walked down the long hallway and passed through a series of doors, each opening only when the orderly had his retina scanned.

Mental note, Sam mused: If I ever have to escape, I'll need to kill one of them and pop his eye out. He shook his head a little and wondered which movie he had seen that would give him such gory thoughts.

They reached a set of elevators and descended six floors to the ground level and into a lobby of sorts. Shortly after, Melinda and a female orderly exited another elevator. She was wearing a similar outfit, but in her case, the effect was quite sensuous. As soon as they saw each other, they rushed to kiss and embrace tightly.

Sam stepped back, still holding her hands in his and looked her up and down, jokingly asking, "Wow, who are you wearing?"

He happened to catch the male orderly who brought him down, glancing at Melinda's cleavage. In your dreams, Sam thought to himself.

Just then, Dr. Young appeared, all smiles.

"Good, you are both here. I thought we should have our meeting in the central courtyard."

He pointed to a set of doors off to the left and moved toward them, expecting the small group to follow. He stopped then, turned to the two orderlies and asked them to wait in the lobby until their return.

Walking out of the building, they emerged into a humongous rectangular space, bordered by the seven-storey building which made up the hospital complex.

"*Whew*," Sam exclaimed, "this is something."

He and Melinda couldn't get over, not only the area, which measured at least three hundred by five hundred metres in size, but the numerous walking paths meandering among beautiful flower and shrub beds, some of which neither had ever seen.

"The flowers are stunning and so colourful," Melinda commented.

"I thought you'd like it," Young said, pleased with their reaction. Perhaps this might help bring their guard down somewhat allowing him to extract more information from them.

"I sensed the two of you were intimidated by the venue of our first meeting," he added.

Melinda gazed at Sam lovingly and moved up to him. She reached up to kiss him on the cheek and seemed to nibble on his ear as she whispered, "Can we trust him?"

Sam pretended to be tickled and did the same to her.

"We have to start trusting someone here," he responded in a soft murmur.

Young started slowly strolling.

"Come along. Let's walk, why don't we?"

The three proceeded at a leisurely pace, taking a variety of paths, stopping every now and then to admire the beauty of the vegetation in the courtyard.

Young began his questioning.

"Have you been able to remember any of the answers to the questions I asked in our first meeting?"

Sam looked at Melinda and then back to the doctor.

"To be truthful, we haven't been completely honest with you."

The expression of surprise on Young's face was obvious. But then, a smile appeared.

"Really. So you do remember who you are and why you were on that highway?"

"We remember who we are, all of it. We aren't totally sure why we were walking on our own on the highway. We may have separated at some time due to our delirium."

He paused and then continued.

"I don't know if you are going to believe us when we tell you our story."

Young chuckled.

"You forget I'm a psychiatrist. I must have heard every crazy story possible. Try me."

That seemed to put Melinda at ease. She nodded to Sam to continue.

Sam began, explaining who they were, when they were from, the work they had done and the invitation to Area 51.

Young listened without saying much, other than asking what Area 51 was and why they were invited to go there.

Melinda filled in that part of the story.

As she described the President's challenge and what they found at the D.U.M.B. site, Young's demeanour changed somewhat.

"So you are saying this craft, thought to be a spaceship, was in fact a time vehicle?"

"How else would we be here?" quipped Sam.

They said nothing about Tong and Voot, nor the fact that they had first gone into the far future. That could only be divulged to the President, assuming they could ever get to meet him or her.

"And you somehow managed to get inside this craft and learned to fly it here?" Young asked, in an incredulous yet slightly mocking tone.

Up until then, he had tended to believe the two, especially after his research on their original clothing and their speech patterns. Now, he was having second thoughts.

"So, where is this craft presently?"

"That is something we can't tell you. Not because we don't want to, but because we truly don't remember," Sam said, with Melinda nodding in agreement.

"And why come here? Now?" Young pressed.

Sam looked at Melinda who shrugged her shoulders and shook her head.

"Another question we can't answer, yet," Sam replied.

"With everything else we've remembered, I think that too will come to us. We need a little more time. But I can say I believe we came in order to talk to someone of importance," he added.

Melinda piped in, "I would imagine that with something this paramount, it would have to be someone high up in the field of Physics or government, such as the President."

The doctor thought for a moment.

"If you are telling me the truth, can you explain why you decided not to advise your own President or talk to the powers that be or were at the time?"

Sam answered without skipping a beat.

"We found out that the military brass in charge of Area 51 wanted to keep the craft for themselves and use it and the technology surrounding it to have the US gain the upper hand in world affairs. We feared what this type of science could do were it to fall into the wrong hands."

Young's eyebrows rose as he pondered the response.

"And you think the people of this timeline won't abuse it as well?"

"I don't know. That's something you will have to tell us. Has society evolved enough to be able to handle this technology as it should be handled?" Sam asked, trying to turn the tide in their discussion.

Simon Young ran his hand through his hair before speaking.

"I think that would depend on who you were to talk to," he said, beginning to believe in the two once more.

"Who is President now?" Melinda asked.

"That would be President Bonita Gonzalez."

Melinda chuckled and said to Sam, "I know of a few conservative Republicans who would roll over in their graves if they knew."

Again, Young's eyes grew larger.

"That's right, they were called Republicans back then," not realizing that he had shifted more into their camp.

"Today, they are known as Traditionalists. For about two hundred years, we've had a multi-party system. We found it to be much more responsive to and representative of the people than the two-party system I assume you were familiar with."

"Why did that system change?" Melinda asked.

"That's a long story and I'll be happy to explain things of today to you at our coming meetings. But the short version of the answer to your question is, the pope."

Now it was Sam and Melinda's turn to be surprised.

"How does, or did, the pope factor into this?" she asked.

Young laughed and said, "I'll keep this concise. Sometime after when you say you are from, the world faced one of its greatest threats: terrorism. . . ."

Melinda absent-mindedly grabbed Sam's forearm, remembering the brief she had prepared for President Alexander, concerning the convergence of chatter between the many terrorist groups around the world.

". . . Every country was besieged by terrorist groups, whether political or religious. It got to the point where governments were starting to turn on their own citizens. That is when Pope Nguyu from Kenya realized that the world was moving toward total anarchy. He reasoned that terrorist groups were rising in numbers and strength because of the poverty in the world and the lack of hope this engendered.

"He decided he had to do something. Bombs would not work, but compassion and kindness might. Though he faced huge opposition within the Church, he issued a papal bull, declaring that the Church would liquidate all of its assets and that the wealth acquired would be managed by the bishops and priests around the world, for projects which would distribute the money raised to feed and house anyone in need, regardless of religion, and to create situations by which the poor could not only find employment, but begin to counter the monopolies of the multinational corporations. It didn't take long for the other major religions to follow suit."

"You're kidding," Sam said in awe, "that's like the pope in the Shoes of the Fisherman."

Young stopped his explanation to ask what that was.

"Just a movie I saw," Sam answered.

Young looked puzzled.

"What's a movie?"

"Now, that's another story that we'll have to get to later," Sam replied, smiling, "but please continue."

"Well, it took the world about ninety years for the process to take place, but by the year 2110, there were no terrorist organizations, anywhere. The people of the world had reason not to upset the new economic reality and protect rather than destroy it."

"Brilliant," Melinda said quietly. "The organization of the Churches could reach down into the communities everywhere, bypassing the usual large charitable organizations and governments which often took the major portion of funds raised for their own administrative needs. Conversely, all the money went directly to where it could do the most good."

Then Melinda looked at Sam and added, "Well, I guess I was right. They were looking at joining forces."

Sam smiled and complimented her, "You're good, sweetheart. I've always said you're the best at what you do."

"My God, she mused. I wonder how Alexander managed through that crisis."

Turning to the doctor, she asked, "And how does that bring us to the term Traditionalist?"

"Oh, right. That's what this was leading to. Just because the world was at peace, it didn't mean the politicians were. One faction in the United States longed for the time before Pope Nguyu. Religion, that is organized religion, waned and became less relevant to many. The Traditionalists catered to those citizens who thought religion and politics were two sides of the same coin."

"A conversation about religion and politics might have been totally different from the one I had with President Alexander about the American obsession with guns," Sam commented.

Young stared at Sam.

"You spoke with your president?" he asked with wonder.

"Yes, a few times, actually."

Young shook his head, in part because he was having as much difficulty assimilating all that the two had told him as they seemed to be having. If they were the real deal, the thought of being able to talk to and learn from people from over three hundred years in the past was just blowing his mind.

"Let's conclude our meeting now. I have so much to think about, as I'm sure both of you have. I would like to meet you again after supper, if you are not too tired?"

Sam and Melinda shook their heads.

"We would love to continue," Melinda said.

"We have so many questions to ask you," she added.

Young paused and then stated, "I've decided to put the two of you in one of our conjugal rooms in a different part of the hospital. You'll find it much more comfortable and I see no reason to keep you apart any longer."

Melinda's face just lit up as she rushed forward, wrapping her arms around the doctor and giving him a big kiss on the cheek.

"Thank you, Doctor."

"OK, OK, enough of that," Sam said, pretending to be jealous, "but thanks, Doc."

The three headed back to the lobby. Young told them it could be a little while before their room would be ready and that they should consider going to the cafeteria to get something to eat. The orderlies would remain with them to escort them there and then to their room.

Chapter 54

About then, CASS informed Doctor Lawson that the call from Lieutenant Saunders in Washington was now available.

"Good. Bring him up, please."

The translucent screen appeared before his eyes and a clear image of the lieutenant magically appeared and seemed to be floating in mid-air.

"How are you, Stormy?" Lawson quizzed.

Lieutenant Leonard Saunders was an old university friend of Lawson's. The two had spent a few years at Harvard, in their respective fields: Lawson in psychiatry and Saunders in political science. They had originally disliked each other, believing the other's field of study to be less important than their own. But after a few evenings in the local pub, drinking and on one occasion, taking a swing at each other over an argument no one remembers, they realized they were much more alike than they were different. The following encounters at the pub became bonding sessions for the two of them.

Saunders' nickname had come about because of an incident in which another student, drunk as a lord, had challenged Lawson over his thoughts about Nietzsche's belief that humans should rise above the fray and act civilly at all times. Saunders thought it could be funny to go into a loud rant in an attempt to intimidate the other, feigning insanity, thus making it difficult to know what he would do next. It worked and the drunk student quietly left the pub. The nickname, Stormy, stuck.

"Great! But tell me, how is it we've never been able to find a good nickname for you?" he asked sarcastically.

"Clean living. Clean living is all I can say," Lawson shot back at him.

"What's up, that you'd call and say it was urgent?"

"I have a situation here that, I believe, merits your attention. One that might help you get the promotions you've been itching for, and the position I've dreamed of in Washington. What I'm about to describe to you might sound crazy, if you'll excuse the pun, but I wouldn't have called unless I was sure."

"Really," responded Saunders, "this sounds interesting. Tell me more."

Lawson described the two cases and the information he had obtained during the interview. He explained what Doctor Young had proposed based on his original research and the similar condition of the patients when they were found.

"I wouldn't have called you unless I thought this could be real. It was when CASS brought up the images of the two people involved that I realized it might not be a hoax. If I am right and I think I am, this could turn out to be the most important event of our time."

Stormy Saunders sat back in his chair and thought.

"Tell me more."

"Not safe over the com. Security records everything," Lawson responded.

"I think it would be wiser if you were to come here and see for yourself."

Lawson knew Saunders would jump at the chance. They had had many discussions over brandy, about the fact that the American military was but a shadow of its former self. With the elimination of international strife, the defence forces had been reduced to the level of a glorified police force. Saunders had long hungered to be able to prove himself somehow. But with few opportunities to shine, chances of advancement were stifled.

"Alright," Saunders said, "I can take the express *Viatube* to Dallas and then transfer to the local network and be there in . . ." looking at the time on the screen, ". . . in three and a half hours."

"Good. You won't regret it," Lawson said with satisfaction.

He decided to head home for a few hours. He knew it would be a long night once Saunders arrived.

****

"CASS," Dr. Young called out while sitting at his desk, having returned from his walk and talk with the Buckners.

He was buoyant, almost jumping out of his skin, with the thought of having stumbled on the event of the century: He could actually have humans from the distant past in his care. The

238

information he could glean from them, from the mores of the past to how they had travelled to his time would prove to be phenomenal.

And yet, he still had questions. If they had access to such an invention, when scientists of the present still did not, then who developed it? the government or some private corporation? or was it as simple as cryogenics?

None of it made sense. But he was determined to get answers.

"Yes, Dr. Young. How can I help you?" responded the bodiless voice.

"Can you give me a summary of the interview this morning, highlighting the physical responses to the questions asked. As well, correlate that with any insight from Dr. Lawson."

"It will be my pleasure. One moment, please," CASS responded.

Young drummed his fingers on the desktop, waiting for the report.

"In brief, the biometrics indicate that there was truth in the assertion of who they are. In fact, Dr. Lawson had me do a deep search in the past for the names of the people they claim to be and I found a few possibilities, of which only one convergence of two people bearing their names happened once."

That caught Young by surprise.

"When was that?" he asked.

"In 2016," she answered.

That seemed to corroborate what the two had discussed with him in the afternoon.

"How did Dr. Lawson react to that information?"

"His response was one of surprise and confusion."

Young sat back in his chair, questioning why Lawson had not revealed that fact to him, all the while realizing that he, too, was withholding information from his boss.

"Has Dr. Lawson made any additions to the file or initiated any follow-up which I should be aware of?" Young asked, feeling a little paranoid.

"He added nothing to the report on the two cases, but he did make a call to a Lieutenant Saunders in Washington."

Young's eyes grew larger and he frowned as the implications of the news began to set in.

"When was the call placed?" he asked with a hint of concern.

"It was placed one hour, forty-six minutes and ten seconds ago," CASS replied.

"And where are Dr. Lawson and this lieutenant now?" Young added.

Again, there was a moment's pause before CASS answered.

"Dr. Lawson is presently at home and the lieutenant is twenty minutes from arriving at the Viatube terminal in Dallas."

"He's coming here," Young exclaimed.

"If one considers the timing of the *image-call* and that of his itinerary, I believe that would be the correct assumption."

Young was beginning to panic. It would seem Lawson was indeed manoeuvring to reclaim the case for himself and the fact he was bringing the military into the picture did not bode well for the two patients.

What could he do? Lawson was the head of psychiatry and had full jurisdiction over any case in the hospital. If Young was to oppose him, it could mean being dismissed, not only from the case, but also from his position.

And yet, what choice did he have? He truly liked Sam and Melinda and knew that if the military was being involved, they would be grilled, dissected and analysed. They would have no life to speak of until, well, forever.

"Would you like to add anything to the report?" CASS asked calmly.

"No, thank you, CASS. That will be all for the moment."

He pushed back from the desk, dropped his head and squeezed his eyes shut, trying to think of what he needed to do next. Deep down, he knew what he had to do. He was merely trying to summon the courage to get it done.

Chapter 55

"Stormy. Where are you?" Lawson asked while riding in his MOT2, shortened version of "Means Of Transportation: two seats" vehicle, on his way to the Viatube terminal. Saunders' image was being projected on the front window of the vehicle he was sitting in. Visible over the lieutenant's shoulders were the other passengers travelling with him, each busy talking to the person next to them, or reading from the monitor attached to the seat in front of them, while a few were trying to get a little shut-eye.

The Viatube system was now the preferred method of transport between cities. It was a marvel of engineering. The technology had actually been available for over three hundred years in office buildings. It was used to convey messages by means of vacuum tubes which connected different offices to one another, but it had never been applied in this manner until now. The long, sleek people movers, which could carry up to eighty passengers, travelled at incredible speeds, inside large vacuum tubes linking every city in the nation. Because of the shape of the vehicles, people had taken to calling them torpedoes.

During the twenty-second century, the five richest men in the world had pooled their excess wealth to fund the development and construction of the first fusion power plant. Because of the technology which they surprisingly made available for any country to use, the need for fossil fuel dropped to almost zero. The deal was simple: The country could build as many reactors as it needed, with technical support from the founding corporation, on the condition that the electricity they produced be used by and at no cost to the citizens of said country. In effect, it was a nationalization of the production of power by the countries of the world.

Every part of the globe now had access to unlimited and free electric power. The standard of living everywhere rose, essentially eliminating poverty. Manufacturing boomed and the economies of the world nations equalized. In spite of that, not everyone was equal financially. There were still many who profited greedily from the free energy source.

The unlimited power revolutionized the world in every way possible, from lighting and heating cities in every corner of the globe, to cleanly exploiting the planet's resources, and altering the form of travel, both on land and at sea. The only dependency on fossil fuels was for powering ramjet airliners on transoceanic flights. The jets took much less time to get from place to place and did so with a minimum of fuel consumption.

"We've begun our deceleration. Should be there within ten minutes," came the answer from the speaker.

"Good. I'll be waiting at the gate," he responded with satisfaction.

Waving the video link off, Lawson eased himself in the comfortable seat of his vehicle. The small electric car was whizzing along the raised highway, one of thousands moving in either direction, each slotted in a particular lane and programmed to take its riders to their destinations without traffic jams, congestion and accidents.

He had reserved a MOT2, as opposed to the one-seater he usually retained from the MOT pool, to allow him to pick up Saunders. No one owned a vehicle anymore. It was cheaper to call for a ride and depending on the number of occupants, to pay more or less to get where one needed to go. All MOTs were owned by the municipal governments which maintained the vehicles and housed them in hundreds of underground garages, spaced out below the city for rapid deployment. It was another win-win situation created by the availability of free electricity: revenue for the cities and cheap, efficient and clean transportation for their citizens.

Lawson stretched his legs and folded his arms, trying to get comfortable for the rest of the ride to the terminal. He shifted his body up against the door of the vehicle and leaned his head onto the glass. As he silently whipped past the countless, brightly lit buildings on his way, he began to fantasize about his future.

Finally, he could leave the hospital and all the crazy inmates which had occupied the past twenty years of his life. Not wanting to think about the impact of what was to come on Sam and Melinda, he began to plan his move to Washington. Saunders could take the credit for the greatest find in the nation's history and go after those hard to get promotions, but he would be the real person behind the revelations that would come. He had no doubt that he could parlay his discovery into a nice cushy position, working with two patients only. He would use every trick in the book to break them and get them to reveal all.

A smile of satisfaction crept onto his face as he closed his eyes, continuing to dream about the life-changing events he was now orchestrating.

"You have arrived at your destination, Dr. Lawson," the vehicle's voice stated, startling him awake from his reverie. He had actually fallen asleep and had to slowly and lazily stretch his body to will the slumber to escape it.

Sure enough, he was nearing, as programmed, the arrival side of the terminal. As he approached the massive circular structure, shaped much like the flying saucers of old science fiction stories, he saw through the ceiling glass all the transparent tubes connected to the building, much like spokes on a bicycle wheel. As the MOT slowed to a stop, he noticed several torpedoes slowly slipping into the building. He assumed one of them was carrying the lieutenant.

Some six minutes later, out came Saunders, in full uniform and carrying a small overnight suitcase.

Lawson ran his hand over the optical sensor on the small armrest next to him and the two gull-winged glass doors lifted open, allowing him to hop out to greet the lieutenant.

"Good of you to come, Stormy," he said, while firmly shaking the man's hand.

There was a slight bit of irritation in Saunders' voice: "Not a problem, but I sure hope this will be worth the four thousand kilometres I just travelled based on your promise that this was important."

****

Simon Young had been quite busy since the revelation of his boss having lied to him about the information he had dug up concerning the couple. He had decided that he needed to protect Sam and Melinda from what he presumed Doctor Lawson and the military would have in store for the two.

He had rushed up to the conjugal room into which they had just moved.

"We have to talk. Now!" he said as they opened the door.

After describing what he had uncovered and explaining what was about to transpire, he pressed them to tell him what they wanted to do. He was ready to jeopardize his job if they trusted him to help them escape. Or, they could go along with Lawson's plans in the hope they would be alright.

Sam and Melinda spoke privately for a moment and then turned to Young.

"I don't think we have a choice," Sam said.

Melinda picked up the discussion.

"There are things we haven't shared with you," she admitted, "but we are here for a reason and this reason is something we can only discuss with the President. We doubt Dr. Lawson has such a consultation in mind. Can you somehow help us get to Washington? From there, we can hopefully arrange to get together with the President."

"Phew," exclaimed Young.

"I can likely help you get there, but I truly do not believe you can ever convene a meeting with the President. The protocol to confer with her is quite rigid."

Young continued.

"Though you probably could not manage to set up a meeting, I think I might know someone who could. One of my university professors was named chair of the National Science Committee. As such, he advises the President on matters dealing with science and technology. I'll bet he would help, but only if I can convince him that you are legitimate and indeed who you claim to be."

Sam and Melinda looked at each other.

"What do you think?" Sam asked.

"I don't know about you, but I think it's our only chance," Melinda responded while adding, "I believe we can provide you with additional information which could prove to be convincing. Besides, you say Dr. Lawson was able to find pictures of us during our time? Can you do the same?"

"I can get CASS to pull them up as well," Young mused.

"Do you think it's a good idea to bring someone else in on this?" Melinda asked with concern.

"Sorry? Oh, you mean CASS. Don't worry, she isn't one of the living," Young said, smiling.

The look of confusion on Sam's and Melinda's faces was ignored by the doctor.

"Now, I have much to get ready. We will require new clothing for you, then we'll need transportation to the Viatube Centre."

He stopped for a moment contemplating something he had just realized, but then went on.

He looked at his watch and almost panicked.

"No time to waste. Please, change into the clothing I'll send to the room and then wait until I come to get you."

Abruptly, he left the two to wait for his return.

Upon entering his office, he accessed CASS and asked her to print off all the pictures of Sam and Melinda she could find.

As if he forgot another issue, he added, "And, could you also download the iris scans for patients Thomson and Jeremiah to my watch? I'll need them for a report I'll be preparing on them."

Then he called on an orderly and told him to bring appropriate travel clothing to Sam's and Melinda's room.

Finally, he touched his watch lightly and engaged the telephone app. He then purposely tapped a number rather than call it out: CASS could be monitoring.

A moment later, the voice of a rather shady character Young had treated a few years before, answered: "Hello, Simon. What's up, man?"

Young got up and walked out into the hallway before he responded.

"George, I need to call in that favour you owe me."

****

An hour later, Dr. Young knocked on the door of the hospital room and had his iris scanned. He knocked again and then walked in.

Sam was standing before him, now dressed in the clothing Young had sent to them.

"Hey, Doc. The duds are really nice," Sam exclaimed.

Young reasoned that that meant the clothing.

"Where is Melinda and is she ready?" he quipped.

"Yes, I am, thank you," Melinda blurted out as she exited the washroom.

The two outfits were relatively similar to the clothing the two were used to, though again, they couldn't tell what they were made of.

"I wanted to assure you wouldn't stand out in public with more fashionable clothing," Young said, looking at Melinda who had on a prim and proper dress, while Sam was sporting cotton-like pants and a short-sleeved shirt.

"We have to leave now. Lawson is at the Viatube terminal and will be on his way here shortly."

Young then pulled out two small boxes from his pocket, opened them and presented them to the couple.

"Have you ever worn these?" he asked.

There, in the boxes were two sets of strange-looking contact lenses.

"You will need to put them in," he said.

"Seriously?" Sam questioned. "Why and where did you get them?"

"The why will become evident shortly. As for the where, well, they came from a former patient who is 'in the business' of providing customers with means to avoid detection, or kids with means to get into concerts or bars, underage. Now, just put these in."

Sam chuckled.

"The more things change, the more they remain the same, don't they, Doc?"

Young nodded, then pulled out a small bottle and handed it to Melinda.

"Use this solution to help insert the lenses. It will aid in keeping your eyes lubricated and ease the sensation," he added in earnest.

The two went to the washroom and complied.

They returned a little later only to find Dr. Young already at the door, eager to rush them out.

All three walked up the hallway and down the two flights of stairs which led toward the main foyer.

Outside, at the entrance, a strange vehicle waited for them.

"Hey, you have a Smart Car?" Sam said with a hearty laugh.

"I love it," and then added, "so I guess you haven't advanced that much in three hundred years."

Young shook his head.

"Actually, it *is* quite smart, as you will learn shortly."

He walked up to the front of the vehicle and waved his hand over the window on what would have been the driver's side in Sam's day. The four glass gull-wing doors shot up.

Sam was impressed.

"Cool," he said, looking at Melinda. "Right, sweetheart?"

Melinda just smiled, happy to see the kid in Sam once more.

No sooner were they in than the doors folded down and a pale grid pattern appeared on each of their faces.

Melinda almost panicked when she saw the pattern on Sam's face.

"What was that?" she asked anxiously.

The vehicle began to move, without anyone at the controls.

"Don't worry. That is why I took the precaution of supplying you with the lenses. Each and every vehicle has biometric sensors which scan every passenger. They check the irises and search the database for a match. In this way, the location and destination of everyone travelling is logged and recorded."

"Sounds like Big Brother, if you ask me," Sam said incredulously.

"Yes and no," Young responded.

"In the extremely rare case of an accident or for critical contact reasons, we've found that the system is useful. One side effect has been a drastic drop in crimes such as thefts or murders," he added with some satisfaction.

"Just as I said," Sam repeated, "Big Brother."

Then he added, "Still. Pretty cool."

****

"Now, no more secrets. What is this about?" Saunders demanded.

Lawson took pains to describe every detail of the events surrounding the case, from the police reports to the interviews and pictures CASS was able to retrieve.

Though somewhat sceptical, Saunders listened carefully, knowing the doctor would not have gone through getting him there unless this was the real deal. The magnitude of the situation wasn't lost on him.

"So you say they could be made to remember everything about how they got here?" he questioned.

With a smug smile on his face, Lawson replied, "I've been doing this for twenty years and with the information we can uncover on them, I'm positive you will have a secret that has been hidden for over three centuries."

"You understand what this would mean, don't you?" Saunders said in a slow and paced whisper.

"We could change history. If they came to the present, they probably could go back. Which means we could do the same."

He paused, deep in thought and excitement.

"Can you imagine the changes we could bring about? We could kill Hitler. Or go into the future, see what will happen and decide if we *want* to let it happen."

Finally, he came back to his own little world and looked at the doctor, saying, "I could become President if I wanted to."

That struck Lawson as being wrong on so many levels, but he forced a smile and tactfully warned, "That would be your choice to make. But you might want to be careful about what you would change in the past. What if you were never to be born?"

The thought hadn't crossed Saunders' mind.

"I see what you are saying," he replied with the realization of the power he could wield, but yes, he would have to be careful and selective.

They arrived at the hospital and headed immediately to the psychiatrist's office.

"CASS. Bring up the pictures you found of the two Buckners."

"Certainly, Dr. Lawson," she responded in a matter-of-fact tone.

There appeared on the holographic screen floating above the doctor's desk, the pictures the search system had uncovered.

"Seriously, these are the same people you say you have sequestered here?" Stormy asked.

"Yes, they are. There are no apparent surgical indications of facial alterations. All biometric scans and comparisons indicate they are identical," Lawson said priggishly.

"Alright, then, let us go meet these two," the lieutenant uttered, in an almost commanding tone.

In an equally authoritarian voice, Lawson said, "CASS, contact the floor attendants in charge and have the two patients brought to the interview rooms."

"They are no longer in individual rooms, Dr. Lawson. They were moved several hours ago to the conjugal wing, room 227."

The doctor was surprised he hadn't been consulted, but he had left the hospital and it wasn't an unusual move to put married couples together, if the situation warranted it.

Looking at Saunders, he asked, "Do you want to go for a walk?"

Then, he paused.

"No. Wait."

"CASS. Where are the patients and Dr. Young?"

"The patients seem to be in their room . . ."

Because the conjugal rooms were for couples who had been deemed *safe*, sensors had not been installed in any of them, for obvious reasons.

". . . but, they did have visitors."

That caught the two by surprise.

"Visitors, you say?" the doctor questioned, "Who?"

Again CASS continued in her dispassionate voice, "There would seem to be a slight discrepancy in my records, but Dr. Young and patients Thomson and Jeremiah were seen leaving the room."

Lawson was beginning to boil.

"Were they seen entering?"

"That is the discrepancy. No, somehow, they were not."

Lawson turned to Saunders.

"They are running!"

"Where are they now? Check your links to the transport system," Lawson roared.

A moment passed and CASS returned.

"They were scanned boarding the Viatube Express Transport to Los Angeles three minutes ago."

Lawson had a frustrated and perplexed look on his face.

Saunders on the contrary, displayed one of extreme disappointment.

He pulled out his communications device, a penlike apparatus and spoke into it, "Lieutenant Leonard Saunders, priority level seven, ID number Delta Alpha 7918. Connect me to Los Angeles central command."

"Yes, sir," was the response, "How can I help?"

"I want a team deployed to the Los Angeles Viatube Terminal, stat!" he said.

"The purpose, sir?"

"I need three individuals stopped and detained."

"Sir, we have a team on site. Give me a moment," the voice said.

****

The threesome were able to position themselves closest to the exit door with Young in the aisle seat. The rest of the passengers were slowly boarding and looking for somewhere to sit.

"I thought we were going to Washington?" Sam asked.

"We are. But trust me," was all the doctor said.

Sam looked over at Melinda and was struck by her calmness in the midst of the chaos of all the events they had gone through this day, not to mention over the past month.

"Are you alright?" he asked.

"Yes. I'm fine," she answered.

"No. I mean," reaching over to touch her stomach, "Are you alright?"

A little irritation painted her face.

"I'm pregnant, not ill," she whispered, remembering having spoken those same words to Sam after being told by Tong and Voot, in another place and time, that she was with child.

Then, a gentle smile replaced the frown.

"But, thank you for asking and caring."

She leaned over and gave him a soft kiss on the cheek.

Dr. Young kept looking at his watch, seemingly anxious about the departure time.

"Is everything OK, Doc?" Sam asked.

"Yes, perfectly. Regardless, I would like you to take the lenses out of your eyes, and have you hold on to them.

Sam and Melinda glanced at each other perplexed, but went along with the request.

Young, in turn, did the opposite. He pulled out another small box from which he removed a pair of lenses, and inserted them into his eyes.

No sooner done, than he rose and told the other two to follow him.

As they left the torpedo and passed the ticket attendant, she called out to them.

"Sir, where are you going?"

Young turned to her as he was walking and said, "Sorry. We have an emergency."

The attendant looked at Sam and Melinda and noticed the two had tears in their eyes due to the removal of the lenses.

"Oh, I'm sorry for you. Good luck."

As the two caught up to the doctor, who was racing for another gate, Sam looked back, noticing the doors closing on the torpedo.

The sign above the gate they were heading to displayed the words "Washington, Departure 1800 hrs."

"Smart move, Doctor," Melinda commented, "a regular James Bond you are."

Young didn't bother asking her who James Bond was, content with the comment he assumed was a compliment.

Halfway to the Washington departure gate, ahead of them and rushing in their direction, were a half dozen men in security uniforms. The three stopped dead in their tracks and gasped with panic.

The funny thing was that none of the officers was looking at them, but rather at something well behind them. So the three simply moved out of the way and the soldiers scurried past them, yelling for the ticket attendant to stop the torpedo from leaving.

It was too late, of course, as the train was already slipping away and would be accelerating to over a thousand kilometres per hour within minutes.

Sam leaned in close to the doctor to whisper something to him.

251

"That was a close call. But why didn't they stop us?"

"They still believe we are on that torpedo. None of the scans will tell them otherwise. By the time they realize they've made a mistake, we will be in Washington. Now, let's not dillydally, shan't we?"

****

"What do you mean, you could not stop them?" screamed Lieutenant Saunders.

"Well, man, alert security in Los Angeles. No, you had better alert all the major terminals on the West Coast. I don't want to lose them again."

He turned to Lawson and scowled.

"So far, I'm not impressed," he said, almost with a hiss.

"Take me to the terminal. I'll take the first tube back to DC and run the search from there."

Lawson's dreams seemed more like nightmares at the moment. One thing was certain: Having experienced it himself, he was now aware of the true reason Stormy had acquired such a nickname.

Chapter 56

They had arrived on schedule at the Viatube terminal in Washington. Shortly after, they were pulling away in a MOT4, heading to Professor Higgins' home.

The iris scan had identified Dr. Young as Phillip Rose, a resident of Las Vegas, while the other two came up as the former patients whose iris patterns had been printed onto the contacts they were wearing once more.

"Aren't you going to call him to tell him we are coming?" Sam asked.

"No. I think it is safer to show up and hope he'll listen long enough for you to make your case," Young answered.

By then, darkness had set in, as it was about eight p.m. The ride took approximately one hour and was spent almost entirely in silence. Each was deciding what they would and wouldn't tell the professor.

The MOT4 sped north along the Capital Beltway around the city and just before it reached what Melinda thought was the Potomac River, it began to manoeuvre to take an exit not far ahead.

"Is that the Potomac coming up?" Melinda asked Dr. Young.

"Yes, it is," he answered.

"Sam, though I don't recognize the area with all the new buildings there, I remember driving here in my old Toyota, looking at and dreaming about all the beautiful mansions in the small secluded subdivisions on either side of the highway. I always hoped I might someday live in one of them."

Sam gently rubbed her hand and said, "We're still young and with Jake on the way, who knows."

The vehicle crossed a long bridge and veered off the beltway. It circled around and under the highway and then went west on what was in Sam's and Melinda's day, the Clara Barton Parkway. It continued on for about two kilometres before turning again to the left, crossing a smaller bridge.

"Are these the islands?" she queried once more.

"Right again," the doctor answered.

"Wow, none of these was developed in our time. Sam, look around. The structures are like the big mansions I spoke of."

Vaso Island was one of about ninety islands which dotted the river and which were now part of the most envied real estate in Washington. It was relatively narrow, measuring only about five hundred metres wide and two thousand long. The road followed the northern shore, next to the small cliffs which dropped off to the river.

Along their right, they passed three beautiful gated estates, set back from the road and largely hidden by the trees surrounding them. Though they were all well lit, they were laid out in such a way as to claim as much privacy as was possible.

"And this is where Professor Higgins lives?" Sam commented.

"It's part of the perks of being one of the foremost neurosurgeons and psychologists of our time. As well, it doesn't hurt that he is also the Chair of the National Science Committee," Young said, not without revealing a trace of envy in his voice.

Melinda almost missed a sign which advertised the private sale of a property, but by the time she tried to get Sam to see it, they had already passed it.

They were nearing the end of the island as they approached the last property on the southeastern tip.

"We're here," Young announced.

Sam was disappointed to find that the house was dark, though the driveway was well lit by low in-ground lights.

"Well, it looks like no one is home," Sam said.

"Not necessarily so," Young replied.

The house was impressive without seeming ostentatious. It was a good-sized two-storey dwelling with a peaked roof and a unique front elevation. The outer skin of the house was made of stone, much like the others on the island. What differentiated it from those were the two tall, one-and-a-half-metre-wide windows which stretched from the ground and rose about eight metres high where they angled to meet in the middle, much like a chevron matching the pitch of the roofline on either side of the peak.

The vehicle drove through the open gate and onto the large semicircular driveway which led to the front of the house. When they got out and walked up to the porch, they realized that the entrance area which had seemed diminutive from afar, was actually quite large, measuring some five metres wide and four deep.

As they stepped into the porch alcove, a motion sensor turned on the outside lights. Before them were three large panels of glass which served as the entrance's outer wall, the centre one being the actual door. They could see nothing of the inside of the house, as they tried to look through the glass. That's when Sam and Melinda noticed that the glass panes appeared to be stained a dark grey.

"Your professor seems somewhat strangely obsessed with his privacy," Sam commented.

"Not really," the doctor said, laughing, "but I can see why you would think that. The reason is that all residential windows are manufactured with liquid crystals sandwiched between the glass panels. This gives the windows a high insulation value and they also become opaque when charged with electricity."

As he was speaking, the grey in the glass wall began to dissolve and light emanated from inside the house. Within two seconds, the glass was clear and they could see a good deal of the interior, including the elderly gentleman who was standing just behind the door.

The professor looked like a well-kept gentleman. He was tall and slender, his face not betraying his age, though the wavy grey hair and wrinkled brow disclosed that he was probably over seventy years of age. Mostly, though, the intensity of his eyes revealed a man of high intellect.

He opened the door and bellowed with a wide grin on his face, "Simon, so good to see you. Why didn't you tell me you were coming?"

He stepped back into the foyer, allowing the three to join him there.

Young entered and walked into the wide, outstretched arms of his mentor.

After the embrace, he turned to Sam and Melinda and then back to the professor,
as he made the introductions.

"This is Sam and Melinda Buckner. They are the reason why I am here. They are also the reason why I could not contact you other than in person."

Higgins looked intrigued, but did not seem surprised.

"By all means, you are all welcome," he said, as he waved his hand over a wall sensor and the glass panels became opaque once more.

They followed the professor down the long, two-storey-high, dark slate-floor hallway. Sam and Melinda marvelled at the space. On the left were two banks of closets separated by a pair of glass-paned French doors, set back between the closets. A quick look within revealed the room to be a den. Directly opposite were two similar solid walnut-panelled doors which Sam assumed to possibly be those of a bedroom.

Strangely enough, above these doors was a protruding walkway with a glass banister but without stairs leading up to it.

The professor noticed the puzzled look on Sam's face.

"Are you wondering how I get up to the bedroom above?" he said, with his own questioning look.

"You read minds, do you?" Sam responded, smiling.

"The lift at the end. They are quite common," he said, pointing to what looked like a trap door in the floor and horseshoe-shaped arms recessed into the wall.

"It's a single-person lift up to the second floor," Higgins explained as they walked into the great room.

Sam was about to question the host on how the lift worked, when he saw the main living space of the house.

It also had two-storey-high ceilings, with four large Caribbean-style fans which helped circulate the air.

The kitchen was situated to the right, boasting long L-shaped granite countertops, stretching along the bedroom wall as well as the right exterior wall. In front of these counters stood an expansive island, with a cooktop and a large inset chopping board. The far end of the rectangular island morphed into a large round tabletop, framed by four stools.

A huge rectangular dining room table, capable of seating as many as twenty people, occupied the centre of the room.

And, to the left, could be found the living room space. Identical sofas, set up in the form of a U and surrounding a large square coffee table on three sides, seemed dwarfed by the tall contemporary marble fireplace which stretched all the way to the ceiling.

Other than that, the room was spartan, without any clutter. There were no carpets: only a continuation of the dark slate from the front hallway.

But most remarkable was the large glass wall which formed the whole rear of the expansive space. It was composed of three large bifold glass patio doors which were open wide against the two pillars, letting in a soft warm breeze. The pillars held up the rest of the square glass panes, making up the wall above, completely translucent at the moment, allowing for an unimpeded view of the lights of the buildings dotting either side of the Potomac and the DC skyline in the distance.

Sam and Melinda were amazed at the simplicity and beauty of the residence.

Melinda commented with awe, "Your home is just incredible, sir."

"Thank you," the professor said with a genuine smile. "It is much too large for me, since my wife passed six years ago. But I can't seem to find the courage to leave."

"I'm sorry to hear about your wife," Melinda said with a pained look on her face.

"Oh, don't worry about me. I've learned to cope with my loss."

"Now," the older gentleman said, wanting to change the subject to the reason of this unexpected visit, "Why don't we sit on the sofas and you can tell me what is happening."

"Before we do," Young interrupted, "I would feel more comfortable if this meeting was private," looking at the glass wall and open doors.

The professor raised his eyebrows but complied by bending somewhat toward the coffee table and swiping his hand over a small sensor: The patio doors began to close. When they were shut, he ran his hand over the same sensor but in the opposite direction and the glass on all the windows turned opaque, wiping out the view.

"Thank you, sir," Simon said as they all sat.

For the next half hour, Dr. Young described everything that had transpired and what he had found out, both as a result of his research and of the interviews, including photos of the couple in the past. He also explained how he had helped them escape and why they had come to Washington, pursued by the National Security Agency.

Higgins sat impassively, listening carefully, not showing any emotion other than at the mention of wanting to speak to the President.

When Young finished, he turned to Sam and Melinda and asked, "Is there anything you would like to add? Perhaps, where you left the ship you travelled in?"

Sam shook his head and answered, "What we can tell you is that the ship you speak of is no longer here . . . now. We are here to stay. There is more information we need to share, but it can only be with the President."

The professor had been leaning forward, arms crossed on his knees. He settled back into the sofa cushions and tried to assess the strangers' claims.

The pause was long enough to be uncomfortable for Sam and Melinda as they waited for what he would say next.

"Let us suppose I believe you. How do you propose I bring the matter to the President? What could I possibly say or do to convince her that you are who you claim to be, other than repeat the information and show her the few bits of proof you've presented to me today?"

Young spoke up first.

"Sir, you are the Chair of the National Science Committee. Do you not have discussions with her on issues of national importance?"

"Yes, I do. I speak with the President at least once per week. Nevertheless, there's quite a difference between advising her on issues dealing with science . . . and science fiction."

Melinda stepped in.

"Sir, let me assure you, this has nothing to do with science fiction. It is science fact in the future."

That stunned Young and Higgins.

Melinda realized she might have said a little too much and looked over to Sam.

"The professor has a point," she said in a low voice. "Do we . . .?"

Sam thought for a moment and nodded his agreement.

"You explain," Melinda suggested.

"I guess we have to trust someone to get us to the President," he said. "Sorry, Doc. Not that we didn't trust you, but I think you'll understand once I've explained our mission here."

It took an hour and a half to make sense of the reason why they were in Area 51, the nature of the EGGs and the presence of Tong and Voot. Also, why they left the way they did and what they experienced in the far future. Finally, he divulged why they were sent back to this particular time and what they were required to do.

All through the explanation, the two doctors asked a myriad of questions, trying to poke holes in the story, in an attempt to reveal that Sam and Melinda were part of a major hoax. They found none and they were left to believe or not believe.

Sam finished with, "So, there you have it. Either we are two crazy individuals trying to pull off the biggest con ever, or, we are telling you the truth."

Higgins simply looked at Young, trying to judge whether or not he had been duped. He knew his protégé and was well aware of his abilities, deciding that if he had believed the two, then he, too, should give them the benefit of the doubt.

"You say this primordial black hole hits the earth in three hundred years?"

Sam nodded.

"That's what we were told."

"I'm aware of the theory of their existence and your description of their global impact is consistent with what would happen if one did strike the earth," the professor acknowledged.

Then he asked another pertinent question.

"Why now? Why were you sent back to this precise time?"

Melinda shook her head and speculated, "We're not completely sure. We know we couldn't have been able to convince the world leaders during our time. There was too much strife and lack of cooperation. Based on what Dr. Young has described of this time, it would seem you are much closer to being able to work together in building all the underground cities which will be needed. Moreover, the gnomans were adamant about this time slot."

The professor mused for a moment and added, "Yes, yes. And three hundred years might be enough time to get the job done."

Sam looked at Melinda and then back to professor Higgins.

"So, are you saying you will help us?"

Higgins didn't answer right away, but took time to think, rubbing his chin with his hand.

Finally, he answered.

"Yes."

Chapter 57

By the time they had finished talking, everyone was exhausted. The professor had suggested Sam and Melinda have the run of the house and be given the upstairs bedroom, above the master in the front hallway. Young would use the bedroom in the basement, next to the games room. It was the room he had been assigned on the few times he had visited the professor and his wife.

Higgins had shown Sam and Melinda how to use the lift: They had to pull the hinged C-shaped arms from the wall and, with both hands, have them join around their waste to engage the lift's motor. The platform glided up, connected to a mechanism behind the wall by a bracket which extended through a long slit in the wall, to the second floor. Sam couldn't help but take it up and down a few times before heading to the bedroom. Melinda commented about boys and their toys.

An hour after they had settled comfortably under the blankets, having talked a little about the next steps they would be taking, Sam found he couldn't sleep. He thought he would head to the kitchen and grab something to eat, so he slipped out of bed silently, careful not to wake Melinda. Before closing the door behind him, he looked into the room to gaze at his wife who was sleeping peacefully. He couldn't help thinking how lucky he was to be married to her--the mother of his child.

As he took the lift for another short ride, the slight hum of the motor alerted the professor who was still awake and in his study.

"Hello," he said loudly enough for the "intruder" to hear him, but not so loudly as to wake the others.

"Who is there?"

Sam arrived, peeking into the study from the hallway, wearing his boxer shorts and T-shirt. As he approached the door, he was surprised by something scurrying on the floor. He actually had to jump sideways not to step on a small vacuum robot, busy prowling for dirt.

"Hello, professor. I see you have assistance with the housekeeping tasks."

"Every little bit helps when you are alone," Higgins responded.

"I'm surprised to see you up," Sam remarked.

"I don't need much sleep. One of the advantages of old age," he said, chuckling.

"I couldn't sleep," Sam admitted, "so I thought I might take you up on your offer to make myself at home and get something to eat."

The professor was sitting in a leather LA-Z-BOY-style chair, a holographic screen hovering before him. He was sipping on a cognac while doing some reading.

A quick look around the room revealed to Sam that this man was special and possessed eclectic taste.

As with the other areas of the house, the den stood two floors high and similar to the hallway, it had an overhanging walkway all around the second floor. Lining every metre of the walls on the second floor were tall walnut bookcases, filled with, from Sam's estimation, at least ten thousand books. The only area not covered with a bookcase was that of the tall window in the centre of the front wall, extending down onto the first floor.

This level was also covered in colonial-style raised walnut panels, lit with candle-shaped light sconces. It was like a throwback to the days of Thomas Jefferson.

"Wow, sir, I love the sense of style and tradition in your den. I am surprised, though, at the fact that, in this day and age, you have hard-copy books."

"One of my many eccentricities," he quipped and then added, "May I ask you to join me for a drink before you get something to eat?"

He pointed to a side table, on which sat a carafe of cognac and several glasses.

"Help yourself."

Then he continued, "I've been able to retrieve and read some of your papers. Quite insightful for the time."

Sam returned with his cognac and sat in an armchair, opposite the professor. He could see him through the hologram of the research he had submitted. Higgins read another word or two, flicked his finger in a sideways motion, forcing the page to flip over. Then, he opened his hand, fingers extended and closed it quickly. The image disappeared and the professor pulled his seat in a more upright position.

"Yes, very insightful for the time in which you lived. Much of your research was later proven to be correct. Did you know that? Being a psychologist, I especially enjoyed your theory about our species and the importance of symbolism. A fair amount of Jung, with a touch of Freud. Did you know they drew a considerable number of their theories from one of the oldest religions in the world: Zoroastrianism."

He stopped himself.

"There I go again. Once a professor, always a professor. I apologize."

"No, please don't," Sam responded. "It makes me feel at home talking about a subject I'm familiar with. I haven't had such a discussion, well, in over three hundred years."

Higgins laughed, rose his glass and said, "Cheers."

Sam raised his glass as well and they both savoured their drink.

The professor's voice changed slightly, sounding much more serious.

"Do you know why I decided you could be telling the truth?"

Sam shook his head.

"Perhaps it would be easier to show you."

He got up from his chair and walked over to the corner, where Sam spotted another lift to the walkway above. The professor seemingly floated up to the walkway and then made his way around to one of the bookcases off to the left. He searched through the books in that section and pulled out a small manuscript. Tucking it under his arm, he returned to the first floor and his chair.

"Of all my purchases, this document ranks among my favourite ones. It took me years to track it down," he said, as he handed it to Sam.

Leafing gently through what seemed to be very old parchment-paper pages, he saw that the language used was a form of early French. There were drawings as well, of old ploughs.

"Written in French," he suggested.

"Actually, they are written in Provençal, a French dialect. What do you make of the drawings?" the professor quizzed.

"They seem well done, with attention to detail. Why do you ask?"

A knowing smile crossed Higgins' face and the teacher in him returned.

"The author of the documents, as you can see on the front page, was someone named Jacques LeSage and it is dated 1307."

Sam made a face that showed he was somewhat interested.

The professor continued.

"The surprising thing about it is that the type of plough he describes wasn't invented until about three hundred years later . . ."

At this point, Sam looked more impressed as he took another sip of his drink.

Higgins continued as if on a hunt.

". . . which would mean this LeSage was either one incredibly smart and talented individual, hundreds of years ahead of his time, or . . ."

He paused to see if Sam understood his meaning.

Sam's eyes grew wide as he began to comprehend what the professor was intimating.

Presently, he was truly awed.

"You're saying this person might have been a time traveller too?"

"The thought crossed my mind as you described your own situation earlier. I put two and two together and realized that if you have travelled in time, could others have done the same?"

The two fell silent, lost in their own reverie.

Higgins cut it short.

"Now, I've been known to make a mean sandwich. Let's go to the kitchen and I'll prove it."

Chapter 58

The next morning, Melinda had to shake Sam a little harder than usual to wake him and it took a long shower to get him to come around completely. He filled her in on his impromptu meeting with Higgins, which convinced her that they had done well in trusting him, as well as Young.

The two headed down to the kitchen, welcomed by the smell of coffee. Professor Higgins and Doctor Young were already sitting at the round end of the counter, drinking their cup of java.

"Ah!" exclaimed the professor as he saw the two and rose from his stool. "Please, join us. I can offer you a great mushroom omelette, croissants or just plain toast and jellies. Tell me, how are you feeling?"

"A little sluggish," Sam admitted.

Melinda responded with, "My stomach is a little queasy."

"I'm sorry to hear that," the professor empathized.

Sam just looked over at his wife with a knowing smile.

****

"No. Stormy, what I'm saying is that they are in Washington."

"Look, John," Lieutenant Saunders said, still angry, "I travelled across the country on a wild goose chase. Now you want me to go looking for them here?"

"Listen. I know it is them and I know where they are," the doctor said earnestly.

He continued, "I had CASS run follow-up searches on the two former patients we thought were with Young. She came up with recent scans of them in two cities: in Vegas and Washington. So I sent security to check on them here and they found both individuals, meaning that the two in Washington have to be the Buckners."

Saunders began to cool down.

"You say you know where they are?"

"Yes, but that could be a problem," Lawson admitted.

"How so?"

Lawson answered, "They were tracked to Professor Jonathan Higgins' home."

"The President's advisor?" bellowed Saunders.

"The one and only Chair of the National Science Committee," the psychiatrist said with despair.

"How the hell do you suppose we handle this?" Stormy said, his anger rising once more. "Do I simply walk up to his door and accuse him of harbouring fugitives or do I just raid his house with a SWAT team?" Saunders hissed.

The doctor thought for a moment and then said, "Not quite. Here is what I suggest you do . . ."

****

The four were laughing and exchanging anecdotes about funny things that had happened to them, as though they had known each other all their lives. The three hundred and fifty years that had separated them seemed to have vanished.

". . . and the President really said that?" Sam asked in astonishment.

Melinda was just as surprised.

"Our President Alexander would never dare," commented Melinda.

"Every word is true," the professor stated, still chortling.

Melinda hadn't yet finished her croissant when she looked out through the rear glass wall of the house. Beyond the wide balcony which stretched across the back of it, overlooking the infinity pool below, she could see all the way down the Potomac to the American Legion Bridge on the 495.

She put her hand over Sam's and whispered, "Sam, look."

He did, followed by Higgins and Young.

Even though they were about two kilometres from the bridge, the flashing lights on half a dozen black vehicles travelling at high speed would draw anyone's attention.

"They aren't MOTs, are they?" Sam asked.

"No," responded the professor, "they are military and if I had to guess, they are coming here. We do not have much time. Five minutes at most," he added.

"Quickly, follow me to the den," he ordered them, a tone of urgency in his voice.

"What about the food and dishes? If they come in to search, won't that be a giveaway?" Melinda asked as they all made their way behind the professor.

Still moving quickly and spryly, he explained that he could easily empty the food in the combustion chamber, an appliance all homes had now, to disintegrate it to ashes within a minute. As for the dishes, had she not heard of dishwashers?

They reached the den and Higgins told Melinda to follow him to the lift on their left, sending Sam and Young to the other one on the opposite corner of the room, and to meet on the next level.

They gathered in front of a series of bookcases. The three guests had a questioning look on their faces as the professor pulled out one of the books up along the right edge and reached into the cavity. A click was heard and the whole bookcase moved forward, forcing everyone to step back against the banister.

Higgins grabbed the side of the bookcase and easily rolled it to the left, revealing a small opening behind it. Sam realized it was a hidden chamber above the hallway closets in the entrance.

"My wife was a little paranoid when I was appointed Chair of the Science Committee due to some of the issues I would be responsible for, so I had this built in case we were threatened. It isn't large, but should be adequate. The light sensor is on the right."

They stepped in, the light turned on and without a word, the bookcase was rolled back into place.

By then, sirens could be heard and Higgins estimated the military vehicles were already on the small bridge leading to the island. He headed back to the kitchen to take care of the evidence.

A thought crossed his mind regarding the bedroom. He might not be able to get to their room to tidy up. He checked his watch: no time!

He was clearing the food and dishes when he heard the front door chime. Hurry, he thought to himself.

He locked the lever on the incinerator and ran his hand in front of the sensor. He heard the sizzle from within as the doorbell rang once more.

He moved quickly up to the hallway, where he slowed his progress as he tried to slow his heart rate.

There on the other side of the glass were six security agents, with a commander waiting impatiently, his hands clasped behind his back. The professor heard a noise somewhere behind him. A quick glance toward the rear of the house told him the rest of the soldiers were surrounding the building.

As he opened the door, he smiled at the commander who was dressed in a black uniform with a matching military officer's cap.

"Yes, Commander. How may I be of service?"

"My name is Lieutenant Saunders of the National Security Agency. May we enter?"

"What is this about?" the professor said convincingly.

"Please, may we enter?"

The professor stepped back, opening the door wider.

"By all means, Lieutenant."

When they were all inside, the lieutenant looked around and with a quick flick of his hand, pointed to the door of the den, the lift at the end of the hallway and the main room, sending several of the soldiers on a search for the fugitives.

"I apologize for the intrusion, Professor. We have received information that you were visited by three individuals late last night. Is that correct?"

"Why, yes. I was visited by my protégé, Dr. Simon Young and two charming friends," he said calmly, smiling.

"Are they still here?" the lieutenant asked.

"Why, no. They left an hour or so after they arrived," the professor said, sounding concerned.

"And, why did they come?" was the next question.

"They said they were in town for a couple of days, for a conference on biogenetics and had not had the time to book a tour of the White House. Knowing I frequently spoke with the President, Dr. Young hoped I could arrange a private tour."

"And, have you?" Saunders asked.

"No, I haven't had the chance to do so. I was about to try, just as you rang the doorbell. But why the concern?"

The lieutenant explained that Security had received intelligence about two individuals who were making plans to assassinate the President and had fooled Dr. Young into coming to see his mentor to get them within the White House.

Dr. Higgins feigned surprise, though a slight bit of doubt about the Buckners did creep into the back of his mind.

By then, the soldiers had returned, each one shaking their heads, meaning they had found nothing. The professor tried not to show his relief at the thought that his guests had been courteous enough to make their beds and tidy up.

The lieutenant could not hide his frustration, a fact which only made the professor more pleased.

Records had shown that the MOT used in getting there, had indeed left about the time that the professor said it had, but the sensors had not recorded there being anyone in the vehicle. Either they had not left or the sensors were defective. No way of knowing in time to arrest the professor and ransack the house to find the three.

"May I offer you some tea?" Higgins asked.

"No, thank you, sir. However, there is one thing I would like you to do," Saunders said, thinking he might still be able to get the Buckners.

"What might that be?"

"I want you to make the call and arrange a tour, as they have asked. You will need to confirm the details with my office," he said, handing the professor his card, "and we will see to it that they are stopped and prosecuted. Can you do that?" the Lieutenant pressed.

Higgins knew he was being set up, but continued with the charade.

"I will certainly cooperate. When I have the particulars, I will contact you."

He paused, looking down while rubbing his chin.

"Oh, my, my," he said. "If I had only known. They were such a nice couple. And to think they were in my house."

"One never knows, Professor. That is why our services to protect you and the public are so essential. Now, if they try to reach you before you call me, do not let on that I've been here."

"Absolutely not. Thank you, Lieutenant," the professor said, sounding very much relieved.

With that, Saunders looked at his men through the rear windows and raised his hand, signalling for them to leave. He did the same for those in the foyer, and then let himself out without saying goodbye to the professor, who was left holding the door open.

He remained that way until he could see the last of the military vehicles disappear down the road. He closed the door, locked it and waved before the sensor to turn the glass opaque. He walked down the hallway and repeated the gesture for the rear windows to change as well.

It took barely thirty seconds for him to get up to the bookcase, behind which his guests were waiting.

As the three exited their hiding spot, the professor said, "I think we have things to talk about."

Chapter 59

The four were huddled once more at the far end of the kitchen island.

"How would you suppose we proceed now, Professor?" Melinda asked.

"Well, the lieutenant is expecting a call from me, informing him of where and when we will be entering the grounds of the White House," he answered, "but, we will need to send him elsewhere."

Sam looked up at Higgins and asked, "You don't think he's going to fall for that, do you?"

"I agree," Melinda chimed in.

"If I were him, I'd have every entrance covered and try to get eyes on us as soon as we enter the city core."

"You are both correct. Which is why we must have a Plan B," responded the professor.

"True," said Sam, "so we need to have a better idea of what makes him tick if we are going to attempt to outthink him."

Higgins turned to Young.

"Now, this should be an interesting case for you. Give me your assessment of the man," he said, in a very teacher-like manner.

Simon thought for a moment, hoping not to disappoint his former mentor.

"I would say he is capable enough to reach the command level he now occupies. He's ambitious: He wouldn't have travelled across the country after simply receiving a video call from Lawson. He is probably protective of his position and mistrustful of his superiors, in that I don't believe he has informed them about the two of you. The fact he came personally to find us here, and with only a small number of security agents, reveals that he is keeping this close to the vest and might not have access to the full support of his department. I would attest his greatest flaw to be his ego, which means we can't underestimate how ruthless he will be in order to get his hands on us."

The expression on Higgins' face indicated he was impressed.

"That is probably an accurate assessment," the professor said, "therefore, I propose we get the MOT to leave us at the Lincoln Memorial and that we walk from there."

Sam looked surprised.

"Has it survived up until now?"

The professor laughed.

"Absolutely. The entire National Mall and White House grounds and buildings were considered priority heritage buildings and are maintained as they were in your time, in part because of the tradition, but also because it is what Americans and tourists want to see."

"If that's the case," Melinda said, "I should be able to help get us around."

"I'm anxious to see the Washington Monument and the Lincoln Memorial again," Sam added.

"What do you mean, again?" Melinda asked, a little incredulous.

"I went to Washington on a school trip when I was in Grade 8," Sam said proudly.

"I worked for months selling raffle tickets with a car as the prize and used my commission to pay for the trip."

"I'll bet you were a handful for the chaperones," she said sarcastically.

"No, not at all. I was good. Well, other than planning the stunt of the water bombs we dropped on the passersby several floors below our rooms."

"I knew it," Melinda blurted out, "trouble from the beginning."

"And this is the man in whose hands rests the fate of humanity," commented professor Higgins.

They all laughed and then got back down to business. The critical part of all of this would be the professor's association with the President and whether he could convince her to meet with Sam and Melinda.

He headed to his den, sat on his office chair, summoned up his holographic monitor and began.

"Priority access, alpha, two, niner, zero, epsilon. Name: Dr. Jonathan Higgins."

The computer voice responded with, "Password, please."

"The hurricane has arrived," the professor answered, thinking to himself that it was a rather stupid phrase to use.

"One moment, please."

Silence.

Then, all of a sudden, "Dr. Higgins. ¿Qué tal, profesor?" President Gonzales said, pleased to hear from her advisor.

"To what or whom do I owe the pleasure of your call?" she said. Then, just as quickly she added, "No matter, you will need to get to the point, pronto. I have a cabinet meeting in fifteen minutes."

"I am sorry for the unscheduled call, Madam President. There is something I need to bring to your attention, something I believe will render moot anything you may have on the agenda with the cabinet," he said, hoping to pique her curiosity.

"Is that so?" she replied. "Well, out with it."

"Are you alone?" Higgins added and then proceeded describing the situation. He brought up the pictures and biographies of the two Buckners, and also sent her copies of Sam's research.

President Gonzales quickly scanned all of the information before her.

"And, you are convinced they are who they claim to be?"

"From my research on them and after having spoken to the couple at length about their own time, I am confident they are, and that their claims about their sojourn in the future are real," he said, with the most convincing tone he could muster.

Gonzales leaned over to the intercom, pressed the button and merely said to her secretary, "Arthur, please advise the attendees that the meeting is cancelled."

Getting back to the professor, she uttered, "How soon can you get here?"

"Within two hours or so, ma'am. But there is a problem."

"And that is?" she asked.

He explained the situation with Lieutenant Saunders.

"That is a problem," Gonzales admitted.

"He has removed the possibility of meeting clandestinely. No one can know we will have met or that these two people exist."

She sat back in her chair and thought about what to do.

"And you say you believe he is acting alone and no one else knows," she questioned.

"That is our assessment, ma'am."

"I have a few calls to make. Leave that to me. In the meantime, I will have four tickets for a private tour available at the

Northwest Gate so if anyone checks, it will look as though nothing is up."

****

"Sir, we've detected communications from the house," an agent reported to the lieutenant.

"Who to?" he asked.

"Sorry, sir. Unfortunately, the communications were encrypted beyond the level we can easily decipher."

"Get on it, stat. But I can guess who the call was made to."

As he got back to the documents at hand, the com next to him on his desk rang. He pressed the "On" button and said, "Yes."

"Lieutenant Saunders?" the voice said.

Saunders stiffened as he recognized the person behind the voice.

"Sir, yes, sir."

It was General Adams, his boss's superior.

"How may I be of service, sir?"

"I've received an interesting communication from the President herself. She asked about information concerning an operation she believed you were running. Is there anything to this?" the general probed.

Saunders winced silently, almost panicking into admission.

He took a deep breath and answered, "No, sir. Nothing out of the ordinary here. If there were, I would have advised Commander Winkle. I don't understand where the President would have heard of such an operation. And, sir, why would she be involved in this fashion?"

"Son, I haven't a clue but I need to get to the bottom of this. I want you to report, along with Winkle, to my office first thing in the morning," the general barked and then hung up.

Saunders sat back in his chair, the blood having drained from his face. Steady yourself, he thought. All isn't lost. When I capture the four, I'll have all the proof and ammunition I will need to absolve myself and make my mark directly with Adams.

Slowly his calm returned and he began to get excited about what lay ahead.

The com device rang once more. Who is it now? he wondered.

It was the professor who said when they were to be at the Northwest Gate of the White House. He thanked him and hung up.

Northwest Gate. Right, he thought. They are going to the South Lawn Gate. But, just in case . . .

Chapter 60

Professor Higgins had called for a MOT1 to be sent to the house. Melinda had assumed it would be watched, so the plan was to have Dr. Young, dressed in the professor's clothing and sporting his trademark fedora, take it into the city in his place.

A moment after it left, they noticed a military vehicle slowly exit the property Melinda had seen for sale and follow the MOT at a distance.

The three of them got ready and about five minutes later, an empty MOT4 approached the professor's driveway. An encrypted call had been made to make the reservation.

Hesitantly and cautiously, the three exited the house and quickly boarded the vehicle.

The MOT1 was supposed to take the 495 south to the suburb of Tysons and then in toward the capital via the 66. The MOT4 was to follow the more picturesque and less public occupied George Washington Memorial Parkway. It would be slower, but more secure.

****

"Good work, Agent Clarke. How long ago did it leave?"

"That was about thirty-five minutes ago, sir," the agent said, bragging.

Saunders felt good. He had them.

"And the other?" Saunders added.

"We are still following in stealth mode. It has just turned onto Highway 66 and heading toward the core," the agent reported.

"And, did you locate the MOT4's ID from the reservation listing?"

"Yes, sir. That would be MOT4-947D. We've begun tracking it. It is presently passing the Chain Bridge on the GWM Parkway. We estimate it should be crossing over into the DC area in about twenty."

"Good. Now, they are usually programmed to come up behind and around the Lincoln Memorial and up to Constitution

Avenue. Send three members of the team to intercept them. Make sure they have pictures of the Buckners. . . .

". . . Once you have, get me access to the MOT's directional software. I want to disable it where and when they reach the team. So, get me that override capability!"

****

"Alright, Professor, we know the lieutenant will not let us get to the White House. He can't afford to take a chance we will reach safety. So how do you suppose he will try to stop us?" Melinda asked.

Sam realized she was in work mode, being the best at what she did.

"I'm afraid you are probably correct," the professor admitted, "but other than the fact he must have your pictures and knows my face well, we should get close enough to walk, hidden by the hundreds of tourists on the Mall."

Sam piped up, "If I were him, I'd want to catch us in the MOT. Can he control it somehow?"

The professor's eyes widened.

"Only if he can access the controls of the vehicle," he said.

"I would imagine that feature has been built in for security reasons," Melinda added.

She continued, "So, if that is the case, and we have to assume it is, we need to get out much sooner than planned."

The other two nodded in agreement.

By then, they were crossing the Potomac via the Theodore Roosevelt Memorial Bridge and the MOT was positioning itself to exit by bearing to the right.

"There," pointed Higgins. "We'll be going off on that exit ramp."

Looking at the Lincoln Memorial and then at the Mall before it, Melinda exclaimed, "You were right. It's exactly as you said. Nothing has changed in over three hundred years. I know exactly where I am and where we need to go. Can you stop the vehicle somewhere on the ramp?"

"Yes, I can," responded the professor.

About a hundred metres farther, he entered his citizen code and told the MOT to pull over to the side.

****

"The MOT has come to a stop, sir," reported the agent watching the bleep on his monitor.

"What?" screamed Stormy. "Are you sure?"

"Yes, sir. They stopped about four hundred metres from the team."

"Damn them! How did they know?" Saunders yelled.

"Tell the team to fan out and head north to intercept them. They'll need backup. Send four more on Constitution Avenue from the east side, to box them in. Stop them at all costs."

****

"I sure hope the grounds are as they were before. Because if they are, just over there, over that small knoll, there should be a walking path which will lead us to Constitution Avenue. From there, it's a good twenty-minute hike to the White House," Melinda estimated.

"My dear," said the professor, "I'm afraid you'll have to add some time to that because of my speed--or lack of it. As well, it might be wise if we were to split up, don't you think?"

"OK, we'll meet up at the guard house. Once there, we should be safe," Sam answered, taking Melinda's arm and pulling her to move faster.

They took off together, but it wasn't long before they had outdistanced the older gentleman.

Sam looked over his shoulder as he ran and saw two uniformed security agents about two hundred metres behind the professor, chasing him with their weapons raised. He could hear shouting and assumed they were yelling for him to stop, which he didn't.

Tough old guy, he thought to himself as he heard a pop. Both Sam and Melinda looked back, only to see the professor fall to the ground.

"No, no," cried Melinda, "this can't be happening."

The two almost stopped running, but then picked up speed, knowing they had no choice.

They got to the end of the pathway and as Melinda had indicated, they were on Constitution Avenue. She yanked Sam by the hand across the street, dodging the vehicles, not realizing they were programmed to dodge them or any pedestrian on the road.

They reached the other side and Sam asked, "OK, where to now?"

They were at 20th Street, moving east and mingling with the crowd of picture-taking tourists. They hated having to slow down, now feeling guilty about the professor who could easily have handled this pace.

"The agents knew we were coming, and from that direction," Melinda replied. "Damn, that lieutenant is good. Which means, if it were me, I'd have more agents coming from up there."

She added, "Keep a sharp lookout."

They walked to 21st Street, trying to blend in. Melinda was the first to see them.

"Don't stare, but up ahead about a hundred metres, over to the right and trotting, along the path next to the Pond: two of them."

They felt exposed, but Sam squeezed her hand and said, "Just in front of us. The tour group with the guide. Let's catch up."

In fact, there was a tour group of about twenty-five people, with a guide holding up a sunflower pinwheel over her head and walking backward giving historical information to the group. Sam and Melinda managed to reach them in time and mingled with the tourists who, they determined by the comments, were German.

"Smile, pretend you're having fun, but don't look at the one approaching the group," Melinda suggested to Sam.

The agent had slowed his pace, trying to make his weapon less visible behind him, while he scanned the group as best he could.

He was moving fairly quickly and happened to pass by Sam and Melinda just as they ducked behind a colossal man. They kept their heads down, all the while peeking about to see where the security agent was.

They saw him pick up speed and continue his high-paced chase westward, while talking on his com.

"Whew, that was too close," Sam said.

"I don't think we're in the clear quite yet," Melinda commented. "There are most likely more of them crawling all around here. I think it's time to head away from the main drag and get onto the streets where we might more easily see our trackers."

They turned up 18th Street, just one block from the Ellipse, the large green area in front of the South Lawn of the White House.

Melinda was right once more. The street proved to be almost empty. Over a block away, they spotted two more agents moving quickly, scoping left and right as they crossed the street, luckily moving back toward 20th Street.

Sam and Melinda came out of the doorway they had ducked into.

"I think we have to move as quickly as possible while we can," Melinda urged. "When we get to New York Avenue, we'll be more exposed, but it should be the best way to get us to within one block of the White House and the Northwest Gate."

"OK, I have your back," Sam said, leaning down to kiss her.

****

"You haven't found them yet?" Saunders bellowed. "They must have gotten past you somehow."

"All teams, head back to the White House. I want half of you at each of the two gates. Don't be too obvious. Team One, what is the status of the professor?"

"We've dressed his leg wound. Not much more than a scratch, sir."

"Good, bring him in. I'm sending a vehicle for you."

****

Sam and Melinda were crouching behind a hedge, across Executive Drive on the corner of Pennsylvania Avenue.

Things seemed very quiet, with nothing to indicate any sort of danger.

Sam turned to Melinda and whispered, "I don't think it's a good idea for the two of us to be seen together. Let me go on my own. One person walking casually toward the guard house shouldn't raise too many questions. There are a good number of tourists there taking pictures. I should fit in."

"OK," Melinda said, "but, keep an eye out."

Sam was just getting up when Melinda grabbed his arm and pulled him back down.

"Look," she whispered.

Sure enough, across the street, a uniformed agent came running to the corner and turned toward the guard house.

"Damn it!" Sam said, "So close. Now, what?"

"I don't know," Melinda answered.

"Well, I do. We have to try. I'm going anyway. I have the advantage of knowing there's a guard there. Maybe, somehow, I can get in. We need the President's help now more than ever. Sit tight. I'll signal you if I think it's safe."

"What do you consider safe?" she said with a smirk.

"OK, if I think we can get in."

He gave her a quick hug and slowly got up, then walked around the hedge onto the sidewalk. He trotted across the street ahead of the traffic.

He was only about fifty metres from the guard house and so far so good, but he couldn't see what was happening on the other side, which was the driveway entrance onto the grounds.

He stopped and pretended to be a tourist among the others and even proceeded to talk to one of them, pointing to different features of the grounds.

That's when he heard a scream. It was Melinda.

He looked and spotted her where he had left her but saw she wasn't alone. Two security agents were also there, trying to grab and immobilize her. Sam noticed they were having a hard time doing so. She managed to elbow the one, almost dropping him to the ground behind the hedge. The other slapped her, only to get a solid punch to the nose in return, a punch which seemingly connected well enough to break it. As she was about to dart off,

Sam saw her fly forward as the first agent grabbed her ankle to retain her, preventing her from sprinting.

Sam stopped, hesitated a moment, wanting to run to her rescue, but realized their only chance resided with the President. He then turned and charged with all his might toward the guard house.

He reached it and made an incredible right turn around the corner onto the driveway leading to the grounds of the White House.

He couldn't stop in time. He crashed full speed into the agent they had seen earlier. He had been talking to the regular guard at the gate, but was suddenly flung up against it, knocking him out cold, and sending him falling on his rear, slumped before the entrance.

The regular guard was taken by surprise and couldn't react fast enough before Sam took a huge swing at him, his fist aligning with the guard's jaw. He dropped where he stood, leaving Sam wondering what he needed to do next.

He walked through the door to the guard house, stepping over the body. He looked around the room and on the counter below the sliding glass window, he noticed the four tickets the President had promised to make available for them. Right, what good are they now, he wondered.

He scrutinized the control panel next to the tickets.

No, it couldn't be that simple, could it? There were four large buttons: two green and two red, with the words Driveway and Sidewalk above each pair.

He became aware of the tourists outside who had witnessed what had happened, and were beginning to panic, running from the fence in front of the grounds, to anywhere they thought would be safer. This drew the attention of the White House guards patrolling the area. They began communicating with house security, different from the NSA, and converging on the guard house.

Sam slammed his hand on the green button labelled Sidewalk.

He stepped out of the house in time to see the gate to the driveway open and the unconscious agent fall onto his back.

Sam realized he had no time to spare. He knew he was taking a chance storming into the White House, but he also knew he had to do it and do it now. He kept thinking, please let them see I don't have a gun . . . I don't have a gun.

He jumped over the security guard and began running. A quick glance back and he saw two more NSA agents turning the corner around the guard house, in hot pursuit, with their weapons up. As he looked around, he saw White House security, dressed in suits and ties, also running toward him, but from the opposite direction. You have to be kidding, he thought to himself: Three hundred plus years and they're still using 'Men in Black'. . . and they're still dressed in suits and neckties!

A line of mini-explosions, creating a series of small craters, ripped across his path, forcing him to stop suddenly. What was that, he wondered. Then he glanced up at the roof of the White House, where to his dismay, stood no fewer than ten SWAT soldiers, all holding high-powered rifles, all of them trained on him.

Just to make their point, another volley of bullets exploded before and on either side of him.

Sam dropped to his knees and put his hands up on his head.

"The President is expecting me," he yelled in desperation.

He closed his eyes hard, assuming he'd be shot. That's it, he thought: I'm done.

Coming from behind, the two NSA agents reached him first, the one planting his right hand firmly on Sam's interlocked hands, making sure he could not move.

"Get up!" the other ordered.

Sam complied.

They had begun putting restraints on his wrists when the White House agents reached the three.

The NSA agents raised their guns, not at Sam, but at the other agents.

"This is a national security issue. Back off. He's coming with us," one of them barked.

The other four agents looked at each other and together raised their deadly looking pistols, aiming them squarely at the two NSA agents.

"Begging your pardon," said the one who was obviously the commander, "but you are on our turf now and this is our collar."

He then whispered into his com.

Returning his attention to the issue at hand, he calmly repeated his demand, "You need to relinquish the intruder."

One of the two, in turn, spoke into his com and listened to the response in his earpiece. The look in his eyes was one of surprise.

They again raised their rifles toward the four and said, "We've been ordered otherwise, sorry."

Sam stood there, not quite sure what was happening. Were it not for the fact that he was in both parties' line of fire, he would have considered this a funny situation.

The White House commander put his hand up against his earpiece and said, "I think we all need to stand down."

As he said that, a small-statured person was just coming out of the White House and moving slowly toward the scene of the standoff.

Upon her approach, she calmly but forcefully said, "Soldier, I need you to release this man," to which the agent responded by quickly cutting the restraints off, while all the guns were lowered or holstered.

The white-haired lady smiled as though this was an everyday occurrence and held her hand out, "I presume you are Dr. Buckner?"

Dumbfounded, Sam reached for the frail-looking hand and shook it, noticing it was much stronger than he had expected it to be.

"Madam President, I am honoured to meet you. Still, I need to talk to you immediately about Melinda, my wife and my friends here, Dr. Higgins and Dr. Young. They are in danger, I believe."

She gestured for him to come with her.

"Do not worry yourself. They will all be joining us very shortly. I've been making a few calls of my own."

No sooner had she uttered the statement, than he heard a familiar voice yell out his name.

He turned to see Melinda dashing toward him. She bolted into his arms and embraced him. He hugged her tightly, and then reluctantly released her.

Melinda made her way to the President and extended her hand.

"Madam President, thank you so much for your efforts to help free me and save Samuel," using a more formal tone.

"We are most grateful to you."

As they stood there, they became aware of a small kerfuffle taking place back at the gate. There was Dr. Young, positioned next to the MOT1 he had taken from Dr. Higgins' home, insisting he needed to be let in.

The President looked behind Sam to see what was happening. She raised her arm and gestured to let the doctor in.

Sam turned to the President.

"There's the issue of Dr. Higgins. I'm afraid he was shot when we first arrived here."

He looked venomously at the two NSA agents and said, "They or part of their team are responsible."

"I know," admitted the President, "but, rest assured that the professor is fine and will be joining us momentarily. Now, please follow me. We have so much to discuss."

****

No more than thirty minutes later, they, as well as Dr. Higgins, were sitting in the Oval Office with the President.

The professor had arrived shortly beforehand and been taken to the Oval Office in a wheelchair. Luckily, his injuries were minor and they didn't prevent him from meeting the others in an upright rather than sitting position, even if he walked with a limp. Be that as it may, he did comment that although his time with the young couple had been interesting, if nothing short of exhilarating, he had had enough of the cloak-and-dagger style of life.

The President ordered tea for everyone while the group sat on the sofas, similar to those Sam and Melinda had sat on when meeting with President Alexander, so long ago.

Melinda looked at this President and tried to compare her to the only other one she had known personally.

The gender difference did not come into play. Both carried themselves with confidence and President Gonzales did so, in spite of her diminutive size of about 150 centimetres. She seemed oblivious to the height of the others, including Melinda.

She had sharply cut facial features and soft white waves in her hair, which was pulled back and tied into a bun at the back of her head.

Melinda liked this woman and felt they could not only confide in her, but could also count on her support. It was a good start to their mission, she thought. She looked at Sam who was partaking in a lively discussion with the other two doctors and the President, about some of the new science of the time. He, too, believed they had found an ally.

The President took advantage of what seemed to be a pregnant pause in the conversation.

"I imagine you must be wondering why I would come to the rescue of individuals involved with what could be the most preposterous story in human history?"

The others remained silent, waiting for the answer to that question.

"I am no fool," she continued, "and if any of this ever became public, I would probably be accused of and impeached for being mentally incompetent."

Instinctively, Sam and Melinda's eyes met and lowered, understanding the position they had put her in.

"I did a fair amount of research after Dr. Higgins contacted me and provided me the information he was privy to. All of it proved to be corroborated. Even so, that wasn't what convinced me you were telling the truth."

The questioning and somewhat confused looked on the faces of everyone was telling.

She continued, "All that information is public knowledge, available to anyone with access to the right databanks. This could all be an incredible hoax, launched by my opponents to embarrass me and to discredit me, if it was to come to light and be proven false."

Her political savvy was not lost on the group.

"This being said, there remains the fact that I have access to information no one else can boast of."

That got her audience's attention.

She resumed her monologue.

"One of the few real perks and responsibilities of the office is the option of being able to leave a message for the next president. Not all have done so and I have yet to decide what I will include in mine, but one leader's message stands out. Your President Alexander left a note, not for the subsequent replacement, but for any of the following presidents."

Now her audience was truly curious.

286

"He left a message three hundred and fifty years ago, which I opened."

She walked to the Resolute desk, which Sam thought had been so well preserved, though the leather inlay on the top had been replaced countless times.

She picked up a folded piece of paper, with the presidential wax seal still attached, but now broken.

Gonzales returned to the group and handed the letter to Sam.

He took it and turned to Melinda, sitting next to him and the two read its contents. On the back, a short message was hand written.

Melinda looked at the handwriting.

"It's Alexander's," she said in awe.

The message said, 'To whichever President is contacted by a Sam and/or Melinda Buckner, you need to listen to them. Not to be opened otherwise.'

Sam turned the letter over and unfolded it.

The room remained hushed as he read.

"I have just approved a mission which could be the most important in human history. I have asked two of the people I trust the most to make a journey no one of our time has ever made. I hope I will be able to destroy this message if they return, but if not, I believe they will try to contact whoever is commander-in-chief at the time. Yes, I do mean, at the time. They have saved my life twice and I don't believe they will lead the reader astray. If you are reading this message, then I know they are there with you. Give them my love and the nation's gratitude. President Felix G. Alexander."

Sam and Melinda were speechless, as were the two doctors.

Melinda's eyes welled up and Sam's weren't too far behind.

He slowly handed the letter back to Gonzales.

"So, I gather you now understand why I will work with you. I am humbled by the thought of what you have agreed to do for humanity. I cannot guarantee that you will be welcomed in every country of the world, but I can promise you that I will open every door possible and lend you all the influence this position allows me to exert."

The full impact of the mission they had agreed to felt like a crushing weight on Sam's and Melinda's shoulders.

"Now, tell me your story and leave no stone unturned," Gonzales requested of the couple.

Chapter 61

The description of events done, there was nothing but silence in the Oval Office, punctuated by the sound of an ambulance siren somewhere close to the White House.

Finally, the President broke the silence with a question to Professor Higgins.

"How real a threat is this primordial black hole?"

"Ma'am," he began, "because we've never encountered one, it remains speculative at best. That being said, they have been predicted for over two hundred years. We have had confirmation of massive black holes in the centre of almost every galaxy we have mapped; therefore, I would heed on the side of caution. Assuming this is possible, we have no choice."

Turning next to Sam and Melinda, Gonzales summarized her concerns.

"You two have placed me in quite a predicament. On one hand, I trust both doctors here and they believe you are telling the truth. As well, there is the issue of the evidence they have provided, which leads my logical side to agree with them. On the other hand, you are asking me to gamble my presidency, my reputation, not to mention billions of dollars in expenditures which can never be explained to Congress and the citizens of the country, to prepare for an event we have no way of knowing will happen or how to prevent.

"So, if I agree to go ahead with this, there still remains the matter of convincing the leaders of the rest of the world that this is true and that they need to take the same gamble I am taking. There has to be something, anything more that you can give me as proof. It would have been simple if you could have produced these EGGs, as you call them. I can't even pull up records from Area 51 concerning these crafts as there aren't any due to the secrecy around the work done at the site.

"Is there anything," she emphasized, "anything you can give me?"

Sam looked at Melinda with a 'should we?' expression.

Melinda understood his question.

"We don't need to hide anything now. On the contrary, total revelation is key," she said.

Sam turned his gaze to the President.

"We have nothing physical to offer. Be that as it may, we do have time itself that we can call upon to prove what we are proposing. Before leaving the far future, I spent a good while in their archives researching this period."

"Please proceed," was all Gonzales said.

Sam asked her to record the information he was about to share.

"You will need this intel when you call your peers. Unfortunately, we can only provide you arguments for but a dozen world leaders, but it should be enough to get started.

"Let's first begin with the Prime Minister of Great Britain . . ."

Sam spent the next hour describing events he had committed to memory and that would happen to each of the world leaders he was to identify. None of these events had occurred yet, but every leader mentioned would be aware of the circumstances surrounding each one. For example, the President of Italy presently had a mistress who, before long, would be exposed as an agent of Egypt. Mysteriously, she would disappear before inflicting too much damage to the president's government.

In another situation, he related that the Prime Minister of Canada would soon be diagnosed with terminal brain cancer and that she would die within three years of the diagnosis.

The President gathered the pertinent facts for each of the world leaders identified.

Professor Higgins interrupted to clear up a thought which bothered him.

"If these individuals are advised of these events and are convinced of your story, what is to prevent them from trying to alter history and change the timeline?"

"Good question," Sam admitted, "but every one of the events I've described has factored in any change they might implement, for instance, the dismissal of the Egyptian agent. For others, such as the cancer case, she already has it and it will be shown to be particularly aggressive and unstoppable.

"The point is," Sam continued, "that you need only advise them and let them do their own follow-up. They will call back for more information. That is when you can tell them of our story. I would assume they will be open to being convinced to take action along with you."

"Dr. Young," the President questioned, "your opinion of this strategy?"

"I have to admit," he said, "I think it is a stroke of genius. This type of information would be a very powerful tool of persuasion. Madam President, how would you react in the same situation?"

"Indeed," she replied, without giving a specific answer.

Turning to Sam, she asked, "Is there such information for me?"

"I don't know how pertinent it will be for you, but, I did come across the names of Doctor Lawson and Lieutenant Saunders while I researched the timeline of the events of today."

All eyes were now set intently on Sam.

"According to the records, the doctor will commit suicide in a psychiatric hospital in three months, while Lieutenant Saunders will be shot, a year from now, while trying to escape a similar military facility."

The President's face went white.

Higgins was concerned.

"Madam President, are you alright?"

"Yes, yes, I am fine," she responded hesitantly.

"What you are not aware of is that while all of this was unfolding and just prior to Sam storming my lawn, I made calls to the lieutenant's superiors, telling them he was unfit for duty because of complaints from Professor Higgins, who had been confronted by Saunders and was concerned about his mental stability due to his raves about an imminent attack on the White House by time travellers. He is at this moment in custody, on his way to a military facility in West Virginia.

"I also made similar calls to authorities in Las Vegas. Dr. Lawson is now a patient within his former hospital."

Melinda wanted to find out what the President would do now that she was aware of the probable outcome.

Gonzales looked at her squarely in the eyes and simply said, "Let us let history take its course, shall we?"

She paused and then continued, "Please, allow me to change the subject for a moment."

She had a mischievous smile on her face.

"As I said earlier, I did some research on your time period and there is one issue I would like you to clear up for me."

Melinda was a bit apprehensive, not quite sure what it was the President thought she could clarify.

"Well," she said, "I understand that one of the politicians of your time tried to run for the presidency on a platform supporting the people's right to bear arms, including high-powered rifles."

Melinda nodded and added, "Yes, it was a rather common platform for one side of the political spectrum."

"Ah, you are a consummate politician, not wanting to raise the issue of which party. But, he also ran with the promise to round up and deport all Mexicans in the United States, did he not? You can understand, considering my heritage, that I would be rather sensitive to that."

Melinda chuckled.

"Yes, Madam President. That goes without saying; but, just to clarify, he wanted to deport those immigrants who had come into the country illegally on the premise of building a better life here. It was incredibly divisive and a sad period for our country."

The President thought for a moment and then simply commented, "He was somewhat of a fascist, wasn't he?"

Epilogue

Five months had passed since the initial meeting in the Oval Office. President Gonzales had begun the process of implementing the plan of building fifteen underground cities on the US mainland, mostly in the eastern and central parts of the country because they were in more stable geological locations.

By then, only three other countries had agreed to work with the US to execute their own construction project. The rest, contacted by Gonzales, were sceptical about the secret information she had provided them. Their scepticism was fuelled either by their belief that the US had somehow spied on them or had manufactured the situations, or because they felt they could resolve their own issues, on their own terms. They were not to be advised about the upcoming cataclysm until they were ready to work with the US on the venture. Most, at any rate, came around within five years.

In Washington, a shadow cabinet had been set up to oversee the whole of the operation. Among its members were the four who had brought the issue to the President's attention.

Melinda, who was now well advanced in her pregnancy, was responsible for coordinating the security surrounding the project. As daunting as this was, she developed a successful strategy of encapsulating information, where each component of the tasks to be accomplished worked separately from the other, never combining operations and never divulging every aspect of the rationale behind the work.

Sam was the director, responsible for developing the technologies they would need to build and maintain the cities. This included the most difficult issue, that of miniaturizing the fusion power plants. Another was creating the construction materials for the underground tunnels and buildings, using only the raw elements available in each of the regions. The transportation of large amounts of these materials had to be minimized to prevent exposing their *raison d'être*. Sam had help from professor Higgins who worked closely on the enterprise for an additional seven years.

The job of setting up the arduous process of selection of the candidates for the future cities fell to Dr. Young. He was able to bring CASS over and introduce it to expand the capabilities of the government's less intuitive computer systems.

Other members of this invisible group were responsible for such things as the replication and substitution of the great works of art, the originals to be stored in the underground cities for posterity. Luckily, when Pope Nguyu liquidated the Vatican assets, including all the artwork in its possession, a great number of the pieces were purchased by American museums. Those bought by private collectors were eventually donated to museums for public viewing. As a result, acquiring the pieces of art was a relatively easy task.

President Gonzales proved to be quite adept at finding the initial funding for the enterprise. She personally invited and then interviewed a number of very wealthy philanthropists and managed to get a good many of them to contribute parts of their wealth, based on their confidence in her position, and on the premise that they were indeed not only helping the country, but also all of humanity with their donations. In some cases, when a very select few were informed of the real reasons behind the launching of this operation, their estates were donated and held in trust to help ensure its success after their deaths.

Over the next couple of centuries, successive presidents were able to raise the needed cash required, sometimes through shady means. One method of choice was liquidating and diverting the seized assets of criminals and their organizations, and then distributing and hiding the proceeds through a maze of government departments, to eventually end up in the project's coffers.

In order to support participating countries, Gonzales had also agreed to share any and all techniques and procedures which they developed. This meant that Sam and Melinda would be travelling a great deal, for years to come, helping these other nations implement their own plans for survival.

As busy as they were, the two always made alone time for themselves. They also wanted to have a normal family life, or as normal as their mission would allow. This was especially important with the arrival of their son.

The property Melinda had seen for sale, just down the lane from the professor's house, was finally sold--to the Buckners. They loved the setting on the Potomac, the large yard for Jake, where Sam could teach him how to catch a baseball, or let him play with Oliver, the large Labrador Retriever they had promised themselves to purchase.

They spent a month designing the house and the construction only took another three, which was a good thing, considering the fact that Melinda was getting close to term.

****

When the big day came, Sam and Melinda behaved like typical parents. As much as Sam knew about the biology associated with delivering a baby, he seemed a little lost, wanting to help but not quite knowing how to do that. Melinda on the other hand, was calm and in control.

They had discussed the birthing of their baby with the doctor, who had raised his eyebrows over the questions about how Sam would manage to get Melinda to the hospital in time. The doctor smiled and then explained that no one, at least in his memory, had given birth in a hospital setting for a very long time, other than cases which clearly indicated the possibility of the mother and or the child dying. He explained that a *BURTH*, or Birthing Unit Response Team in Home, fully capable of dealing with the majority of potential complications, would come to the home and set up a sterile enclosure in which the event would occur.

Sam's job was to clear a room, large enough to accommodate the transparent and plastic-like tent, complete with a large tub, in whose warm water the mother would sit to deliver the child.

Melinda started her labour at about five thirty in the morning, at which point the Birthing Unit was notified and a separate call was made to Professor Higgins. He had insisted on being told when she began, night or day.

Within the hour, the unit had arrived and commandeered the empty room Sam had prepared several days prior. While the doctor and midwife looked after Melinda, Sam helped the third member of the team, a technician, prepare the specialized unit.

There wasn't much to do to get it ready since the whole of it was completely collapsible, with the walls and ceiling neatly folded inside the acrylic tub. A simple outlet was tapped and the tub's electronics started a blower which inflated the enclosure to its final shape. On the walls was a series of transparent pockets holding everything required of a delivery room, from sterile gauze, to saline water bags, to surgical equipment if needed.

Water was introduced through a connection to a water hose and the tub was filled. The water would then be kept warm and maintained at the correct temperature during the whole procedure.

A small electronic device containing digital audio files was turned on and began playing music specifically chosen by the couple to help Melinda relax and to welcome Jake melodiously into the world.

After about four hours of labour, Melinda was ready to deliver and brought to the tub. She slipped into the warm water, lovingly helped by Sam who remained at her side throughout the whole process. The doctor had fully checked Melinda while the other two were setting up the birthing room and concluded she was healthy and in no danger of complications. She turned over the reins to the midwife, who was a doctor in his own right.

Melinda delivered Jake who did not hesitate to let his presence be known to everyone there. The baby, still attached to the umbilical cord, was placed on her belly with his head just over her heart. To Sam's surprise, the midwife turned to him and asked if he wanted to cut the cord, saying, "It should be the father's task to help launch his child's independence."

After having done so, he turned to look at Melinda who was holding Jake, rubbing his back gently and cupping warm water with her hands over his skin. Although exhausted, she was glowing with love and tenderness, and Sam was overwhelmed thinking how lucky he was to have her as his wife and how lucky Jake was to have her as his mother. The baby then turned his head, found his way to Melinda's breast and began suckling. Sometime later, with pride and with care, Same carried his son while escorting Melinda to their bedroom.

All of the equipment to help deliver the baby had been efficiently packed, reversing the earlier process of installing it and carried out of the house. It had only taken the burly technician an hour to leave the designated room as empty as he had found it.

Sam and Melinda were lying on their bed, with Jake tucked in between them, swaddled and sleeping peacefully.

The doorbell rang and Sam reluctantly left his family's side.

Opening the door, he was greeted by Professor Higgins and Doctor Young, both practising the age-old tradition of sporting a large cigar in their mouths, neither of which was lit, handing one to Sam along with a bottle of very expensive Scotch whiskey. There were also plenty of congratulatory bear hugs all round.

Sam had given Higgins a quick call to let him know that the baby had arrived and that all was well. That's when Higgins had placed his own call to Young, relaying the good news.

The two asked if they could see the baby and Melinda. After checking with her, Sam led the two up to the bedroom and they spent the next hour whispering praise for both mother and child, already planning, much as a grandfather and favourite uncle would, the wonderful life Jake would have.

****

Weeks and months passed, and Sam and Melinda quickly settled into a routine which included plenty of time with Jake.

Much of their work was done from home, over encrypted Internet connections, linking them covertly with all of the managers of the project. Though both sometimes had to travel, they made sure they were never away at the same time, so that one of them was always with Jake.

As the years flew by, Sam and Melinda continued the monumental task of preserving the world's collective knowledge, safeguarding the great works of art and music, and creating an environment in which a future humanity would find refuge, all the while raising an amazing son.

The boy developed into a very curious and active child. He loved to tinker and investigate the workings of anything he could get his hands on. The times he heard his mom or dad call out, "Jacob T. Buckner! Get your butt down here," warning him he was again in trouble for taking apart something he shouldn't have, were too numerous to count.

Jake had inherited Melinda's piercing blue eyes and black hair but Sam's unruly curls. His skin colour was a blend of the two, making him look as though he had a permanent tan. Up to the age of fifteen he had been fairly small, but then he experienced a sudden growth spurt and by the time he turned seventeen, he had gotten to within a couple of centimetres of Sam's height and had filled out sufficiently to boast an imposing and athletic body.

Although he had acquired Sam's tendencies toward the sciences, he gravitated to the area of engineering and chemistry, rather than biology and genetics. He took full advantage of the technologies and advancements this society had created and made available to him, and which constantly astonished Sam. Jake became somewhat jaded with the number of times Sam would recall how primitive such things as the Internet were back in his time and Jake's favourite comeback was that he wasn't surprised given both his parents were almost four hundred years old.

Since the age of fourteen, when Sam and Melinda had taken him aside and told him the whole story, he had changed in a subtle way. The change was prompted not by disbelief or rebellion, which the two parents had worried about, but more by an even deeper respect and admiration for them because of the sacrifice they had made for humankind. This fostered in him a stronger sense of responsibility and purpose, in an effort to be more like them. Not surprisingly, by the time he was twenty-one, he had already earned a Bachelors and a Masters in Applied and Theoretical Engineering.

Not long after his graduation and before he began his doctoral programme, Melinda had called him down for breakfast, as she had every morning. But, on this particular morning, there was only silence from the intercom system.

Slightly annoyed, she walked up to his bedroom and knocked. There was no response. So, she knocked again and then opened the door, wincing as if trying not to invade his space or find him walking out of the washroom in his birthday suit.

His bed had not been slept in.

She screamed for Sam to come up to the bedroom.

When he got there, he found Melinda crying and standing next to Jake's bed, looking at something she was holding in her hand.

Bewildered, Sam asked, "What is it, sweetheart?"

She looked up at him, tears running down her cheeks and then raised her hand.

There, dangling from her fingers was the chain with the Ammolite pendant she had given Voot just before having left for this time period.

Sam's look changed from one of concern, to surprise, to understanding.

He reached for Melinda and wrapped his arms around her, as she sobbed into his shoulder.

They stood there for a long time, trying to internalize what they knew had happened but found difficult to accept.

Finally, Sam whispered, "You know he's OK, don't you?"

It was now apparent to them that Jake had been visited by Tong and Voot, and the pendant revealed the truth of his disappearance: He was probably in the far future, one of the chosen few being recruited to help repopulate the surface world.

They continued to hold each other tightly, at once grieving the loss of their son and rejoicing in the knowledge that he and his progeny had a better chance of survival.

Now, they felt alone once more, much as they had so many years back, when they had first arrived in this timeline. They strengthened their embrace in an effort to reaffirm their love for each other, in a moment so few people would ever experience, then or at any other time.

And how to explain Jake's disappearance?

Due to the secrecy of their work, they needed to answer to very few people. The story would be that Jake had gone abroad to complete his doctoral degree. The only people they confided in were Dr. Young and Professor Higgins.

The professor had actually become quite close to the Buckners. He would take his afternoon walk down the road to their house almost every afternoon for a cup of tea and to discuss the progress of their work with them. That was when he wasn't conferencing with the President or when Sam and Melinda were off somewhere in a foreign capital, coordinating their parts of the endeavour. His role had been reversed: Once the teacher, he was now the student, with the couple becoming the source of information linking him to the past and the future he so longed to know about.

He had developed a genuine fondness for Jake. He saw in him the grandson he had never had. He admired the boy's thirst for knowledge, love of learning and incessant curiosity. Higgins had introduced Jake to his book collection, allowing him to pick and choose whichever volume he wanted to read. He was amused when, at first, Jake had feigned thinking that paper books were 'uncool'. It wasn't long, however, that he was repeatedly knocking at his door asking if he could find and read yet another.

Although the professor understood where Jake had gone when he disappeared, he couldn't help but feel a pain in the pit of his stomach whenever he thought of his absence.

One day, about a year and a half after that event, Higgins strolled over to the Buckners' house and knocked on the door. He would usually get a reply over the intercom to let himself in, but today there was nothing. He checked the doorknob and was surprised to see that it wasn't locked. He rang once more and still getting no response, entered and yelled hello. Silence.

He found all of this very strange, since they had always let him know ahead of time whenever they would be away. He began to panic, hoping nothing had happened to them. He quickly walked through the house to see if anything was out of place or if he could find some evidence of trouble. He was relieved that everything appeared normal, including their clothing and personal effects which were still in place.

He decided not to jump to conclusions and supposed they had probably gone out to run some errands and would return shortly. So, he headed to the kitchen to make himself his usual cup of tea and then settle in the sunroom to wait for them.

He walked over to the cupboard where he knew they kept the tea, only to find the canister already on the counter. He noticed a slip of paper poking out from the bottom of it. He lifted the container, pulled out the note and looked at it, thinking he had perhaps overreacted and that this was their way of telling him of their whereabouts and the time of their return.

He unfolded the note and read the content. It was short and, at first, the professor seemed somewhat confused. The meaning of the message which simply stated that they had gone to meet Jake, finally dawned on him.

He turned and leaned against the counter, feeling a little dizzy, realizing that they would not return and he would probably never see them again. Much like he had experienced when he lost his wife and then Jake, he felt a profound emptiness in his heart and tears welled up in his eyes.

It took but a few hours for the news of Sam and Melinda's disappearance to reach the President.

As the President sat in her chair behind the Resolute desk, assessing the impact of the Buckners' vanishing act, she came to two conclusions: The first was that with some adjustments, the project would continue without major problems. The second was that she envied Sam and Melinda.

Shaking her head in wonder, she thought she would give anything to be where they were . . . or should that be, when.